Armando Bizzarri

The Curse of the Chains

To my wife, for pushing me to take this back up after twenty years.
And to the fascinating and beloved nerd world,
in all its forms.

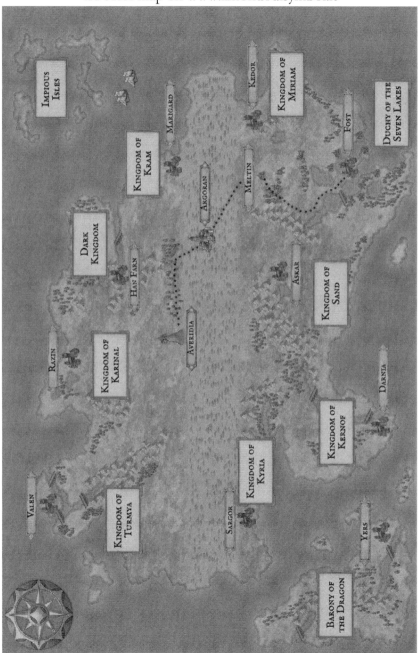

CHAPTER 1 (The World of Symbol)

Time passes.
Every existence contains within itself the forces of good and evil related to human nature, but nature is fickle.

I tell of a time when the natural balance was destroyed, men yielded to oblivion and a terrible evil was unleashed.

It is in a dusty room in the prison-city of Argoran that I tell this story, and even now the evil I mentioned returns to spread.

Everyone needs to do something to prevent failure again, and you too, whoever you are, will have a role after me.

I have already done my part! Damned if I did.

My name is Silven, and if you are reading these words, it means that I am dead.

To save the innocent, the elders of that world hid the Relic.

Therefore, for five hundred decades it remained buried.

The light disappeared as the darkness outlined the figure of a twisted man.

The souls that were not seduced by his power were bridled with pain until their spirits were broken.

His deformed body was a testament to the wickedness that consumed him. Even the blood curdled as it coursed through his empty veins, keeping the heart pumping dry.

In a dimension and in a lost and distant time, between myths, Gods and magic, there was a planet named Symbol.

This is a world illuminated by two stars crossing in the middle hour of the day, stopping all human activity because of the excessive heat.

The light and heat were so intense that the known world was strewn with small deserts from North to South and from East to West, so much so that they seemed to act as an antechamber to the great central desert, where it was claimed that every kind of nightmare could take shape, and where the presence of the Gods was amplified by the silence and desolation that the increasingly chaotic cities could not offer.

In the middle season, the two suns lengthened the days so much that life was almost exclusively bearable along the rivers and coasts.

All this was contrasted by a dark night, without stars and moons, as if to mock the bright days present throughout the year.

In a world of deserts and barren plains, rivers and coasts soon became the cause of battles between neighbors, which led to wars between kingdoms.

The blood of entire generations was shed to conquer small stretches of sea that could guarantee a valid resource for the sustenance of their civilization.

Thus, it was that one kingdom erased others, exhausted by famine and war, which already bordered it on the prosperous coast.

In a few tens of years, it came to the point that the internal ones were completely incorporated by the neighbors with the sea and came to a relative stability, at least from the military point of view, since now the tension was exclusively between North and South, meaning between the kingdoms above and below the belt formed by the great desert itself.

One day, something strange happened.

All the rulers of the planet died on the same day, drawing terribly between unspeakable cries of pain, until every single bone was broken by the demonic force that had taken possession of their now dying body.

This was the episode that marked the beginning of the invasion of the Sleepless Ones throughout the known world.

Starting mysteriously right from the central desert, two huge armies of zombies, skeletons and ethereal presences began their fan-shaped advance towards the North and South.

Months passed before it was possible to realize the real danger that the whole planet was running, until one day, a general on a diplomatic visit to an allied kingdom, was greeted by an ethereal presence that blew his life away in his sleep with a gesture of its hand, right in front of his astonished escort.

Only one of them managed to return home and report the incident to the wizards and clerics of the court.

The entire kingdom was wiped out in a few days.

The powerful soulless armies, led by demon generals, found easy targets unprepared to face such an emergency, made worse by the death of all the rulers hastily replaced by weak souls in search of easy glory and power.

With unusual speed, an agreement was reached that would put an end to all kinds of hostility between kingdoms, at least until the common enemy was finally overthrown.

The allied soldiers managed to hold the Sleepless Ones in a vice, but the price of such confinement was very high. They no longer enjoyed numerical superiority and had to garrison the area still in danger.

Many were the deserters at this juncture who had seen zombies fighting even without arms, skeletons that seemed to engage in dances of death on the few remaining mangled bones, and ethereal spirits swirling around and reaping death just as a farmer cuts wheat with his scythe.

Desolation and despondency soon took hold of the soldiers, who held the demonic horde in apparent check.

It was then that the wizards discovered that the enemy's weak point was the demon generals themselves, to whom all their subjects were magically bound.

You had to hit them one by one if you wanted to dissolve this bond.

At dawn the next day, the knights went to meet their fate.

The clash lasted hours, during which none of the troops took a single step. It was not their day, but that of the deeds of heroes with scars of innate courage.

They fought against spells of all kinds with the sole force of the sword. Many of them did not even realize that life was abandoning them.

They were still there, standing and proud to fight a common enemy and no longer to deprive a village of its livelihood for the benefit of their own.

Many of these heroes died even before they touched the ground and before they struck a single blow, but no one has forgotten their courage that freed Symbol from atrocious agonies and unspeakable suffering by soulless bodies.

The last demon was taken down and torn to pieces. An instant later, the Sleepless Ones' army broke the magical bond.

The ethereal presences vanished into light breaths of wind, while skeletons and zombies collapsed on themselves in a terrifying din of millions of bones breaking and disarticulating.

Therefore, the danger was averted thanks to warriors who fought like lions for freedom.

That day is remembered as that of the triumph of good over evil, and its anniversary is still celebrated with a week of dances and songs that resonate in all the kingdoms in unison.

When everything was accomplished, soldiers and magicians were rewarded with all kinds of wealth and the seven surviving knights were also assigned a small fief each.

For the rest, everything returned as before in a short time, and with the arrival of the torrid middle season, the quarrels began again.

The seven heroes soon consolidated their friendship that had the sole purpose of taking mutual benefit from their new possessions, so they decided to unite their fiefdoms into a single small kingdom.

Thus was born what is still remembered today as the Duchy of the Seven Lakes, where life is serene, quiet and flourishing.

The Duchy stands on the south coast of the known world, and fortunately almost one third of the land is bathed by one of the most fish-rich seas on the planet. In fact, it is on this that its economy is based, and it is thanks to the abundance of fish and seafood that the small kingdom still exists.

In addition, its lands, consisting of gentle hills and dense woods, are bathed by a navigable river that crosses the Duchy from North-West to South, to flow into the sea, but not before having made the lands crossed fertile.

Politically the Small Kingdom, as it is usually called, is divided into seven fiefdoms characterized by good independence and governed by their respective knights, who each reside in a large city, but all linked to the central one that serves as both administrative and economic capital.

The six fiefdoms, in fact, stand all around the one in the middle.

Despite its modest size, which can apparently induce the larger and most combative kingdoms to an easy conquest, the Duchy is militarily powerful.

Its strength, more than in its number, lies in the excellent training and good equipment that every soldier can have.

As if the sea and the river were not enough to wet it, each fiefdom has a lake near which the cities have arisen, something that has always bolstered the already high morale of all the citizens who continue to increase, attracted by the riches of the lands and the justice with which they are governed.

CHAPTER 2 (To the Market)

"Have a good day, father!" said the young Jelko Neville with joy.

"Good day to you, son. Try to make good deals at the market and remember to always be on your guard in bargaining with the dwarves of Ulrin. It is an art in which they have no rivals!" replied Faxel, as he clutched his belt with sword and dagger with real symbols at his waist.

He pinned his blue cloak and went out to pick up the horse at the stable to go to the city palace, as he did every day.

Faxel, Jelko's father, was a skilled warrior of the small group of royal guards, who had the task of supervising the safety of the highest officials who carried out their work in Fost, the central capital of the Duchy of the Seven Lakes.

In particular, Faxel was assigned for fifteen years to personally protect the court magician Zimas, the greatest in the kingdom, and not just there.

He was a tall man, with very white hair gathered in a braid that fell to the middle of his shoulder blades and a long white beard also made of many braids. He was thin and old, but his eyes betrayed his age by giving his face a hint of extraordinary intelligence that concealed his old age.

But this did not matter.

No one was interested in how old he was and apart from the small circle of people who had directly to do with him, no one dared to speak to him.

Zimas was said to be crazy, and the poorest and most humble people who crossed him on the street made way for him for fear that madness would take over, turning his renowned magical power against them.

In fact, he interspersed moments of extraordinary lucidity with others of terrible madness.

But this was normal, as every great magician since ancient times, to be such, had to bear the signs of three mental and bodily scars: humiliation and ablation of feelings, physical disfigurement and finally madness.

Zimas had completed his journey for several years now, a path that began when he was still a little boy and saw himself mercilessly rejected by the only person he ever loved. This led him to harbor such a grudge that it took him years to find himself before the one who held his lover's heart in his hand.

That was the day he suffered the second scar.

In fact, in the furious fight that followed, he was blinded by the anger and thirst for revenge that clouded his mind. He could not help but fall to the ground almost dead, and missing a hand.

The years that followed were of intense study of the art of magic, and over time came the madness that made him one of the most feared magicians in the whole known world.

Faxel contrasted with the appearance of Zimas. He was a little taller but much more robust. He had long black hair with some gray veins here and there that gave him a noble and resolute touch.

He was forty years old, but his physique, powerful and agile like that of all the royal guards, was enough to keep away the lowly who believed they could overwhelm him only by being half his age and a little bolder.

Faxel had a good job that allowed him to have a certain economic freedom, yet neither he nor his son was interested in living better than that.

He recounted that his wife had died when Jelko was just born, torn apart by a demon during the invasion of the Sleepless Ones in a strenuous attempt to save her only child.

Since then, father and son began to feel a strange disinterest in material things moving elsewhere in search of greater fortune, until they arrived in the Duchy of the Seven Lakes, where they settled permanently.

Jelko collected all his merchandise in a canvas, made bundles of it and left the house.

For several weeks now, he had locked himself up there to devote himself to his favorite pastime: working metals to make rings and pendants of all shapes.

Those who succeeded best depicted animals, so in the small oven he had built with his father, he forged snakes that twisted around his fingers and mythological dragons immortalized in medallions.

This time he had worked hard as the day dedicated to the God of commerce Venakin approached, who was honored with three days of intense haggling. Merchants also came every year from neighboring kingdoms for the occasion.

And those days came.

Jelko left the house and already from afar, in the direction of the large central square, he heard confused cries that bypassed each other in an attempt to make their goods gain value with their voice.

This infused in Jelko even more enthusiasm: seeing so many people of different races, some small quarrels and exotic goods of all kinds, made him feel a strange feeling that pervaded him completely, like the heat of a fire on a cold and rainy day.

He headed to the stable where he kept his mule.

Faxel tried many times to give him a horse, but he was now resigned after seeing Jelko's attachment to the animal he had given to him about ten years earlier.

He was kept together with his steed in a kind of guesthouse where the people of the neighborhood could shelter their quadrupeds cheaply.

"Today is a really nice day to do business!" said the old groom who had seen the boy come in while he was brushing one of the horses.

"You are right! I came to pick up my mule just to go to the market."

"You'd better go on foot. If it's a beautiful day for us, it's not for your mule. This morning it has not yet touched its hay, it is old and maybe it will die even before me!" he said jokingly.

"Then I will do as you say, but I recommend you take care of it."

Jelko finally headed towards the heart of the capital where the square had been used as a large market for the occasion.

At every step, he felt the desire to reach his destination grow within himself, not even realizing how, on that beautiful day, the streets he traveled were adorned with yellow flowers to honor the God Venakin.

The central streets were all well paved and, as they approached the square, widened like rivers do as they reach the sea.

Finally, he arrived at the entrance of the great market.

The noises were almost deafening: there were dwarves, dark-skinned humans and a funny race with the features and size of a child, although the age was certainly not that of a beardless boy.

These were all things that Jelko had already seen, but each time it was as if it were a completely new situation: the cries, the races, the guards at the corners, the square itself.

He immediately put his merchandise still wrapped in his lap, because he knew that in such places and confusion, thieves abounded, hiding behind seemingly harmless faces and striking with a light and velvety hand.

He shook himself out of his stupor of contemplation and began to look for a place to rest his forged metals.

He walked through the crowd, bumping into it left and right, until a stall of beautiful weapons lured him.

He could not overcome the temptation, so he approached and noticed that behind them were two tall, dark-skinned merchants. He had already heard of that breed, but had never seen it so closely. These were elves from the desert regions of the center, which explained the color of their skin.

Jelko stopped for a moment.

He also remembered that someone talking to him about it, had assured him that those elves were to be kept away because they belonged to a ruthless race prone to violence, after centuries and centuries of generations who had to fight every day for survival in arid territories.

He thought about it for a moment and said to himself: —I am in the midst of so many people, with guards everywhere and in a fortified city. What can they ever do to me? I don't think they have come this far in search of trouble, at least not now.—

He arrived at the stall and was immediately attracted by a beautiful sword with a finely worked hilt and a wide shimmering blade with two half-length tips.

He knew something about weapons, and even more about metals, so it was not difficult for him to understand that it was an excellent sword, but looking at it well he recognized it as one of those supplied to the royal guards of one of the coastal fiefdoms of the Duchy. The hilt, engraved and decorated with galleons and ships, was unmistakable.

He remembered it because when he had to go two years earlier with his father to establish an embassy in those lands, the guards regularly carried the sword by their side.

He also knew that royal weapons could not be sold or given to anyone, except to another guard of the same rank.

If his father had seen it, he would have requisitioned it and asked a bunch of questions to those dark-skinned merchants, so he began to wonder what such a sword was doing there and in those hands.

"Are you here to buy it?" said a subtle female voice, bringing Jelko back to reality.

He had not noticed in the slightest that now there was someone watching him by his side.

He turned to answer, but the words died in his throat when he saw the beauty of that young girl.

She was at least a palm shorter than him, with very black and straight hair that fell compositely on her shoulders straight as if they had weights on their tips. She had two large eyes as green as emeralds, a clear face with fine and graceful features that foreshadowed a future beauty even more splendid than the current one.

Looking at her well, Jelko noticed that the tips of her ears were sticking out of her hair and realized that she was a wood elf. He also realized with some discomfort that, although she seemed to be no more than sixteen years old, she actually had to be older, since elves could live even ten times longer than humans.

"No, I was just looking at it... It's very beautiful" he replied, recovering.

"Do you think it was stolen from someone?"

"Why do you ask me? It's a sword like any other. There will be thousands like that."

The wood elf looked him intensely in the eyes: "Until recently you were not so sure, anyway... What is your name?"

"Jelko. What about yours?"

"My name is Elyn" she said.

Meanwhile, the two dark elves seemed to continue to bargain, disinterested in the discussion behind their backs, not rightly believing that one could conclude the deal of that sword he was looking at with a little boy.

Out of curiosity, Jelko started to ask Elyn what a young wood elf was doing in the company of two dark elves, but the girl interrupted him, upset: "Please don't ask me, I don't want to talk about it. And if you don't decide to buy something, I'll have to take care of another customer, otherwise my friends will get angry if they see that I am wasting time."

Suddenly a gloomy voice thundered over their heads: "Elyn, why are you sitting on your hands? Don't you see that the guy is not interested in buying? Don't waste time and serve the buyer I was talking to."

"Immediately!" she replied, running towards the customer who was already grumbling loudly about the delay in concluding the negotiation.

A slight gust of wind moved her black hair, uncovering a tattoo behind the nape of her neck depicting a chrysalis trapped in a spider web.

Jelko remained one-on-one with the dark elf towering over him in height and size, making him uncomfortable.

"Sorry" he said, "I didn't mean to waste your time, much less your helper's."

"There's just trouble here for you boy. Go away."

And so he did.

He walked away and turned just a moment to see Elyn again, then continued to look for a free place for his merchandise.

He found a corner between two fat spice merchants and began to discard and neatly arrange his merchandise, after having spread the cloth that wrapped it.

It was a good day of business for Jelko, worthy of the God Venakin who was honored, but for him it was always like this.

His processed metals were snapped up and even if there was not much profit, he always managed to make good deals to buy what he had already spotted some time before.

And this time, he decided that sword of mysterious origin would be his.

The whole day passed quickly, but not without some usual brawl between merchants, promptly quelled by the guards who were deployed in force that day, mindful of previous years.

Jelko had now sold everything he had worked hard for in the previous weeks. Crowds began to thin and buyers became scarce.

He stood on his toes on a black stone placed to delimit the corner of the square and looked over the heads to see if the merchants from the desert were also about to leave. He saw them still intent on their business, but he could not see the little wood elf.

He had sold almost everything and decided not to run the risk of them leaving before him.

He collected his few remaining items and headed for the price of the sword that had fascinated him.

He walked with a brisk pace until he saw that the sword was still there, but slowed down upon not seeing Elyn behind the bench.

It was said that he would ask after her, when the deal was concluded.

He crossed gaze with one of the dark elves and said: "I would like to take a look at that sword at the bottom of the bench" trying to give the voice a sure tone to hide the light and ringing timbre of his age.

"You wouldn't even be able to lift that one, but I have here a long-bladed dagger worthy of the greatest murderers" said the elf, trying to sweeten the last words so that they would make an impression on Jelko's mind.

"I don't care sir. I'm here for that sword."

"And let's feel a bit boyish. How much can you offer?" replied the elf in an ironic tone since the discussion was almost amusing him.

"Forty gold coins. The steel at the tip is poorly polished and the hilt is encrusted with sand."

"I see that you have observed it well, but for forty gold coins I would not even sell you the dagger that I had proposed to you in the beginning! Go away, you're tiring me. Don't waste my time anymore."

"Fifty gold coins, not one more" Jelko replied resolutely and not at all intimidated.

"I said leave or you will regret it."

A pause followed that for the dark elf seemed to last an eternity.

The eyes of that boy were fixed on him as if they were scrutinizing that poor merchant to the bone, displaced by so much audacity.

It was Jelko who put an end to that inner discomfort by saying in a firm voice: "Do you prefer to sell that sword and earn fifty gold coins, or to see it requisitioned while you and your friend are placed under interrogation by the court magistrates? I know very well where that sword came from, and I also know that neither you nor I should have it."

The dark elf was suddenly seized by great embarrassment.

The other companion was busy on the opposite side of the stall and could not help him in that unexpected discussion.

Trying not to reveal the inner contrast, he said: "You are just a stupid presumptuous boy. That sword has belonged to my clan for generations. That's why I will not sell it for only fifty gold coins!"

"I don't think your clan comes from the maritime fiefdoms of the South. There are no dark elves there."

"You're wrong! Go away or you will regret it, I have already told you!"

"I repeat that it is a serious crime to possess that sword if you are not a royal guard. Sell it to me and you will wash your hands completely. No one will know that it was in your possession. Today the square was full of merchants all day" he replied marveling both at his brazenness and at the way in which the words flowed from his mouth according to a formidable scheme and timing.

The elf, taking advantage of the fact that his companion had freed himself at that moment, approached him and spoke with him in a low voice in an unknown and harsh language.

Meanwhile, Jelko did not know whether to give it to himself or continue to flaunt his security and mastery of the situation.

He was terrified of having combined it big, verbally defying two dark elves who would not hesitate to move on to the facts if they could.

But the square was emptying and the crowds of guards increased more and more.

The elf nodded at the other, went to the sword, took it and wrapped it in a canvas now reduced to shreds, returned to the boy and placed it in the bench in front of him.

"Here is your sword, boy. You can take it away for fifty gold coins."

Jelko was more than satisfied and hastened to cut off the deal to avoid complications. He was aware that this time he had gone far beyond the mark; he had almost ridiculed the dreaded dark elves. In addition, he now possessed a sword that did not belong to him according to the laws of the Duchy.

He quickly moved away with a brisk pace, trying to avoid low traffic.

He did not dare to turn even once, and with his sword wrapped and half-hidden under the robe, he reached the area of the square used as a base camp by the patrol guards.

Suddenly a roar echoed from one wall to another of the large buildings that delimited the perimeter of the square.

He was slammed by the displacement of air against the bench of the captain of the guards, fell to the ground and before losing consciousness he could only see a reddish glow overlooking an entire sector of the square.

He woke up two hours later in his bed.

At his side was Faxel, giving him air with a large leaf while he sat in a small wooden chair.

He tried to get up, but his father's hand held him back: "Don't be in a hurry son, you are still pale and too weak to stand."

His father's voice seemed strangely harsh and icy to Jelko's ears, but he didn't pay it too much attention and asked: "What happened, father? The last thing I remember is that I was at the central square. Who brought me here? And where is my..."

Here he suddenly took awareness that even his father did not have to know what he had bought. He would never have approved of it, and if everything went according to plan, he would had hidden the sword before returning home to a safe place that only he knew.

Faxel's face was impassive. His voice flaunted a patience held back by force, even at that juncture when his only son was recovering after having a hard time.

"You were asking me where your royal sword is?"

Jelko lowered his eyes and said nothing. Now he was in a sea of trouble, he would rather face a hundred dark elves than his father.

"I'll tell you what happened so you can see for yourself. I was returning to the palace with Zimas when a roar caught my attention. I pushed him into the door and rushed to a part of the square that was on fire following a violent explosion. After a moment of silence, there were screams of frightened and wounded people. I don't want to tell you the most chilling details. Suffice it to say that twenty-two people died almost instantly, including all six guards assigned to supervise that area."

Jelko, who was listening carefully to him, interrupted him impatiently: "What was the cause of everything?"

"When I got to the point where I think the explosion originated, I found something incredible. A young wood elf was holding a golden ring with a large red stone set in the shape of a tongue of fire, and the strange thing was why she was there on the ground with her eyes wide open, safe and sound, while around her there was destruction and death."

Jelko moved, recognizing the young Elyn in that elf: "Has nothing been done? Where is she now?"

"She was arrested on charges of being the architect of the explosion. The ring she held in her hand will be examined by the court magicians, then her fate will be decided."

"I can't believe it… Elyn..." he left the sentence hanging to think of when he had met her a few hours earlier, her hair, her green eyes.

Faxel took a long breath then said: "What were you doing with a royal sword? When I found you, you held it tightly to your chest."

"I didn't know it was such a sword. I liked it and I bought it, as I couldn't get it out of my head all day. I'm sorry father, now that I know what sword it was, I understand that I should not have bought it. What has happened?"

Faxel first smiled during that discussion: "It's here under your bed."

Jelko was suddenly enveloped by a hot flash with the thrill of hearing such unexpected and unpredictable news.

After four days in captivity, Elyn was tried and found guilty.

The ring she held in her hand that damned day turned out to be a powerful magical object capable of generating a large explosive fireball.

The same ring that caused the death of innocent people, now, was the reason for her guilt and death.

Having killed for no reason, and moreover of the guards, did not give her any extenuating circumstances.

She would have died the next day on top of a pyre in the public square, the same as the accident, slowly devoured by the flames burned by Faxel, in charge of setting fire to the driest and finest wood placed at the base.

Jelko begged his father not to do so and to try to have the court review the position taken, but every attempt was in vain.

Faxel did not like to attend these executions, much less participate in them, but he would never back down in the face of his duty.

Since he had sworn allegiance as a royal guard, he had never disobeyed an order and did not intend to do so even at the insistence of his son, who was convinced of the girl's innocence.

A friend who had recently studied the art of magic told him that to work, those kinds of rings, must be stuck to the fingers and not simply held in the hand.

But how was it possible that this detail had escaped a court of experts?

Maybe his friend was wrong, but he preferred to believe the opposite.

He tried in various ways to point it out to his father, but he completely put the decision back in the hands of those who knew more about the matter. In any case, he could not do anything and Jelko, on the last day, only begged him not to set the fire.

"How will I be able to look you in the eye after you have killed an innocent woman?" he said in a voice broken by tears.

"Son, that elf is guilty, and if a court of experts and sages says so, it must be true. I will only do what needs to be done, I have not decided to blame her and I would not even want to set fire to the pyre, but this is my job, and in all these years of service I have never failed in my duty."

Jelko could not understand why a just man like his father had to bend before a law that would make him a murderer in a few hours.

Why not rebel? How could he remain so calm knowing what he would do the next day?

Faced with such firmness, he could not say anything else and went to bed with his eyes swollen with tears and a heart full of mixed feelings for Elyn and his father, that if he refused that assignment, he would gain the love of a son he would never lose.

The night was sleepless, thoughts chased each other and sensations expanded.

How did Elyn feel when she was locked up in a damp cell, knowing that the next day she would be taken from there to be burned at the stake?

If only he had been older and had some power, he would never have allowed it, but he could not help but resign himself and helplessly watch the umpteenth error of heartless minds.

That damned day came and seemed to drag on forever.

The square was full of curious and ruthless people. In the center there was the pyre with a large wooden pole in the middle to which the young witch would be tied, and all around was a cordon of guards in a double row.

When the door of the building was opened, which had a few cells inside where the condemned were transferred shortly before their execution, the screams increased in intensity.

Elyn came out with her hands tied, accompanied by two big guards.

She wore a thin white linen dress that highlighted her perfect young body. Her gaze was firm and impassive, almost contemptuous of the death she was facing.

Jelko was far away and in the crowd, but her eyes found him and he felt himself dying inside when she smiled at him.

The cries all around had disappeared. Her eyes squinted and for a moment he seemed to hear Elyn's voice, as weak as that of the sailors' spirits in the brackish winds, tell him something incomprehensible, but extremely reassuring that gave him a feeling of inner peace.

The return to reality was hard.

The young wood elf was at the foot of the pyre where there was also Faxel with a large torch lit.

She was raised and tied to the pole, then wood was accumulated around her. The terrible cry of the crowd now echoed in unison and Faxel set fire to the pyre under the helpless eyes of his son.

Elyn screamed as she burned.

For a moment she could no longer be seen and in her place there was only a dense cloud of smoke, then only flames.

Jelko never forgot that day.

Every time he closed his eyes, he saw her coming out from behind the market stall with her smiling face, the thin body under her tight white robe and her hands outstretched towards him to hug him.

He could not hear the cry of a seagull without seeing her with the eye of the mind.

He thought it would be like this until the day of his death, and even after that, wherever his soul went, she would be there, a little girl burned by order of a ruler, according to the laws, in the splendid Duchy of the Seven Lakes.

CHAPTER 3 (Dreams)

Jelko wandered all day around the city with his eyes lost in the void. The killing of Elyn had shaken him deeply.

He could not think of anything other than that young wood elf who died shortly before, yet already forgotten by all.

The capital was now deserted. The two suns were about to set and his shadow was long and sad. It was getting dark and it was time to go home, but he couldn't find the courage to do so knowing that his father was waiting for him.

It was almost night when he decided to return.

From a distance, he saw the light of a weak lamp. He imagined that Faxel had stood up to tell him something, but he was still too disappointed and angry to speak to him, and he hoped to himself that looking into his father's eyes would not hurt him even more.

He entered, gave a melancholy look at the author of his pain, then walked to the bedroom.

Faxel was about to start a speech. He had spent all evening waiting for his return, but he gave up seeing the sadness and bitterness that invaded the face of his son.

Jelko immediately went to bed without even taking off his clothes, extinguished the two candles hoping to fall asleep as soon as possible so as not to think about that day anymore, trying to erase it from his mind and memories.

He fell asleep almost immediately, but the dream phase was no less painful than when he was awake and conscious.

Now he was on the ground floor, used as a tavern of an inn.

He was at a table alone, and he had to be a few years older because he did not recognize himself in the traits of that young man. He smelled a sudden smell of damp grass, as if he were in the middle of a meadow after a rainy day.

He turned around and realized that, behind him, there was a mysterious tall and slender figure with a large hood that descended on her face, leaving it in dim light.

She moved a few steps towards him and with her hands she made to uncover her face. Then she was shaken by an unknown force, it was as if someone whipped her and gave her powerful slaps from the inside.

Now she was turned away, the wide hood slipped down her back uncovering her neck and nape.

Jelko recognized Elyn by the tattoo in the shape of an imprisoned chrysalis, even more beautiful than he had known her.

This time she was tall and blonde, but she writhed in pain and even her delicate and clear face was all contracted.

In a short time she was completely enveloped by a large tongue of fire, her skin was blackening and her clothes were burning.

Elyn screamed like the day she was burned at the stake, but when she made a louder cry, the flames disappeared.

The girl returned white, almost seeming to emit a faint light of her own as her body slowly levitated upwards.

Jelko got up because he wanted to hold her back and never let her leave, but a mysterious force sat him down and he felt that the forces were slowly abandoning him.

Thoughts were twirling, his eyes closed, yet Elyn was still there watching him from above, then he never saw her again.

He only heard her echoing voice repeat softly: "...*min rakasin... min rakasin...*"

He woke up in shock in his bed all sweaty and with those unknown words still in his head.

The candles were lit.

The window was not well fixed and had opened and now slammed against the wooden wall of the house.

He remained motionless for a moment to recover, then got up, pinned those words in his inseparable leather-lined notebook, closed the window and extinguished the two candles again.

Yet he could no longer fall asleep.

He was constantly thinking about the dream, the meaning it could have, the consolation he had felt in seeing Elyn again, those words of unknown meaning spoken by the girl in a warm and sweet voice.

Thoughts also fell on the previous day.

The pain was still alive. It would leave a scar that perhaps would never heal, and it was like a cross that his heart would carry for the rest of his life.

He thought about why he had become so attached to that elf he hardly even knew, and found himself immersed in the tears of his conscience and without answers.

And his father? What would he tell him the next day?

He still didn't feel like talking to him and maybe his forgiveness would never come.

Confusion took hold of him and his thoughts became turbid.

In such a state of mind, he decided that he would not spend another day under that roof and in that city.

The memory would have been too great and unbearable: every day the same, full of pain and bitterness towards his father and those citizens he had seen with ferocious eyes and veins full of adrenaline for an execution that did not touch them even remotely.

In the middle of the night, he collected in an old backpack the things he considered most useful without making the slightest noise. Every object deemed indispensable was carefully stored. He took the leather water bottle, his notebook and finally pulled out his sword from under the bed.

He looked at it in the faint light of the candles and paused to wonder if that weapon was the cause of everything.

He wrapped the hilt to hide the royal symbols with canvas tape, doing so with extreme care so that the cover was perfect and the grip, in case of need, firm and secure.

Then, he harnessed it with a rope and lowered it from the window so that, if his father heard him immediately afterwards and saw him go down the stairs of the house, it would have been easier to find an excuse, rather than doing the same thing with the backpack on his shoulder.

He walked out of the room and headed for the staircase leading to the ground floor, passed in front of Faxel's door and stopped for a moment, seized by a whirlwind of mixed feelings.

For Jelko, his father had always been everything, from an early age, decisive and tender at the same time, and he was about to break his heart.

What was he to do? He could not resign himself. He was free and without constraints. His father himself had taught him this from an early age.

He gained strength and went down the ladder to get to the door.

He opened it and outside it was just dawn. The air that entered was light and sparkling, which shook him, giving him courage even if soon it would be very hot. Yet in the distance he could see large black clouds that did not portend anything good.

If it had started to rain, it would have been the same thing. In his heart it was already raining and he would wonder if somewhere there was a rain that could wash away his pain.

Backpack on and sword at his side, he headed to the nearest door of the city, without looking back for fear of bursting into tears like a child, and for fear that doubt would catch him for taking too large of a step, for which he would pay the consequences.

He passed in front of the stable where the mule of which he was so fond was kept, he thought of taking it away with him as if it were a memory and a comfort of the life he abandoned, but he would have lost too much time.

The city was slowly awakening. Moreover, his mule was now old and he could not have given it the proper care along the aimless road that he had decided to travel.

He passed by and finally arrived at a city gate. The sentinels were on the two side towers guarding them.

They watched Jelko pass by without question and he imagined that it would not be difficult for his father to track him down there, since probably the guards could not forget that that day, early in the morning, a little boy went out of that door alone.

Not far away flowed the big river that crossed the entire capital and part of the Duchy. It was called 'Xanalea', which in the elven language means 'river of life.'

He had not left the capital in a long time, and in any case never alone.

Fost was a fortified and safe city, and he had never felt the feeling of pondering his every gesture as he did then.

The city was as if it clouded many of his instincts, and he thought that it probably must be so for all the inhabitants.

He had always noticed something more in those merchant travelers who constantly moved from one place to another, who knew how many unexpected events they encountered on the way, yet every year they were there.

This was something that fascinated him, and even more so now that he was alone and outside the solid city walls.

It was as if suddenly the instinct for adventure had strongly awakened in him, and he also thought that perhaps city life was like a cage for all humankind, while that in contact with the world and nature, was real life.

As he walked, he realized that with those thoughts and on that warm morning, his heart had lightened a little.

Now he was truly convinced that he was doing the right thing and he meditated to find a goal and purpose for his escape, as soon as possible.

Absorbed in those thoughts, he walked non-stop until he decided to eat.

The suns were high and the city had become small and distant. He wondered what Faxel was doing and this thought disturbed him a lot.

He approached the bank of the river trying to drive the image of his father out of his mind, imprisoning the water in his spoon-locked hands and throwing it in his face.

He paused for a moment to look at his silhouette reflected in the water.

Jelko was just eighteen years old. His features were almost princely.

He had dark eyes and straight light brown hair that fell just below his chin. He was of medium height and the body outlined agility and strength, thanks also to the training that his father had given him from time to time, to ensure that his son knew how to get by with the sword, at least in the simplest situations.

He took a ration of food from his backpack and ate with healthy voraciousness.

He was still too close to the capital and decided not to stay too long.

He spent the whole afternoon walking.

He never looked back and with every step freedom grew within him, keeping him from feeling tired. Yet he felt strange, because ever since he had left Fost, something inside told him to go North.

It was almost evening when he arrived at a point where the river went into a dense forest, so he decided to enter it continuing to skirt the shore a little more, before stopping to have dinner and spend the night.

Tired, he fell asleep and dreamed of something vague about demons or something similar, or maybe even some tale of the past that resurfaced.

Suddenly a noise aroused him.

His senses were at their best, alone and in a forest on one of the usual nights without stars and moons to illuminate them a little.

Instinct told him not to move.

He listened, it could easily be a nocturnal animal. He waited, holding his breath as much as possible so as not to make noise.

He heard a rustle. Something went away and he started breathing again.

He held the sword tightly to himself, let time pass, and with the slightest noise tried to relax to fall asleep again.

Now it was not long before dawn.

He heard another close noise and was amazed at how even this time he managed not to get too agitated. When he opened his eyes he seemed to see two tall figures, not far away, hiding behind two distinct trees.

It was still night, yet he saw something over there.

Perhaps the two figures had a small torch that they then immediately put out, otherwise it was not possible to see someone in the totally dark nights of that world.

He seemed to suffocate. He began to breathe again and to think about what to do.

He warned slowly that any blows could come from any side.

He saw absolutely nothing. Hearing was the only sense to rely on.

A time passed that seemed eternal to him and finally a slight glow began to peep out on the horizon. Now it was dawn and he seemed to be reborn after a wait that never ended.

With that faint light, he looked better in the direction where he had seemed to see something not so long before.

There was nothing strange. He got up, and always on guard, he cautiously approached those two trees.

There was nothing.

He did not want to give particular weight to the thing. It was only the first night away from home. At this rate, his adventure would not last long and he would have been forced to go back reluctantly, only for fear of something that in the end he had only seemed to see.

See? In the nights of that world, if there had been someone, he had to have a light source. Otherwise, it was inexplicable how it was possible to see something in total darkness.

He chased away that thought and to reassure himself, he thought that maybe it was just the aftermath of a nightmare.

After all, he had dreamed of demons that night, fished out of who knows what stories, probably of when the planet was invaded more than ten years before.

He promised himself to look for some safer place for the following night, hopefully near a village if only he had found one, or maybe right inside it somewhere, even in the street or in a barn, it would not have been a problem.

He checked what he had taken. From home he had taken all his coins. It was good that, just days before, he had sold almost all his rings and medallions.

Even he had brought a good supply of food. He could have bought it along the way in some inn, or he could have tried to collect or hunt something.

He set out again, continuing to keep an eye on the river as a landmark.

He was going North. For now he just wanted to get as far as possible from the capital of the Duchy. In fact, he believed he was still too close. At the time this destination was enough for him.

The Duchy was just a beautiful place.

Its lakes and large river made it rich in vegetation, a precious asset in a rather arid and hot planet like that.

Life was certainly much more bearable here.

Who knows what those places that he had heard of were like, those close to the great central desert, certainly much less livable and extreme than here.

Maybe he would have seen them, after all from the South coast he was going in that direction, even though the distance, especially on foot, was huge.

If he had a horse, it would have been different, he thought, he who owned only a mule on whose back he was barely able to stand.

He wasn't able to ride, and only now he regretted never having considered it important.

CHAPTER 4 (The Chosen Ones)

The tall blonde elf was hit in the side by a small tongue of fire. The blow interrupted her concentration and the sphere of protection around her vanished.

The great invasion of the Sleepless Ones had ended not even a year earlier. Symbol was still in turmoil.

On the other side of the containment pentacle, drawn on the floor of the tower room on which they were standing, a tall, blonde elf like her was preparing to cast another spell.

The elf closed her eyes for a moment, drawing a circle in the air with one arm. Again, a bubble sparkling like metal reappeared, enveloping the space immediately around her body.

She nodded her head and threw a ray as black as night towards the enemy.

He dodged it and the blow ended up against the wall behind him, destroying a piece.

Shaking his hands, the elf threw a new fiery tongue that struck the sphere of protection surrounding the rival, causing it to dissolve again.

She took a wavy-bladed dagger from a boot and hurled herself at him, injuring him in the shoulder.

He said: "You have come a long way. Your void magic is powerful, from nothing to the Chosen One of our people in such a short time. It is not for everyone. Or now do I have to call you my Lady?"

She did not answer. She tried to hit him again with the dagger, but this time in vain.

He said again: "You won't be able to defeat me, I'm stronger than you. Admit it!"

He hit her with a kick and walked a few steps away.

She stood on the ground, closed her eyes and concentrated.

As during an earthquake, all the books and objects on the shelves began to tremble and fall on the floor.

Now he seemed almost paralyzed.

She controlled him and tried to slow him down until he was still, but it was difficult, too difficult. His mind was as strong as hers and she felt that she was about to lose concentration.

She barely had time to get on her feet before losing control.

Nodding lightly with her head, she threw another beam of black energy the instant she lost mental contact.

The elf was shot in the chest and the backlash threw him against a table, overturning it.

She was tired. Mind control required enormous stress, and the mind of her brother, a Chosen One like her, was hardly trivial.

He got up, threw again a tongue of fire that fully struck her, throwing her ruinously out of the pentacle and almost unconscious.

From a distance, he gestured.

An intense red light immediately came around her, raised both arms and lifted her off the ground, causing her to float slowly towards him.

—It's over— she thought, facing her brother.

He said: "You can say goodbye to your people who have so benevolently denied me. I will have no mercy for you either, even though I cannot kill you. You all will never find a new place to settle."

The elf began a kind of litany.

She felt that her forces were slowly abandoning her. It was pleasant after so much physical and mental exertion. It was like relaxing after an exhausting day.

She recognized those words spoken by her brother as the terrible Curse of the Chains.

She didn't care, her mind was now empty, she knew what she was up against, but now she was relaxed, she was fine, she almost felt the warmth of a fireplace in the middle of winter.

She liked that feeling, and she surrendered completely to the ritual that was given to her.

CHAPTER 5 (Blood)

A few days had passed since Jelko had set out on a journey. His food was starting to run out and he had moved far enough from the capital.

He had to find a way to get it or to find at least a village and an inn to stock up on. He had always skirted the river overcoming the last of the seven lakes North of the Duchy.

The Xanalea river, his reference, would continue until it left the borders to get to its source in the mountains of the peaceful Kingdom of Kernof.

Where would he go? He thought about it every day.

He knew that on the border there were villages on the banks of the river inhabited mainly by merchants. He thought that he would stop there at least for a day, for supplies and to decide the next destination.

To be honest, he also felt the need to see human beings in the flesh.

He calculated that the next day he would probably be near those commercial villages, where goods from other kingdoms were stored and then gradually descended to the South to be sold.

A few hours ago he had begun to see the outermost wall that isolated the Duchy from the rest of the world, so they should not have been very far away. One last night, probably.

After five days and five nights, in the evening now he had his ritual.

Shortly before sunset he carefully looked for a sheltered and hidden place in the dense forest where he was, always near the river. He put everything down carefully, clutched his sword to himself and fell asleep without waiting long.

He walked all day, so fatigue was a good ally in this regard.

The first day he had dreamed of demons. The next day he dreamed that what he thought was his mother, whom he had never known, had been killed by the same demons as the day before.

The other dreams he was too tired to remember.

Crack!

He woke up in shock after clearly hearing a twig break under the weight of something.

In the usual pitch dark, he slowly managed to focus, glimpsing a plump figure moving with little dexterity and seeking shelter behind a rock.

—For all the Gods! There are no lights, but I can see!— he thought, bewildered.

He was sure of it: the humanoid figure just beyond did not have a torch in its hand. It was neither dawn nor sunset, so there could be no other light sources. It was not a perfect vision as in the daytime, but he could catch a glimpse just enough to have the right perception of what surrounded him.

He was upset by this thing, but at that moment he was more worried about who that figure was. Maybe it had not even noticed that he was there, but then why was it hiding?

Maybe it too saw in the dark to wander around at night in a forest?

He took up his sword with all the courage he had and rose up calmly.

The sight came and went, but it was enough to understand how to put his feet.

He took a few steps towards that boulder and when he was a short distance away, he said: "Who is behind it? I know you're there. Come out slowly and nothing bad will happen!"

No one answered.

He went around the rock and saw a figure curled up on himself as if to protect himself, and finally said: "Do not hurt me, I am unarmed, please!"

"Get up slowly and keep your hands in plain sight. I must be able to see them well at the top, do you understand?" Jelko told him.

"And how do you deal with this darkness? I have a small torch with me. Do I have to light it so that I can see you too?"

It was true. He could not explain it either, but this at the time gave him a big advantage. He had no idea who he was and what intentions that little man in front of him had.

"No, no torch, they would see us from afar. For now it is not needed, as long as you stay exactly where you are. Sit slowly, I do not think you are armed."

"Yes, of course, but please don't hurt me."

Jelko asked: "Who are you and what are you doing here in the middle of the night?"

The sight kept coming and going.

"My name is Peryl. I was trying to reach the villages nearby, but I must have got lost and ended up here by mistake. I thought I still had some light to move, but in such a dense forest, I overestimated the time I had available and the night caught me off guard."

"You don't have any kind of travel equipment" Jelko noted, "just a small bag with something inside. Where do you come from? With just the torch you said you had, you wouldn't have gone far."

"Oh yes, of course. I live a few hours from here, I'm a merchant. Yesterday we celebrated a big sale of fabrics. We definitely drank too much and honestly, I don't even remember how I got here."

He laughed a little laugh and continued: "If you need something, tomorrow I can take you to the village where I live and offer you a hot meal. Here with me I only have cookies."

"Great!" thought Jelko, a hot meal would not have displeased him at all.

He said: "I was just going to one of the villages on the border. If yours is one of those it is right where I am headed."

"Perfect then! Very gladly! Can I know your name?"

"My name is Jelko. There are a couple of hours left until dawn, let's rest a little more and wait for tomorrow morning to move."

"Of course" said Peryl, "I wouldn't want to end up even further than I already am. Would you like a couple of cookies in the meantime?"

Jelko was hungry since morning, he had begun to ration the little food he had left, so he accepted and ate those cookies offered in one bite.

He got half-lying not far away. He actually smelled the scent of those who drank too much coming from Peryl. He looked lucid when they had spoken just before, but evidently he was still drunk because he fell asleep immediately.

—Why can I see him?— he wondered, —why?—

There was no peace, such a thing was not normal, it had never happened to him when he was at home since he had memory.

—But then even the first night, when I seemed to see those two tall figures hiding behind the trees, I was not mistaken!—

This didn't really explain it, even if it was like seeing little more than shadows. No, it was definitely not normal.

He closed his eyes, now it was dark and fell asleep.

Even that night he returned to dream of demons in a very chaotic way, without any logical thread between one part of the dream and the other. It was now quite recurrent.

At one point he seemed to feel something hot dripping on his face and a feeling of physical discomfort.

He slowly opened his eyes. It had been dawn for a while and he was amazed that he had slept so much.

Peryl was above him with a hellish look and drool in his mouth: "End of the games, my friend. It's time to fulfill my mission!"

Jelko noticed that his hands were tied with a thin, but sturdy lace behind his back. His head was ringing and he was definitely dazed.

"Those cookies were good, weren't they? They always do their dirty work without any problem. Too bad you'll never find anyone to share any impressions with."

Jelko, still shaken, began to gather his thoughts and said: "Tonight we agreed that we would go to your village in the morning. What the hell is going on with you? I don't recognize you, you look like another person. Take the gold I have if you want and free me!"

"Do you see this?" said Peryl.

Even his voice seemed slightly different: "It is my Lord who commands me!"

He pulled out a small amethyst amulet that he had around his neck.

The stone was beautiful. The purple almost seemed to pulsate with its own light.

Peryl suddenly pulled a small dagger out of his sleeve. It was easily concealed, which is why Jelko had not seen it the night before.

He cursed himself for being stupid enough not to search him, and for trusting a complete stranger wandering alone in a forest in the middle of the night.

The merchant was still on top of him. He was lying on the ground supine. He had already tried in the meantime to free himself with a few tugs, but those laces, although thin, were very resistant.

Jelko exclaimed: "What are you saying? Take everything I have and free me!"

The situation began to become critical. The man seemed really convinced that he had to carry out the order given to him by his Lord.

He began to agitate and Jelko feared he was becoming uncontrollable.

Peryl approached the dagger to Jelko's eye.

His gaze was fierce and impassive: "I could have killed you before you woke up without even needing to tie you up, but seeing you suffer will repay some of my sadistic instincts that I have always had. And then He needs to know a few things."

He dangerously brought the blade closer to one eye.

"No!" shouted Jelko, turning his head as he could to one side, and the dagger wounded him in the cheek.

Peryl seemed even more out of his mind for missing and said: "Stand still, you cursed fool! I will make you suffer even more and you will also pay for the fact that you rebelled against His will!"

Jelko felt something strange growing inside him.

It was not fear, which he had had for a long time, and it was almost unmanageable.

It was something else, uncontrollable, something that made him jump, but much faster than fear.

He felt his heart running wildly, breathing fast, blood swelling every single vein in his body, a sensation never experienced before.

With last tug on the ties that he had on his wrists and with an unexpected force, he broke them, freeing himself, took Peryl's head, approached it with a lightning gesture and detached a piece of his ear with a bite.

The man rolled to his side, bleeding and cursing.

Jelko in a moment was on him again, he could not control himself. He took another bite into one of the fleshy cheeks, making him scream in pain.

This time it was Peryl who was petrified by the unexpected evolution of the situation.

"Stop! I didn't want to! Don't hurt me please!" the voice was trembling with fear and it seemed that the timbre was that of the night before.

Jelko didn't even hear him, he could hold him still with the strength of one arm. Maybe adrenaline or something inexplicable made him extraordinarily strong.

He took him by the neck and slowly lifted just off the ground.

—What's happening to me?— he thought, only for a moment. The blood on that face deformed by fear pleased him and excited him.

He wanted to see him dead. Right now.

He threw him without any effort against the rock behind which he had fallen asleep the night before. The poor man slammed ruinously against it, falling to the ground without strength.

Jelko, almost in a trance, picked up the small dagger with which Peryl had wounded him just before and slowly approached him.

He hurled it with great force with one arm. He thought he could tear him to pieces with his bare hands. He felt strange, strong, invincible but not lucid, at least not for how he intended to be lucid and rational.

He took his head with one hand while the man was trying to get up painfully, perhaps even this time with too much strength because it almost broke his neck.

He passed the blade across his throat from side to side. Blood splashed profusely in his face and the thing infused him with a strange feeling of macabre pleasure.

He remembered having a ring-shaped seal with him. He had forged it himself in his small forge at the house.

His father had told him a story of a glorious guild of merchants now fallen, they had as a symbol an oak leaf and they called themselves the Merchants of Leaves.

He reproduced the coat of arms of that guild looking for some images in the library of the capital.

He took it from his backpack, bathed it with Peryl's blood and in the middle of that man's forehead imprinted that mark with ease and coldness.

Then he fell to his knees almost exhausted, sweat mixed with blood: —What have I done? I've killed a man!—

He couldn't explain it. It couldn't have been him, not the one he knew at least.

Very little time had passed.

Peryl was still there on the ground, dead for a few minutes now, yet it seemed to have happened a lifetime ago.

He was slowly coming to his senses, sat a little further, took a series of deep breaths and tried to calm down.

—And now what do I do? It wasn't me! It couldn't be me! I defended myself, it's his fault. He drugged me, he tried to kill me and I lost my mind!—

A set of thoughts overwhelmed him. He remembered that this man wanted to take him out, he remembered those laces that first kept his wrists tied behind his back and from which he had freed himself with unexpected strength.

He remembered the demonic look above him, the dagger that wounded him by order of his Lord, then anger, then again anger, then almost nothing.

Far from there, in the faint light of a candle, a worn face watched through the thin veil of amber water inside a large bowl of black stone.

The plan hadn't worked, but it wasn't a problem, he had plenty of time to try again.

CHAPTER 6 (The Caravan)

He spent almost the whole afternoon away from the site of the clash.

He found a small hill where the trees were more sparse at the top. He had run out of what little food he had left, finding a few berries here and there that left his stomach emptier than before. He certainly could not have replaced the meals with those in the long run.

Even while he was looking for something to put under his teeth, his thoughts were always turned to what had happened on the morning of that same day: —Incredible, I still can't believe it. It wasn't me. No, I can't have killed that man.—

He did not give himself peace. He thought while picking the berries to eat, eating them absorbed in a thousand thoughts.

He did not know how to hunt. Hunger could have pushed him to one of the villages nearby, but he was afraid.

—What if that something took hold of me while I was among the villagers?— he kept repeating to himself as his hunger grew.

He camped near the clearing at the top of the hill.

As night fell he saw, not far away, some lights were lit at the nearest settlement, which gave him some warmth while he felt infinitely alone.

The village was really a stone's throw away and he wanted to go there with all of himself.

He had money. He would eat everything his empty stomach could contain.

But he still could not take that step. He was afraid. Who knows if someone would come to look for the man he had killed with anger and bestial ferocity that morning, and who knows how he would have reacted to any accusations?

And who was that Lord of which Peryl spoke?

It was very strange that someone wanted him dead. He had never left the capital, except with his father sometimes, and he did not remember ever doing such a great wrong to anyone.

He was sure there had to be a mix-up or a misunderstanding.

—Ah! If I had never left home! I would be safe in my usual life without a care!—

He repeated it often and even thought of going back, but the food was still a problem. He was about a week away from home. He had to fix it somehow, then he would decide what to do.

The sunset was almost over and the darkness began to come forward. Even the lights of the village that he kept an eye on and that kept him company, began to go dark until only a few remained glowing, here and there.

—I have to sleep. Everything will be fine. I just have to sleep and not think about anything— he repeated while lying on the fresh grass.

He opened and closed his eyes continuously to see if he could see even shadows. For him it was now the signal that something was inside him.

And yes, even if not clearly, when there was no longer any light around him, he could see what surrounded him.

—But why? It's not good. It's not good at all, that something is here tonight too!—

He curled up as much as possible on himself and tried to relax as best he could. Finally, thanks to the unusual day, hunger and fatigue, he managed to fall asleep laboriously.

That night he did not dream of the usual demons in a chaotic, meaningless way. This time he dreamed again of that hooded and tall female figure, like the night before leaving home.

She was seated, her hands tied behind the chair with large, heavy chains, her head lowered to her chest.

On the ground, there were traces of blood.

She seemed to be in a room, yet he could not see where the walls ended, the whole thing was wrapped in a strange foggy penumbra.

The hooded figure slowly raised its head and Jelko once again recognized Elyn, tall and blonde as in the dream of a week before.

Her face, despite everything recalling the torture that took place shortly before, was as always relaxed and of a disarming serenity.

He tried to get closer, but the distance did not decrease despite him was walking faster and faster towards her.

At one point he stopped. She looked at him intensely and he heard words enter his head: *"... vanimar laita... vanimar laita..."*

He woke up in shock, wrapped in the smell of freshly cut damp grass, just like every time he dreamed of her.

It was just dawn. He looked around quickly. He did not notice anything strange, the night had passed without anything happening, apart from the dream. He calmed down.

The hunger cramps were getting stronger and stronger, and he had nothing left to eat.

—I'm going crazy!— he thought as he pinned down the words in his inseparable leather-covered notebook.

—Even dreams torture me.—

He glanced at the village from the clearing not far from where he had slept and said to himself: —Let's go and look for food, nothing bad can happen.—

He repeated those words continuously while storing his things and preparing the small travel backpack. He pinned his sword to his side and walked with those words in his head to gain strength.

—Nothing bad can happen.—

He arrived at the gates of the village at mid-morning, a small wooden palisade surrounded it. He headed towards what looked like one of the entrance doors.

He immediately noticed that there was a lot of hustle and bustle. The village was probably awake from the first light of dawn, it was very alive and busy already from outside.

There were wagons full of goods, people on foot and on horseback, a few guards here and there.

In short, he would certainly not have imagined so much movement in a small place like that.

Yet he should have expected it. After all, it was one of the many merchants' trading villages that were on the border with the other kingdoms, and he understood that probably the rhythm of those places was like that more or less all year round.

He passed the door for arranging the goods.

No one controlled who entered or left, it would not have been easy with all those people. He headed towards what he believed to be the center of the village, as did most of the people around him.

—Finally, a bit of life— he thought.

At every step, he felt better. He was in a decidedly more comfortable place, even if he did not know anyone. He was in the midst of civilization, and no longer alone in a forest among murderers or dreaming of demons or hooded elves.

As in the days of market for the God of trade Venakin, which was celebrated for days in the capital from which he came, here too there were different races, probably from various remote places, all with the aim of selling or buying exotic goods to take elsewhere.

It was the most home-like place he could have seen since he had left a week earlier, though unknown and much smaller.

In one of the streets overlooking the main square, which for the size of the village was actually quite large, he finally noticed an inn.

The sign was made of wood and a bit run down. It bore the inscription 'The Squire.' He hastened his step as he could put something in his stomach, opened the door and entered.

The inn, dark like most of them, had some dark wooden tables in the center and stools along the walls with shelves on which patrons could satisfy their hunger.

Only one table was occupied by two people from behind, they were eating something and had two large mugs nearby.

For the rest it was empty. On the other hand, it was mid-morning and probably would have filled up later. It was a little outside the normal eating hours, but he had been hungry from the day before so he did not pay too much attention to it.

The innkeeper, a man of medium stature, thin and with a long black beard, was placing bowls behind the counter. Next to him was a thin woman, probably his wife, who instead was intent on drying some wooden mugs with a not-too-clean cloth.

They both looked at Jelko without saying a word.

It was he who said: "Good morning! I would like to eat immediately and if possible also buy something to take away."

"Good morning boy" said the man behind the counter, "sit wherever you want, my wife will bring you the dish of the day as soon as it is ready."

He noticed stairs going upstairs and said: "Perfect, thank you. Do you also have rooms to spend a night or two?"

"Yes of course, there are a couple of free ones if you want. Where are you headed? Are you an apprentice merchant? Obviously, you cannot answer. We of the trade always see a lot of people and we always ask the usual questions" said the innkeeper with a slight joking smile.

"No, I'm not a merchant, I'm just passing through, I'm going back to the South to the capital, Fost."

He told him that he was going to the opposite side. He did not want him to know too much about his plans, also because in reality he did not have well-defined ones and not telling the exact truth seemed to him the wisest thing.

"Do you need a stable for your horse? Or maybe even for your friends if you're not alone? There's one back here."

Jelko was almost tripped up by all those questions, but promptly replied: "No need, my friends camped just outside the village. My horse is there with them. I just came to eat and look for some food to take away for the next few days."

"Well" said the innkeeper, "I would like to ask you why you asked me a little while ago if there were rooms for the night. If your friends are outside, you could sleep with them, unless bad blood flows between you! But let's leave it alone, it's not my business. Sit down, my wife is going to serve you."

—How stupid of me. I have to speak less— he thought to himself as he sat down.

One of the two men at the table further on looked like he was laughing.

The innkeeper's wife arrived with two bowls, one with some bread and spicy game, the other with fresh fruit.

"What do you want to drink?" she asked without pleasantries.

"Only water, thank you."

The woman turned around and went back to the kitchen. The man who sneered earlier did it again.

Shortly afterwards, the two patrons got up and after paying the innkeeper they left.

Jelko ate everything and felt much better. He stocked up on travel food and decided to book a bed.

At least for that night, he wanted to sleep on something other than grass in a forest.

He came out of the inn, he wanted to take another look out there at that village teeming with busy people. The Squire was a stone's throw from the main square and in a very short time he was in the middle of it.

He realized how crowded it was. Everywhere there were people bargaining and observing people evaluating goods, weapons, embroidered fabrics, rather valuable pottery and even footwear.

He also noticed three carriages reinforced with metal bars.

Ten guards were standing all around them. He imagined they were transporting prisoners to who-knows-where and meeting who-knows-what fate.

They too had made a brief stop in the village before leaving.

One of these guards, perhaps the lieutenant, often spoke with citizens who approached him to ask him questions.

He did not hear what was being said. Some looked like the same merchants who were there in the square. Others were couples holding children's hands. Some were simply alone.

Intrigued, Jelko approached a man and a woman with two children, a boy and a girl, and asked: "Excuse me! I arrived a little while ago in this village. I noticed those three reinforced carriages, can you tell me if they carry prisoners?"

"Oh yes" replied the man, "they are headed to Argoran prison. They will leave tomorrow morning and a caravan is forming. We and many others are heading North, so we are organizing to join them."

"I understand. Can everyone join?" asked Jelko curiously.

"Yes of course, you can join the caravan whenever you want and jump down as soon as you get close to your destination. It is much safer to travel in a group and this time there are prisoners and therefore armed guards. The important thing is that you are self-sufficient. Probably others will be added along the way, but you will not find people willing to feed you or quench your thirst, and if you are left behind no one will wait for you, unless you have some kind-hearted travel companion."

"It seems right to me. You will all be on horseback or with wagons I guess."

"Not at all" said the man, "you travel on foot, or rather, if you have a horse you can take it and ride it. If you have a chariot come with that, but you will still go at the lowest pace."

"I understand. Thanks for the information and have a good day!"

He spent the afternoon in the streets of that village.

He was amazed once again at how it was always constantly active almost everywhere, and he decided to join the caravan that would leave the next day from the main square.

There was no point in staying there. He would go to the last city to the North before the caravan disbanded to let the guards with the tanks of prisoners continue alone towards Argoran.

It was in fact forbidden to bring any civilian there. On the last day of march to the prisons it was mandatory that only soldiers, prisoners and any officials were sent there for any reason.

Merchants continued to fascinate him. He had always been curious to see goods from who-knows-where or with particular features.

In every corner, there was someone bargaining. Nobody seemed to have time to lose. Each sale seemed to be noisier than that of the previous street, especially when they arrived at the price shortly after establishing the quantity.

From what he had seen, the merchants were like that, animatedly boisterous.

At dinner time, he decided to return to the inn where he had also booked a bed to spend the night. He was already quite tired.

When he entered this time, he found it crowded and the voices bypassed each other forcefully.

He greeted the busy innkeeper with a nod and sat on a stool against the wall where there were shelves to place the bowls with food.

The innkeeper's wife noticed that he had arrived and headed to the kitchen.

"They found him with a blood mark on the forehead of the Merchants of Leaves!" he heard from a table with six diners.

"His throat was cut from ear to ear, and the hunters who found him say that his face had been torn to shreds, as if an animal had raged and cut it to pieces in bites."

"But how is this possible?" said the alarmed neighbor, "the Merchants of Leaves have not existed for at least twenty years. It must be a macabre joke, or a ritual for who-knows-what deity!"

Next to him was a small square table with two well-dressed men: "Poor Peryl. He was a good man."

There was no talk of anything else. Each table had its own theory, some bizarre, others the result of really exaggerated fantasies.

Evidently Peryl was quite well known in the village.

—They found the body of the man who tried to kill me!—Jelko thought, stretching his ears as much as possible, but trying to pretend not to be interested and making himself small on his stool.

The innkeeper's wife brought him food and water. He began to eat as if it were the only thing that interested him.

—If only they knew that it was he who bound me and tried to murder me in my sleep— he thought, freezing in remembrance of how he had killed him, with how much ferocity and superhuman strength he had discovered with amazement that he had at that moment.

He had repeated to himself a thousand times that something had happened to him and that he could not be the boy he knew he was. A mysterious force had taken hold of him. He remembered that anger was uncontrollable, there was something strange about it.

—But how did it occur to me to mark that man with his own blood with the symbol of the Merchants of Leaves?—

He knew summarily who the members of that guild were.

They were unscrupulous merchants, often indirectly violent, who had control over the markets of half the world.

Almost everything passed through their hands. They decided the good and bad weather regarding the affairs of any kind of goods. Having them against someone was a big problem, and if they had an obstacle, they would eliminate it somehow.

It disintegrated within a couple of years, following feuds between the same members after many years of glorious activity.

The guild had become too powerful and the members too numerous and greedy.

By now, all that remained was a memory, for many even painfully mortal.

Slowly, the speeches began to divert on the day just passed, on what to do the next day and small anecdotes that the patrons, almost all merchants, told each other between the tables.

Finally, the man he had murdered in defense was no longer the main topic. He finished eating and went to the counter to pay and ask for access to the upper floor to go to sleep.

After taking the money, the innkeeper said: "Your room is the one at the top of the stairs on the left. There are three beds, take whatever you want. Unless someone arrives shortly, you will be alone."

"Very well" answered Jelko, "I'll pay for the bed now. I'll leave very early in the morning."

"Okay, as you like. In any case, you will find me here early tomorrow morning too. Sleep well boy."

He went upstairs and entered the room that had been assigned to him: a small room with three straw beds. The blankets on top were worn and not exactly clean. It was a very common inn and he certainly couldn't expect who-knows-what.

He could hear the shouting in the distance coming from downstairs.

He put his backpack and sword under the bed and hoped to have a good sleep until dawn. After all, he was in a more comfortable place than the woods, where he had slept for a week.

—I hope not to have strange dreams tonight. I need to rest— he told himself.

He took his notebook, wrote down the day, the name of the inn he was in, and reread the words that Elyn had always repeated twice in his dreams.

—Who knows if they have a meaning or is it just a figment of my imagination? It sounds like an elven language, but I don't know a word. If I were at home, I would have had my father ask the court wizards. After what has been happening to me in so few days, I would no longer be surprised by anything.—

Tired and tried by the emotions of recent events, he fell asleep immediately.

He did not even notice that someone closed the door of his own room after entering it silently.

CHAPTER 7 (Heading to Argoran)

The next morning he woke up very early. He felt rested, as he had finally had a peaceful sleep.

Outside, he could already hear voices, even if not as in broad daylight.

No one had joined him in that room. It was just like when he fell asleep. He got up, put on his boots and pulled out his backpack and sword from under the bed.

He immediately realized, however, that something was wrong.

He was very meticulous in arranging his things. He knew that it was important. His father had taught him that, saying that the ability of a good soldier can also be seen in how he shines and takes care of his equipment.

He looked at the door and noticed that it was open.

He had forgotten to pull it shut. He had been too tired and those voices coming from downstairs kept him company as he fell asleep. Even if he could not have covered it, it would have been better to close it. If someone had entered, perhaps he would have made more noise.

He emptied on the worn wooden floor all the contents of the backpack. Nothing was missing. Yet he was sure that he had not put it in that position with the sword under the backpack.

He always put it on top, so that it was easier to take in case of need. The night before he had been very tired, and perhaps since he felt safe, he had committed the sin of not paying too much attention to the arrangement of the backpack and sword.

He went down to the ground floor and, although it was very early, the innkeeper was already in his place as announced the night before: "Good morning!" the man anticipated him from behind the counter.

"Good morning" replied Jelko, "I forgot to fill up my water bottle. Is there a fountain nearby?"

"Yes of course. You'll find one in one of the corners of the main square."

"Perfect. I was going right there."

The innkeeper pulled out two eggs from under the counter and said: "Our present: a nice breakfast is what it takes, come back soon to visit us!"

"If I pass by this way, very gladly! Your cooking is not bad."

He took the eggs and went out.

The square was not far away and when he arrived it was already crowded with wagons full of goods, others with entire families on top. A good part was on foot like him, all headed somewhere to the North forming a caravan of a hundred people and about thirty wagons and shabby carts.

At the head were those of the prisoners, with the guards around intent on checking the horses and the very doors of the carriages that were all at the back. On the sides, but only on one side, iron bars served as the only intake of air and light for the inmates who were inside.

He quickly headed to the fountain that he identified in one of the corners of the square to fill the water bottle and returned more or less halfway through the long snake that the caravan formed, twisting on itself due to the little space left available.

He noticed a little further on the couple who had given him information the day before with the two children, nodded his head, and they reciprocated by greeting with their hands. He did not immediately approach them. He did not want to be too intrusive, but he decided to keep an eye on them, since they were the only known people who, like him, were leaving.

The caravan never seemed to leave.

He decided to walk it to the head. He was intrigued by those reinforced carriages, which were not far ahead of where he was.

"Hey! Not so close. You can't stay there, go back to your place!" thundered a guard who was between the second and third chariots.

He quickly approached him and said: "Did you hear me or are you deaf?"

From inside the last carriage, he heard that someone moved to run to the bars and look. He could not see his or her face in dim light.

He only saw the hands clinging to the bars.

"Please, excuse me sir, it was not my intention to get so close. I walked overthinking and I did not notice it" he lied promptly.

"You can't get close, it's already too much that our lieutenant allows you yokels to form a caravan with us. Go back to your place and stay there!"

"It won't happen again" Jelko said, turning in his footsteps.

As he walked back, he heard the order to leave from the head of the caravan, and finally the long snake of people and wagons began to move.

Initially there was a continuous starting and stopping soon after, but just outside the village, the march began to be regular, even if slow.

Three days passed.

The three chariots of prisoners were always at the head slightly spaced from the rest of the caravan, as they proceeded someone detached because they arrived close to their destination, and others aggregated.

Jelko had exchanged a few words with the neighbors, and slowly he had approached the man and the woman with the two children with whom he had certainly become more in tune since the day before departure.

During the journey, from time to time, he played with the couple's children, albeit quietly so as not to disturb the rest of the caravan.

All in all, they proceeded in silence. It was never wise to get noticed by making too much noise. Even if they were many, you could never know how many brigands could be out there, and a caravan of such a size could not easily go unnoticed.

Every night he went to sleep a little further, behind some trees when they were close enough. He was still afraid that something would take hold of him. For now, the previous nights had passed without problems and he did not want to risk it.

Seeing in the dark was becoming easier and easier. The images became sharper, as if he were practicing with his new inexplicable ability.

On the fourth night he took advantage of it and approached the three reinforced carriages.

The guards kept very small lights lit on the ground under dark domes all around the wagons. They were not easily visible from a distance given the size, but in case of need it was enough to discover them to be able to see in the dark night without stars and moons of that world.

He did not want to risk getting too close. He was left with curiosity about those silent prisoners inside the carriages. They seemed almost empty, but in the last one he had seen with his own eyes that at least one detainee was there when they had left the village square a few days before.

—They don't necessarily want to talk— he thought, —they are taking them to Argoran. They will probably never return from that place, who knows what they have done to deserve such a sentence.—

Argoran was a completely unusual prison.

It had no perimeter walls, as they were not needed, it stood in the only existing oasis of the great central desert.

Those who escaped would die by the end of the following day from too much heat. To get to safety, it took at least three days of marching, but no one had ever survived the second.

There were no guards in Argoran and the prisoners were abandoned not far away.

The jailers, on the last day of the march, had to proceed without civilians.

It was the rule that everyone was given a ring to wear infused with a magical power that, together with the others, conferred an aura of impenetrable protection. The soldiers only then freed the prisoners, who were pushed out of the aura and could no longer return.

Any assaults by the other convicts, who saw the reinforced tanks with the new prisoners coming from afar, were useless.

The magical aura could not be overcome and the guards went back quietly once their delivery was completed.

By now Argoran was no longer controlled by the troops of the various kingdoms. It had become a kind of dump of humans and other races.

Over time it became a real city.

The condemned residents, men and women, had organized themselves, giving life to a kind of society apart. Slowly, castes had formed among the various most violent and elderly prisoners.

The leader had long called himself the "Yalla."

It was he who decided everything, surrounded by brigands and criminals, the worst of the whole oasis.

The Yalla was the only cornerstone in a community that would otherwise have been even more anarchic.

For years now, the only commitment of the neighboring kingdoms was to bring food from time to time, even if Argoran itself had its own modest and rudimentary food production.

Argoran did not have to disappear. After all, it could be convenient for some king to get rid of someone forever without having to get their hands dirty with blood.

It was said that many desperate people had tried to escape.

No one held them back, and all the guards who had brought the detainees, told of a huge amount of human remains all around the oasis within a day's march.

Once there, you were forgotten by the rest of the world.

From Argoran you did not leave, much less alive, if not by order of some king, who for an absurd reason wanted to grant an unexpected grace to a condemned in exile.

CHAPTER 8 (Revelations)

Meanwhile, somewhere far away...

"It's time. At the first light of dawn, you will complete your task, you cannot fail."

"We shall not fail, my Lord. And all the others? We can't think of them either."

"I'll take care of the rest..."

On the fifth day of the trip, the caravan found itself skirting the mountains that divide the Kingdom of Miriam from the Kingdom of Sand.

It entered a rather vast forest, but with not very dense trees, yet sufficient to give a little coolness. The journey began to be heavy for those who, like Jelko, had been on the march from day one.

The number of travelers was always more or less the same.

Many had arrived near their destinations and had detached themselves from the caravan. As many had joined, now half the faces were new.

"In two days at this time we will have arrived at our destination. And what will you do? When will you get to yours?" said the man as he and his wife helped the children wash near a small stream they were crossing.

"I don't know yet" said Jelko, "to tell the truth, I don't have a real goal." He felt he could trust that family, they were always very humble and kind to him.

"Why don't you stay a few days with us? We are going to my father, he has a big farm. We have room and we would be happy to host you, we will move there for a while."

Jelko liked the idea. It seemed like a sincere proposal and maybe he could really relax, even if just for a couple of days.

"If I don't disturb, gladly! I will not stay more than a few days, I promise! So I'll also stock up on food, I'm almost done with it."

"Ah well, at my father's farm there is always something to do. If there is no more left to do, we find it, food included!"

Jelko took the couple's little girl on his shoulders, took her for a ride as if she were riding a horse and then let her down near the small fire that her parents had prepared to cook some food.

That evening he had dinner with them and told something about him, without going into details.

He talked more about the work his father did, he had always had a great admiration for him and missed him from day one.

He had no other relatives and was so far from home that he really felt alone. The four were amazed by his stories, they had never been to the capital.

While having dinner, they saw that from the head of the caravan, the lieutenant of the guards and a figure with a gray tunic, were walking all the serpentine shape of the wagons towards the tail, announcing something to the wayfarers as they walked.

They also came near them and heard them proclaiming: "Beware! In three days no one will be allowed to continue the march with us. Let everyone consider this order and organize themselves according to what has just been said."

"He is the cleric of the group of men transporting the prisoners to Argoran, he is responsible for the magical protections of the guards. The soldiers always travel with at least one of them, every time" said the man who was eating with Jelko and who had just hosted him.

"But it is not a problem for us. We will detach ourselves from the caravan the day before, so it doesn't concern us."

After finishing dinner and saying goodbye, Jelko found two trees very close to each other and settled for the night behind them.

He was increasingly convinced that stopping by for a little at the farm of the father of those new friends, could be a good solution. He promised himself that calmly, once there, since he did not have to worry too much about food or places to sleep, he would also re-evaluate the possibility of returning home.

He had almost rid himself of the disappointment felt after the unjust execution of that wood elf. Who knows if his father would have welcomed him in a bad way after having run away from home for about ten days now, without saying anything and moreover in the middle of the night.

He fell asleep very relieved. It had been a smooth day and apart from the growing heat, the daily march had continued smoothly.

He dreamed of Elyn again, as always with the appearance of a tall and blonde elf compared to when he had met her at the Fost market, shorter and with very black hair.

She was sitting on a travel trunk and her hood was lowered around her shoulders. She looked at both palms of her hands, then looked up at him.

She seemed very thoughtful and a moment later she squinted as she did every time. Unknown words echoed in Jelko's head with the usual warm and reassuring voice: *"sama alea... sama alea..."*

The dream was very short this time, and he woke up with the usual strong smell of wet grass all around.

He quickly wrote down those words in his travel notebook.

It was good that he could see in the dark, as it was not necessary to light any torch to do so, and he fell asleep soon after.

In the morning, he reread those three sentences that he had previously written down and thought: —I wonder if that cleric can help me find a solution to these words and if they make sense. At most he will tell me no.—

Even before eating something, and since the caravan was not ready to resume the march, he picked up his belongings and headed for the three reinforced wagons.

A guard approached, he kept an eye on him, and seeing that Jelko was heading at a brisk pace towards him, he went to meet him: "What happened to you boy? You can't get too close. Stop here."

Jelko obeyed and replied: "Good morning, sir. I know, I have no intention of bothering you, I would just need to ask your cleric something. It is a very simple question, maybe he can help me. It is very important for me and it will only take a moment, is it possible?"

"No, it's not possible. Take your place, we're about to leave."

Jelko could not miss that opportunity. He tried the only card that came to mind and quickly unrolled a corner of the hilt of his sword with the real symbols he had covered with a ribbon.

"Hey! What are you doing with that sword?"

"That's exactly what I'd like to discuss with the cleric. Maybe I know who it belongs to and I'd like clarification on how to give it to the right people."

"Wait here" said the guard.

From the bars of the last chariot of prisoners, he again saw someone in the twilight watching in his direction as on the first day they left the village.

After a very short time, the soldier was already back with the cleric, a man in his thirties of medium stature with short hair without a beard. Up close his gray tunic had decorations, they looked like runes embroidered with a silver thread.

"Tell me quickly what you have to ask me, we are about to leave."

Jelko made a small bow and replied: "Good morning. I will be very brief. I need to know to whom I can deliver this royal sword of the South of our Duchy. You are going to Argoran and you will have more for a while, but after a couple of days at the home of my uncles nearby, I will return to Fost. Do you know by chance who is the most suitable person to deliver it to? I know I can't keep it and as beautiful as it is, I would like for it to end up in the right hands."

"No, I don't know" replied the cleric, "since you are returning to the capital, it will not be difficult for you to go to the palace and ask anyone. They will be able to give you instructions on the matter. That's all?"

Jelko, who instead of putting his notebook in his backpack had kept it in his pocket, quickly pulled it out and read: *"min rakasin, vanimar laita, sama alea."*

The cleric and the soldier looked at him bewildered.

The guard was getting annoyed for all that wasted time and said: "What the hell are you saying? Enough, go back to your place. Don't let me repeat it twice!"

"Wait" said the cleric, silencing him with a wave of his hand, "Is it elven, or am I wrong? I know it quite well, but what does it have to do with anything? And who are you to come here to tell me these words?"

Jelko was also amazed. He expected the discussion with the two to be a little friendlier, he was not asking who-knows-what and his tones were calm, but evidently for the two it was just a waste of time out of their schedule.

He was amazed at how his answer was instinctively prompt: "An elven merchant, during the market days for the commemoration of the God Venakin, told me these words. Since I did not buy what he wanted to sell me insistently, I left and heard him screaming behind my back. I immediately thought they were insults to me. Do you know by chance what they mean, exactly? Probably he had not taken well to my non-purchase, I penned them immediately so as not to forget them, it is just my curiosity and nothing else."

The two seemed to have believed the story invented instantly and they wanted to quickly end that discussion to return to the ranks.

"I will lead you. Look for me. I am here" said the cleric.

"Enough is enough. I have no more time to lose, and possibly will not let you see me anymore, your business and your stories do not interest me."

Jelko had stood there impaled.

"Did you hear that? Go away and don't be seen again. Go back to your place immediately!" the guard shouted at him, approaching menacingly.

"Immediately" Jelko replied in a choked voice.

He walked back to his place in the caravan. He looked stunned, it was as if they had punched him in the stomach.

—Well— he thought, —I don't know what those words really mean, but how is it possible to dream of elven phrases that have a very specific meaning if I don't know a single word of the language of the elves?—

He walked and thought. Every time he dreamed, Elyn told him a different phrase. It had happened three times and in each dream she seemed tormented. While remaining extremely calm, her soul looked as if she did not give herself peace for something.

During every dream he had, had this impression.

—They would take me for a fool if I said such a thing: a wood elf burned at the stake who speaks to me in elven in dreams, and moreover in a language that I do not know. Yes, maybe I've gone crazy in the last ten days, and I'm only realizing it now.—

He spent the whole day walking alone, immersed in his thoughts, on what to do, on what was happening to him.

Since he had left his home, he had killed a man, discovered that he saw in the dark more and more clearly and dreamed of elven words without ever having studied them.

It was time to seriously consider whether it was time to return home. He would surely find his father and friends ready to help him, or at least he hoped so.

In Fost he felt safe.

Like every evening at sunset, he decided this time to seclude himself a little further for the night.

The next day, they would probably come out of that sparse forest as he heard from other travelers, it began to be quite hot during the day.

They had been away from the coast for some time, and that grove was in all probability the last before the great central desert.

Fortunately, the following day he too would have a destination. He was tired of walking, seven days had passed since he had left the village.

On the farm where he had been invited, he would seriously re-evaluate everything with more calmness and lucidity.

—I will lead you. Look for me. I'm here.—

And he fell asleep.

CHAPTER 9 (A New Friend)

He woke up in the middle of the night. From the bottom of the caravan, he heard some travelers mumbling, complaining about too much noise that had woken them up.

No one lit the torches.

Jelko rubbed his eyes a little and slowly managed to see the point from which those complaints came. From the penultimate chariot he saw a very high silhouette go down and tinker with something under the carriage with a light.

Shortly thereafter another figure, also high, went down and went around the other side. They seemed to be tightening the ropes better.

He wasn't sure, but it seemed to him that at least one had dark skin.

The mumbling slowly ceased and everything returned to normal in a short time. The two climbed back on their carriage in silence.

Jelko could no longer fall asleep. Fortunately, not long after one of the two suns peeped out, just ahead of the other, and in an instant the caravan came alive.

Jelko had just finished fixing his backpack and sword, he was still not far away among the sparse trees. Then he heard cries coming from the caravan.

The screams grew and enveloped all the travelers.

"Help!"

"They're attacking us! They are monsters!"

"They are the Sleepless Ones!"

—Sleepless Ones?— thought Jelko, shaken, —that's impossible. They were defeated fifteen years ago!—

Instinctively he immediately drew his sword.

The caravan was out of control from fear. The women tried to hide the children behind and under the wagons, the men protected them by pulling out daggers, pitchforks and simple spiked sticks.

The guards at the top seemed to be the only ones to have adopted an effective line of defense.

Even the only family he had known was trying to shelter as it could.

He cautiously began to walk in their direction, holding his sword firmly between fear and uncertainty. He was approaching the caravan, and beyond it he saw the assailants moving.

He hoped that the rumors that said they were the Sleepless Ones were not true, but no, they were. A disjointed array of humanoids quickly approached, there were about fifty of them.

The Sleepless Ones had human features, but they seemed deformed and as if they were in a perpetual advanced state of decomposition. They were similar to zombies, but fast. They were not armed, but they had long gnarled fingers with razor-sharp claws. Those were their deadliest weapons.

The ten guards at the head of the caravan did not move yet.

The cleric behind them had begun to cast protective spells on his comrades.

The lieutenant shouted: "The rings! Someone retrieve the rings!"

He was referring to the rings that were delivered in a casket to the group of men heading to Argoran at the start of each journey, those that served to create an impenetrable shield around the possessor once inserted on the finger.

He seemed the only lucid person. His men, including the cleric, were almost petrified on the spot. No one moved and just held position.

The small horde of Sleepless Ones was now on the caravan.

It was really scary. Most of those travelers had only just heard of them, much less seen them in person.

They had rags on them now reduced to shreds. Underneath you could see the grayish skin almost rotting and slime filled their hungry mouths.

They began to reap their first victims with extreme ease.

Civilians, mostly ordinary people and merchants, defended themselves as they could, but all were paralyzed by fear.

After shooting down five of them, the lieutenant was the first to fall among his frightened soldiers, torn apart by claws.

Jelko did not know what to do, perhaps it was better to run away. Even he had never seen the Sleepless Ones before. They were really many and frighteningly bestial, and above all, the caravan was not able to offer a minimum of resistance.

Among the ranks of the attackers, a member of the horde quickly broke off.

In a moment he was in front of Jelko. With amazement he realized that he was a human being with an athletic physique, holding two war axes in his hands.

"Invoke your Gods, boy. Soon you will meet them" he pounced strongly.

He was very agile and fast. With an axe he tried to open the guard that Jelko held with his sword and then hit him with the other. He did not succeed, but Jelko fell backwards anyway.

"Jelko, help! Someone help us!"

The family, his friend, was a little further away. The woman called him, as her husband was trying to keep at bay a Sleepless Ones with a spiked stick and a hatchet in his other hand.

Jelko avoided another blow by rolling on one side. The axe stuck in the ground very close to his ear.

He managed to get up and tried to hit his aggressor.

The stab came up empty, the man easily dodged him and counterattacked with the same tactics as before. This time he managed to open Jelko's guard and hit him in the left forearm.

He screamed in pain, his cry mixed with those of terror that came all around.

"I will kill you, it is only a matter of time. I cannot return to my Lord without having fulfilled the mission" said the man.

The woman from before called him again, begging: "Jelko, help! We are here, please help us!"

His attacker quickly tore a button off the light robe, felt warm, and discovered an amulet that he was holding around his neck.

With amazement he recognized the same pulsating purple stone that Peryl had when he woke up with him on top, in an attempt to kill him.

The royal sword he had was really well balanced and maneuverable, the blows were light. He dodged and gave a heavy blow to the axes that the man had crossed in front of him to parry the blow.

For the moment he resisted the attacks, but his rival seemed to know his stuff. He was certainly much more prepared and trained than him, Jelko did not know how much longer he would be able to resist. He did not have any military preparation, he was not a soldier and he had never really fought. This time, however, he had to do it to save his skin.

The caravan had already been decimated. The guards at a quick glance could no longer see them, they were probably all already dead.

The few horses had been killed first so that no one could escape except on foot, so as to be easily accessible.

"Jelko! Jelko!"

The woman kept calling him.

He turned for a moment and saw her fall to the ground, torn to pieces. A little further on was her husband and two children, killed and torn to pieces too.

"No!" he shouted desperately with all his breath left.

And it happened again...

He began to no longer feel tired, anger and strength grew hand in hand. His blows became more and more powerful and he no longer even felt the pain in his injured arm.

He was afraid that his own sword would break, so much was the strength he put into it.

His rival now defended himself with difficulty. Jelko looked like a fury, striking like a war machine.

A Sleepless One rushed to give a strong hand, among the blows inflicted in rapid succession. Yet with one hit to the humanoid, who did not even have time to try to dodge the blow, it fell dead immediately after.

Jelko had a demonic look.

He struck with superhuman strength, the handle of one of the two axes of his opponent broke under the incessant blows of his sword.

The man began to look at him, terrified. Now he was in trouble and had no breath to resist. He tried to escape, but stopped to parry another blow, tried to escape soon after, turned around to surprise the boy, but Jelko passed him with the sword from side to side.

He had not yet extracted it from his body when he took his neck with one hand and broke it with incredible ease, even if by now he had already mortally wounded him.

The lifeless body fell to the ground with a dull thud. Jelko opened his mouth and stuck the sword that came out of the skull at the rear, sticking into the ground.

All that blood was exalting him.

Two other Sleepless Ones pounced on him. He parried their claw blows and a moment later he cut the heads off both.

"Hey! Set me free! I'm in here! I can help!"

The voice came from the last reinforced wagon. Fighting, he had not noticed that he had almost reached the top of the caravan.

The person to speak was probably that figure that he always saw in dim light in the only one of the three wagons that really seemed to carry someone.

Another humanoid tried to surprise him from behind. A claw ripped through his robe at the height of his side. A trickle of blood came out, but he seemed not to have even noticed.

He turned around and struck a blow. The Sleepless One parried it, but it was so powerful that the claws, placed to protect above the head, broke and the blade penetrated the head killing it instantly.

"There is no time. Free me! These carriages can only be opened from the outside! Break the lock!"

Jelko was not very lucid, he did not have full control of his actions when he was in such a state. He thought that a hand would be useful at that juncture. Too bad that he would have killed him, too. He was sure.

With a large stone, he gave a powerful blow to the padlock that tightened the rear door of the reinforced wagon. The door opened.

"Thank you, friend. My name is Nolan, I am indebted to you."

He was a well-placed boy, a little taller than Jelko, and almost the same age, though probably a couple of years older. His brown hair was long up to his shoulder blades and he had his beard tied in a palm-length braid.

He immediately picked up a sword from the ground of one of the dead guards, who until recently had been among his jailers.

"They didn't see us" said Nolan, "let's try to escape, follow me. Let's hurry!"

"No" he replied in an icy voice, "first I have to kill them all."

"But what are you saying? There are still dozens of them. The caravan is lost. If we run away now, maybe we will save ourselves!"

Jelko seemed absent. His gaze was fixed on the assailants, who traveled the caravan towards the tail, killing all those who tried to escape desperately.

"Ah! But you're wounded!" exclaimed Nolan, observing him better, "let's take shelter somewhere far from here, I know some spell that can heal you. Come away from there!"

Jelko didn't even seem to hear him and began to walk faster and faster towards the Sleepless Ones, as if attracted to them.

"Damn you" Nolan told him as he chased him, "I thought I was safe from the prison of Argoran, you will have us both killed! Stop for a moment."

Nolan stood right in front of him and stopped him with his size, blocking his way, then recited some strange and fast litany with unknown words. He touched Jelko's wounds with his hand and they stopped bleeding and started healing quickly.

"I will come with you, I have no other choice. I hope you know how to fight better than you know how to have an argument."

Two humanoids noticed them and rushed back, drooling and emitting frightening guttural noises.

The one who pounced on Jelko extended its claws.

Jelko dodged them and struck it on the head, piercing it with the force of the thrust. Right away, the blade ended the clash.

Nolan skillfully dodged the blows of the one who was attacking him, he was quite agile and he seemed to know his stuff.

He slipped to dodge another blow from the ground with a kick to the enemy's legs that made it fall. He quickly got up and stuck the sword in its chest, killing it while the enemy was still trying to get back on its feet.

The caravan had now been wiped out.

He no longer saw any human being trying to fight or try to run, in a desperate escape to that point where the forest was not even so dense.

They were all dead.

The Sleepless Ones remained. There were still about thirty of them, who seemed to have stopped once they arrived at the tail of the snake of wagons.

Nolan pushed Jelko behind one of them out of their sight.

"Hey! Listen to me, we are still in time. You will not want to continue advancing towards them! Apparently, we are the only survivors. We wait for them to leave. If we are lucky, they did not see us from over there."

Jelko was breathing heavily, he looked stunned and was slowly coming to his senses. Some muscles began to tremble after the long effort they had been subjected to.

"Stay calm and breathe, you've been furious all the time. Catch your breath."

"May I know your name?" asked Nolan.

"My name is Jelko Neville. I come from the Duchy of the Seven Lakes."

"Well, Jelko, maybe they are leaving. They are too many, we'll try not to make noise and we will get by. We cannot face them in two."

"Okay, you're right" Jelko replied as he took long breaths.

The two leaned out slightly to see what the Sleepless Ones were doing at the back of the caravan.

Jelko said: "I killed a man who was with them, maybe he led them and now they are without a guide. Maybe they will leave shortly."

Instead, they lingered. They did not move from where they were as if they were guarding something.

From the penultimate carriage two tall figures came down and took off their hoods. They were two dark elves.

Jelko recognized them.

"Damn dogs! They are the two dark elves I met at the market of the capital where I come from. They sold me this sword at my insistence. Because of them, an innocent wood elf was burned at the stake!"

"They seem to be friends" Nolan said, "apparently, they don't attack each other. Let's not move from here."

The Sleepless Ones lined up all around the carriage as if to protect it. The dark elves loosened the ropes and pulled down a large chest.

The two opened it.

There was someone inside it, and with tugs and very little delicacy they pulled it out and put it on its feet.

From a distance, she looked like a petite female figure. Her height was more or less that of a child.

She was wearing a very beautiful and fine emerald-green velvet dress, of those usually seen at court, with elegant golden decorations in the hems.

Maybe she was a princess, she definitely had nothing to do with that place.

Seen from behind, her hair was straight and very black.

She turned to Jelko, Nolan suddenly withdrew so as not to be seen.

She squinted, concentrating as she stared at him as if in a dream: *"Sama alea... I'm here!"* said Elyn with the strength of her mind.

Around it smelled of wet grass.

CHAPTER 10 (On the Tracks)

"Elyn?" thought Jelko, stunned.

"They have the wood elf with them, Elyn is alive!"

"But what are you talking about?" replied Nolan, "and who is Elyn?"

"She's the elf they burned at the stake about ten days ago in Fost."

Nolan looked at him thoughtfully: "They burned her days ago in your capital and now she's here? Alive? Do you realize what you are saying? You still seem a bit confused."

The two leaned a little more, to see better from the wagon where they had found shelter.

"They are moving" Nolan said.

Even the horse of the dark elves' carriage had been killed during the clash, probably accidentally at some frantic moment of the assault, so they could no longer proceed, except on foot.

The Sleepless Ones split into two groups: one forward and one behind the two dark elves with Elyn in their midst. They walked in the same direction from which the attack on the caravan had just started.

The elf had no chain or rope that would force her in any way.

She walked with her gaze turned to the ground, in silence.

Jelko did not lose sight of them and said: "We must follow them and free her."

"Yes, of course! And how do you plan to eliminate about thirty Sleepless Ones with two dark elves? I don't know if you noticed, but only you and I are alive."

"Then we will do it ourselves! We must free her at all costs, she has guided me so far for this."

Nolan approached him: "You are making fun of me. An elf who must have died has guided you here to free her, how can I believe such a story?"

"I don't know either. As soon as possible, I will tell you how things went, I know very well that they may seem confusing. They are not clear even to me. For now, let's just follow them."

"Okay. Just because if you hadn't freed myself from that carriage, I probably would have died. I would have preferred to answer you that our paths separate here, but I can't. I am indebted to you."

Nolan stood up bent down so as not to be seen and said: "Wait here, first I have to retrieve some things. I'll come back right away."

He stealthily moved away in the direction of the head of the caravan where they came from. Jelko saw him disappear for a moment and shortly after reappeared to return to his place next to him.

"Take this" Nolan said, "it could come in handy."

He passed him one of the protective rings that the guards had used to enter and exit Argoran unharmed.

They waited for the small group to advance a good distance, before moving from behind the wagon to follow it.

And so they did throughout the day.

They did not stop even in the hottest hours and never spoke, but just communicated in a few nods. The trees thinned out more and more and in order not to be seen. They had to increase the distance that separated them while always staying concentrated.

They went East.

When one of the two suns set, the dark elves with Elyn finally decided to stop at the foot of a large boulder, several dozen feet high and wide.

Some Sleepless Ones climbed up to about half the height, where the rock formed a sort of terrace on which three of them lurked to enjoy a better view, at least until the second sun had also set shortly thereafter.

The two pursuers instead, found a very distant and much smaller boulder behind which to shelter. There were no trees in that area. From there, they could not hear them, but they still preferred to speak quietly for safety.

"Let's get ready for the night and eat something" said Jelko, and with his back resting on the rock he pulled out some food.

"It's not much, I almost finished it and I didn't expect there would be two of us. We will have to replace it in some way."

Before it was completely dark, Jelko finished telling how things had gone that day when he met Elyn at the market, until she was burned at the stake following the explosion that caused death and panic in the large square of the capital.

Nolan asked him: "But what was the point of that explosion? What could it have been used for?"

"I've always wondered that too, I've never found any answer. What I do know is that since then, I started dreaming of her. She speaks to me in elvish and is always tall and blonde, I am convinced that she somehow led me to her to help her."

Nolan listened to him with great interest, he had not missed a single word: "From how you describe this, it seems that every time you dreamed of a member of the race of the Arcane Elves. They are made like that: tall and blond. They are a nomadic people with a huge magical aura and wherever they settle, they normally always bring peace and prosperity."

"I don't know, It's all so confusing. As soon as we have the chance, it would be appropriate to warn the sovereigns that the Sleepless Ones have returned before it is too late. I could send a message to my father, then he would take care of it to warn those in charge, which seems very serious to me."

"And the food! Let's not forget the food!" said Nolan jokingly, loosening up the gloomy atmosphere a bit.

"Tell me about yourself rather" Jelko said, "can I trust someone who was headed to Argoran as a condemned person? Or will you try to break my neck before dawn?"

"I am very far from home, I come from the Barony of the Dragon."

"Ah!" exclaimed Jelko, holding back his amazement by force, "the only kingdom South of the great desert to be perpetually hostile to all the others! Your ships are famous for constantly raiding everything that moves, and luckily there is a huge stretch of sea in between. If you were not an islander, you would also raid by land!"

"I know, we don't have a good reputation and I personally don't share the aggressive attitude of my kingdom."

"Don't tell me you've been condemned because you don't think like them!"

Nolan sketched a smile: "Of course not. I was part, indeed I am still part, of a new order. An order that does not believe in your multitude of useless Gods, but in one God, the God who can and sees everything with his great eye. I have been lucky, many of my confreres have been barbarously slaughtered after being declared heretics."

Jelko listened very carefully, he had never heard of such an order. He had always been open-minded, so he did not feel like demonizing such a monotheistic idea and simply listened to his animated exposition without commenting.

Night came. The group with Elyn was silent.

Jelko said: "From here they cannot hear us, but let's be careful all the same. At least thirty of them will not sleep, they do not need it. You rest and I will stand the guard shift tonight."

"Wake me up when you're tired, you have to rest. You can't see them and if they get closer, we'll hear them."

Jelko sighed: "Since I left home, strange things have been happening to me in addition to the dreams I told you. Every night, I can see better and better in the dark."

Nolan, who had just lay down, pointed his elbows and rose up: "Are you a demon? Don't make fun of me, even though as

I've seen you fight, you might as well be." Then he turned the other way.

Jelko looked in the direction of the elf.

They were very far away, he could barely see her. At that moment, he did not feel her in his head as when he dreamed of her, but he was convinced that she was facing his direction.

The night passed quietly, only a little wind broke that tomb-like silence from time to time.

He also managed to take a nap, albeit a very short one.

His companion slept through the night and when he woke up, he said: "You stubborn fellow! Why didn't you call me to give you the change? Have you been able to sleep at least a little?"

"Don't worry, I rested anyway."

Nolan approached him and said: "How are the wounds going? Let me see."

Jelko discovered his arm. The wound was nothing more than a small scratch, and the one in his side was almost invisible after just one day.

"See? Thank my God, he used me to cure you."

"For now I thank you! I don't feel any pain, your spell was powerful! As for your God, we will see. For now, I'll keep mine, I seem to understand that I will really need them so much."

The group later resumed the march, always towards the East.

The two gave it further advantage and began to stalk it again.

"On that side there is the city of Kedor. Maybe they're headed there" Jelko said, "but I have no idea where we are exactly, so I don't know if we're close by or not."

They walked all day, eating a few quick bites of the little food that was left in Jelko's backpack without stopping. The march proceeded smoothly, they were quite tired and moreover moving on a semi-empty stomach.

It was not long before sunset, when from a distance they were able to see a village in their direction. As they approached, it seemed to be much larger than a simple village.

Nolan said: "Finally, a town. I don't think it's Kedor, it doesn't seem so big. It's probably a town whose name I don't know."

Jelko replied: "I don't think I do either. If the elves don't stop, one of us should jump in to quickly buy some food. I still have enough money with me."

They noticed that when the city was still little more than visible on the horizon, all the Sleepless Ones broke away from the dark elves, leaving them alone with Elyn, to quickly move away to the North.

Nolan said: "They're going to go into town. Their escort is leaving, of course they don't have to be seen by anyone."

Jelko commented: "I think they want to pass the walls by nightfall. We are not far away now and they are picking up the pace."

"What if we attacked them now?" proposed Nolan.

"Mhmm... I do not know, surely we would attract the attention of the guards. Even if we had the upper hand how would we justify what happened? After all, they could very well say that they are merchants on the road and have been attacked."

"You're right" Nolan said, "we'd risk getting arrested and then we're not even sure we'd get the better of those two. Dark elves are quite famous for being good fighters."

Jelko replied: "In the city, maybe it will be easier to follow them. There will be more movement, but we could better blend in among the people. It would be perfect to be able to free Elyn without having to resort to force."

Nolan looked at him and said laughing: "You're optimistic, my friend."

Even the second sun was now setting.

The dark elves with the young wood elf crossed the West gate of the city briefly, exchanging a few words with the guards at the entrance.

Soon after, Jelko and Nolan did the same.

It was almost dark when they entered the town of Meltin.

CHAPTER 11 (Meltin the Corrupt)

The town had stone walls, although they were not very high. The sentinels did not ask questions. They just looked at them from head to toe and immediately closed the doors they guarded, probably like every evening at sunset.

There were only two sentinels. There were no real wars between kingdoms in those years, so the few soldiers employed in the normal control of the cities were sufficient without having to support them with other conscripts.

They wore the shield on their shoulders as if it were a backpack. The coat of arms of the Kingdom of Miriam, in which they were located, was a red sun on a yellow background. Only one had those banners, the other carried a rather shabby round wooden shield without emblems. Even their light armor looked battered and worn out.

For Jelko, this was inadmissible. In the Duchy from which he came, even a low-ranking soldier was dressed impeccably. His armor and even simply the tunic worn under it, was kept maniacally clean and ordered.

Moreover, the two sentinels seemed to have an absent look in their eyes. Surely they were tired and at the end of their shift.

On the other hand, they did the same things every day and for who-knows-how-long.

There was little movement around, now those few people left on the streets were returning home or going to the taverns to have a drink in company.

"Do you see them?" asked Jelko.

"No, damn. We were too far away and who knows where they are now. This city is not really small, let's try to go straight on this road that leads to the center, and hopefully we'll be lucky. Maybe they are looking for an inn to spend the night."

They walked quickly, looking at all the various branches that the main road made at each intersection, but it seemed that Elyn and the dark elves had vanished into thin air.

The road, leading to the city center, at one point curved slightly to the right. A man on a wooden bench was lighting an oil lamp hanging on a wall of a house.

Behind him, a door was closing.

"Here they are! I saw them go in!" gasped Jelko.

"I also think I saw the little wood elf enter last, what do we do?" asked Nolan.

Jelko said: "I'll wait here. They could recognize me if they have a good memory, but they have never seen you before. Try to pass in front of that door and take a quick look. Hurry up, however, it will soon be dark."

"I will do as you say. At the first intersection, I will go back through the parallel road. You stand aside, pull up the hood and do not call attention to yourself."

Nolan walked around, looking with an innocent air as if he took that road every day. Meanwhile, Jelko stood aside against the wall of what looked like a closed shop, pretending to look for something in his small backpack.

Shortly thereafter, Nolan came out of a side street and said: "I don't think it's an inn. The shutters of the windows are closed, even those on the upper floor, and I have not heard any voices coming from inside or seen any lights. I have not noticed any other entrances and on the door there is a small lightning bolt. I have seen several drawn or engraved on other exits along the short path I have taken."

The man who had previously lit a lamp took his stool, moved to the other side of the road and climbed to light another one, this time a little closer to Jelko and Nolan.

The man saw them but did not say a word. Nolan approached him and asked: "Hello, sir. Can you tell us somewhere to spend the night, possibly a few steps from here?"

He looked at him for a moment and shook his head.

"Is it possible that there isn't an inn nearby? We have just arrived and would like to rest for a while, what is the name of this city?"

The man did not answer and this time he did not even turn to look him in the face. He seemed totally absorbed in the mechanical gestures that he meticulously made, as if he were performing a ritual.

Nolan returned to his companion, who was a few steps behind: "The inhabitants of this place are very friendly, no doubt about it. Do you have an alternative?"

Near the city gate from which they had entered, there was a small house. The sentries had just entered.

Jelko spoke softly: "Let's get under the walls near the gatehouse. We will be uncomfortable, but we will be close to the sentries and from there we can keep an eye on the house where the dark elves have entered and a good stretch of this road. We cannot risk to lose sight of them."

"I slept in a prisoner wagon for days and days. It's not a problem for me, I haven't known what comfort is for a long time now."

The two went back a little further, taking as a reference a stretch of wall from which they could watch the road, where there was the door into which Elyn had entered.

By now night had fallen, but thanks to the lamps lit by that silent man, they could still see something.

Nolan sat with his back to the wall, put his knees in his arms and asked in a low voice: "Do you have a plan in mind?"

Jelko replied: "Not yet, but we have all night to think about it. The first thing in the morning, we'll have to get some food, but someone has to stay here and check their movements."

"Yes, you're right" Nolan agreed, "they could leave right away and we can't afford to lose sight of them or travel again for who-knows-how-long without food."

"And how do you think you can free this elf we are chasing for no apparent reason?" he continued.

"I have no idea, we'll have to invent something. Maybe when they leave the city for a first stretch, they will be alone again. The Sleepless Ones, if they are out there waiting, will not join them too close to the city with the risk of being seen by patrols on the walls."

Nolan seemed to agree with the hypothesis: "This could be a good idea. The problem is that we are not fighters with who-knows-what experience, not to mention that we don't even have a shred of armor. To tell the truth, I can manage a bit, and I have seen that you are a fury with the sword, but the dark elves are not to be underestimated at all."

Jelko said: "We must also find a way to warn the mayor of this citadel that we have seen the Sleepless Ones, without being taken for fools. It would be even better if I could send a message to my father down at the Duchy, I would have no problem making him believe the story of what we saw."

The man, who lit the oil lamps hanging on the walls of the houses that lined the main road, seemed to have finished his job. He got off his wooden bench, coughed noisily, staggered around a closed door, started to sit on the ground but fell with a thud.

"What the hell is he doing?" Jelko said, amazed.

"He died?" Nolan exclaimed.

He was not far from them and a moment later they heard his deep breathing.

"He fell asleep there all of a sudden. Maybe he's drunk, even though when I approached him to ask him for information, I didn't think I smelled any beer or wine."

Nolan continued: "Now sleep, there are lights here and I can see in the dim light. Last night you stood watch, tonight, I'll do it. Don't worry, and we hope that the elf will give you some advice in a dream."

"Okay, I need to get some sleep. We should be safe here."

The night passed quietly and in great silence.

As soon as it was day, the two gathered the few things they had, trying not to arouse any particular attention. The soldiers had come out of the guardhouse, and after a moment they were replaced by two others.

Jelko said: "The pace here is undoubtedly a lot slower than in the busy merchant village I left with the caravan."

"Yes, the city gates are still closed and I don't think there is any rush to open them."

The oil lamps, which the man of the previous evening had lit, had not yet been extinguished and he was there on the ground where he had collapsed.

As Jelko and Nolan finished settling down and stretching, they noticed that more and more people were crowding right around that man.

"He died!" exclaimed a woman carrying a bucket of water.

"He died the same as the others! But what's going on?" said a boy who tugged at the woman to take her away from there.

"Let's go and see, hurry up!" Jelko said hastily.

The two approached. They were not far from where they had settled for the night and in a moment they were close to the crowd of people that had formed.

The man on the ground had froth on his mouth and his skin was greenish.

Other passersby stopped, some didn't say a word and left a moment later as if everything were normal.

"Nobody is taking him away? They are barbarians here, they have strange customs" Nolan whispered in Jelko's ear.

Finally, two stout people made their way through the crowd, took the lifeless body and carried it away.

"You two, follow me! Quick!"

Behind them, a medium-sized man with a beard and gray hair seemed to be addressing just Jelko and Nolan.

"Yes, I say to you: come with me. Enter my shop, it's the door next door. It's all right, I just have to talk to you, quick!"

Seeing that the two were reluctant to carry out the order, he approached and pushed them forcefully towards the door of his shop.

Jelko instinctively put his hand on the hilt of the sword he had at his side. Nolan did the same.

Someone, from inside the shop, opened the door and in a moment all three found themselves inside it.

The smell of freshly baked bread was everywhere. Inside there was a girl, probably it was she who had opened it.

"Get us out of here immediately!" Jelko yelled, drawing his sword. Nolan was about to do the same.

"Calm down, we're unarmed. I just have to talk to you. Believe me, you're safer here than out there" the man said.

"My name is Lusva and this is my daughter, Triny. We are bakers."

"What do you want from us?" Nolan interrupted him.

Jelko let his guard down.

"We saw you enter last night before sunset. You were behind three other figures, at one of the windows of our shop, right at the West door here" Lusva said, "those doors haven't opened for more than ten days and just we heard the sound of the bolts, we got curious and my daughter and I ran to the window."

"How come the doors stay closed? Are we in a plague city perhaps?" Jelko asked, sheathing his sword.

"Oh no, Meltin is not a quarantined city, but strange things are happening and I wanted to warn you. Perhaps you can help us, we can no longer trust anyone. Many citizens are now corrupt, as I call them, you cannot be yet, as you have just arrived."

"Help you to do what? And what does it mean that the city is corrupt?" Nolan asked.

The baker replied: "The mayor suddenly decided that there would be free food in the main square every day. He said that the harvest of the whole kingdom this year was far above expectations, and therefore our town was also exempted from having to hand over its part to the capital for redistribution."

"That's a good thing" Jelko pointed out.

"Yes, sure, but from the next day, without any explanation, he gave the order to close all the entrances to the city. No one could enter or leave."

"But then, why were the doors open last night? We had no problems getting in?" Jelko said.

"We wondered about that too" Lusva replied, "you five who entered yesterday are the first since the edict of food and the closing of the doors. But where are the others?"

"They are not with us. Now I understand, they let us in because they thought we were with the first three that passed just before" Jelko said, "the guards seemed rather strange and bewildered."

Lusva looked at his daughter and continued: "Since then, everyone is strange here, or almost. We have never eaten that food, but most of them do. That's why people seem absent, and every now and then someone goes the way of that poor man out here."

Nolan intervened and said: "That food must be poisoned, but why would the mayor do such a thing to his own town? It makes no sense."

Triny spoke for the first time: "That's why we say the city is corrupt. You have to leave as soon as possible, but it won't be easy. We still have a lot of raw materials, and with the oven we manage to get by, but as the population runs out of food, they take advantage of what is provided for free in the square every day. Since they cannot go out into the fields outside the walls, each family's supplies are increasingly scarce."

There was a pause. Jelko and Nolan looked at each other in bewilderment.

Triny continued: "Some days I bring the bread to a family friend of ours a little further on. I keep it hidden in a basket wrapped in scented sheets, so as not to let the smell of it escape. I'm always afraid that someone will attack me."

Nolan watched in rapture. She spoke very politely and he was sure that if at that moment they were in a tavern, among mugs of beer and in the company of noisy friends, he would not hesitate to speak to her to get to know her better. That girl intrigued him, but it wasn't the time to think about it. Not now.

Jelko said: "Regarding the three you saw enter just before us last night, they were two dark elves and a wood elf. They locked themselves up in a house a little further on. It's still not clear why the guards opened the doors for them, since they have orders to keep them tightly closed, from what I understand."

"Perhaps they are accomplices" observed Lusva.

"How can we trust you?" Nolan said, "what can tell us that you're not telling lies for some reason?"

"Nobody can stop you from believing that" Triny said quietly, "you are free to leave and go wherever you want."

Nolan asked: "I noticed that most of the doors, whether they are houses or shops, have a lightning bolt. What does that mean?"

It was Triny again who spoke: "They appeared as the days passed after the edict of food. Every day there are more, we believe it is a sign of recognition that the house is corrupt. If you look out, ours does not bear that symbol. Maybe this can help you to trust us."

"Why a bolt of lightning? Did you understand if it has any particular meaning?" Jelko asked.

It was Lusva who replied: "Maybe it's an ancient rune. My daughter is studying the magical arts in one of the maritime fiefs of the Duchy of the Seven Lakes, but we don't know its meaning. We inherited a small fortune and me and my wife didn't want her to end up being a baker for the rest of her life."

"I come from Fost!" Jelko exclaimed enthusiastically at the news that brought him home for a moment.

"Great place" said the baker, "my daughter would have had to leave at just this time to go back to study in the Duchy. She came back because of my wife's death less than a month ago. She helped me to get things done and now she's stuck here."

Triny, the baker's daughter, was of medium height and normal build, her brown hair pulled back into a ponytail, her dark eyes were very lively and attentive. She did not seem at all naive.

With more elegant clothes and a more refined hairstyle, she would probably have turned out to be a beautiful girl too.

Both she and her father, did not seem to have that blank stare they noticed in many faces encountered outside that door.

"Can we buy some food while we're here?" Nolan asked, "I'm not going to stay in this town of stragglers, and if I can find a way out, I don't want to go without something to eat until the next village or town."

Lusva replied: "You can take whatever you can carry, and if you want you can sleep in the back. Here you are safe, I only ask for one thing in return, if possible."

Jelko and Nolan exchanged a glance and said almost in chorus: "Let's hear it."

"If you can find a way to get through those doors, I just ask you to get my daughter out of here."

Triny approached her father and took his hand: "I won't leave knowing the situation here."

Her father looked at her with sad eyes and said: "I'll be fine, but you must continue your studies. That's what your mother and I wanted."

Jelko said: "Okay, we'll find a way out and we'll try to get you both out of here, just think about getting ready. If that happens, there won't be time to waste."

"Thank you" Lusva replied.

"Jelko" Nolan said, "maybe we should go out, we're losing sight of our dark friends."

"Damn, you're right. We have to go now, get your things ready. We don't know when we'll be back."

"All right" Triny said, "knock slowly three times and we'll know it's you. Be careful."

Meanwhile, the father had quickly wrapped some fresh bread in a cloth and threw it to Jelko. He caught it and put it in his backpack, thanking him.

Nolan opened the door and they went out into the street.

Similarly to what was said in the shop, the atmosphere out there was surreal.

Most people seemed to wander rather than walk. Everyone did the same things they probably used to do every day, but more slowly. The whole city was moving as if in slow motion.

Every now and then, someone could be seen moving faster, perhaps it was one of those few who remained who were not corrupt, as Lusva said shortly before. They could almost recognize each other, they simply seemed normal compared to the other inhabitants.

The two left the baker's shop just as one of the dark elves was doing the same thing a few doors ahead. He walked to the opposite side, turning his back on the two boys.

"Here is one" Jelko said softly, "let's follow him. You move across the street, we won't walk together."

Both pulled up their hoods, covering their faces as much as possible, and stalked the elf from a distance.

At one point, Jelko crossed the street and joined his friend, saying: "Go on alone. I'll stop here, otherwise I'll lose sight of the house where Elyn is. If the other dark elf were to come out, we wouldn't see him."

"Okay, stick around and don't worry. I won't take my eyes off him."

Jelko stopped at that exact spot.

Looking back, he could see the house where, according to their calculations, Elyn and the other elf were still inside, and at the same time for a while he managed to keep an eye on Nolan stalking the other. The two slowly disappeared from view, turning down a street on the left.

Jelko forcibly restrained himself. He was dying to break down that damn door and enter, but he did not know what he would find. As far as he knew, there could be other dark elves hidden inside. It was too risky.

Like most of the people who populated the city, he too walked slowly up and down the street patrolling it. It wasn't long before he recognized Nolan walking towards him from afar.

"He entered a house on a side street not very far from here, that also had a lightning bolt engraved on the door jamb. Everyone is in league here, we have to leave while we have time."

Jelko said: "We have to come up with something quickly. I don't like this situation at all, the city will become unmanageable in a short time, in my opinion."

"Yeah" Nolan replied, "we risk getting trapped among these half-zombie people. What do we do?"

"I absolutely must find a way to get into that house there. If there are no surprises now, apart from Elyn, there should only be the other dark elf with her, and that's already something."

"What if it isn't?" Nolan pointed out to him, "we don't know anything about how many are in there. We can't risk a fight in the middle of the city. There are still guards around, although most of them seem stunned by some mysterious drug."

Jelko was agitated, he couldn't find a way out of the situation.

Elyn was in that house just a stone's throw away, but he didn't know how to get her out of there.

"I have to be able to get in" he repeated, "we have to find a way to bring the other dark elf out, hoping that the other doesn't come back immediately and that there aren't others inside."

Nolan forcibly restrained himself to keep his voice low: "A series of coincidences, not a small one! Just skip one and we're in trouble."

"Unfortunately, we don't have many choices. They could stay here until the citadel becomes uncontrollable, and for us it would be even worse. I understand that the return of the Sleepless Ones and what is happening here inside the walls, are related."

"We are practically at their house!" Nolan exclaimed without being able to control himself.

He immediately calmed down and lowered his voice: "We have to do something, and we have to do it during the day. Otherwise, it is impossible. At night, they are almost all holed up inside the houses and there is too much silence to do one thing stealthily. We don't know how people would react, there are lightning bolts on almost every damn door!"

Jelko's eyes sparkled for a second: "Come on! I got an idea. Let's go back to the bakers' shop."

They knocked slowly three times and a moment later the door opened.

The four talked with each other for a long time. From time to time, Nolan peeked out to keep the situation under control.

Father and daughter did not hesitate to offer their help and set up a plan.

Triny concluded by saying: "It seems like it will work. Now it remains to be seen whether, as my masters teach, practice will prove the theory right."

CHAPTER 12 (Curses)

Nolan and Lusva left the shop, headed for the first street on the right and started chatting at a point from which they could see the house where Elyn was kept.

Triny filled a large basket with bread and left shortly after.

Jelko was the only one to stay inside. From the window overlooking the street, he could barely see Nolan and the baker talking.

After receiving information about which door was the right one, a little further on and on the same side as that of the oven, the girl reached it and knocked on it hard.

Nobody opened. She knocked again. Nothing.

"I'm the daughter of the baker nearby!" she said, knocking a third time with all the strength she had.

The door opened and a dark elf appeared. He was quite tall and slender with black hair and a small scar under his right eye.

"What do you want? I'll cut off your hands if you don't stop knocking."

"Excuse me, sir. I didn't want to bother you. My father sent me to deliver what you asked for: the Jellan family heard that you ordered all this fresh bread and decided to offer it to you. You don't owe me any coins."

The elf came out on the threshold, opening the door completely: "What are you saying? I didn't order anything, you're wrong, stupid girl. Damn you and your useless human race."

"But..."

"I said go away! And never knock on this door again, do we understand each other?"

Lusva broke away from Nolan, leaving him alone.

He almost ran up to his daughter and said: "What the hell are you doing, stupid apprentice? This is not where you have to deliver the bread paid for by the Jellan family! Stop bothering this gentleman. Damn you!"

He turned to the elf who was, to say the least, furious at that waste of time: "Please excuse her, sir. She hasn't lived here for very long and she hasn't quite understood how to get around the city yet."

He gave a nasty push to his daughter, who nearly fell.

Triny almost overturned the basket and said: "I humbly beg your pardon. Mrs. Jellan had talked about a dark elf like you, that's why I insisted when I saw you. I thought I had knocked on the right door, otherwise, I would have left immediately."

Nolan had meanwhile gone up the road a little and was walking hastily among the other townspeople in the direction of the three.

When he reached them, Lusva exclaimed with perfect surprise: "Oh, here is one of the sons who was with Mrs. Jellan when she came to the shop! Excuse me, Mr. Jellan, can you stop for a moment please?"

"Good morning, Lusva. Only if it's quick. I'm in a hurry, I'm already late" Nolan said.

If it had been up to the dark elf, he would have already cut the heads off all three.

The baker said: "Can you confirm to the gentleman that your family has decided to pay for the bread that my apprentice brought to them?"

"Of course, but the delivery was not here. It is two streets further, from what I understand."

"Last night, my family heard of your arrival sir, and this morning the dark elf, who I believe is your friend, passed by the Lusva bakery to ask for a basket of fresh bread to be delivered. My mother and I were at the shop, she decided to pay for it and have it delivered to you as soon as it was ready. They seemed to know each other well, even if your partner was not of many words. It is a sign of friendship and welcome, nothing more."

Triny interjected: "Could you accompany me? I wouldn't want to get lost and make another mistake."

Nolan replied: "Absolutely not! I have to rush, I was al-ready late when I left the house!"

He bowed low and ran away.

The dark elf said in a cold and hard voice: "Your race must disappear from this world."

"I beg you" said Lusva, "the Jellan family are good customers for me, just a poor baker. Take my apprentice to your friend. From what I understand, he is not far and it won't take long. Since he asked for it, I wouldn't want him to be angry about not receiving it."

"Damn you" insulted the dark elf, "and you, follow me! Stu-pid idiot!"

He opened the door ajar and walked off, cursing with every step. Triny immediately stepped behind him and followed.

Lusva did the same, but stayed further away.

Meanwhile, Nolan was observing the scene from afar, peer-ing from a corner of a house. As soon as he saw that the elf and the baker's daughter were leaving, he ran to the shop.

He almost broke down the door, yelling: "Go! Go! Go! Hurry up! We will take care to keep them away as much as possible!"

Jelko was tense. He did not say a word and went out into the street.

In no time at all he was at the door where Elyn was sup-posed to be inside, probably alone.

He opened it and entered.

The room was enveloped in dim light, lit only by a few can-dles here and there. The entrance opened onto a fairly large room.

Opposite, in front of the fireplace, there was a battered square wooden table with three chairs. The only window was on the same side of the door that overlooked the street and it was closed.

On the right side, there was what might have looked like a small kitchen. It was more like a counter, on which food was prepared and then eventually cooked in the fireplace.

Finally, on the left, there was a small and narrow corridor.

From here, light footsteps were heard and the little wood elf appeared in her beautiful elegant and finely-decorated emerald-green dress.

"Jelko!" she exclaimed. She ran to him and hugged him.

He was blown away for a moment. He had seen her die, burnt at the stake, and now he had her in his arms.

"Elyn! Are you alive? How is it possible? That day, I..."

As she had done in the market the first day they met, she anticipated him and said: "You saw me burn at the stake. I know, I'll explain everything."

Jelko gently pushed her away to be able to see her better, he remembered her as very beautiful and indeed she was.

Being locked up in a trunk during the journey with the caravan, and the long days of march, had not affected her at all.

Evidently, the two dark elves had not even touched a hair on her head. Her beautiful dress was neat and clean.

Suddenly, Jelko recovered from that state of contemplation and said: "We don't have much time. Come on! Let's get out of here, my friends and I have come to take you away from those two. If you have something, take it now and let's go out."

Elyn looked at him with the sweetest look he had ever seen in his life: "Jelko, listen to me. I cannot leave this house. I have been bound by the Curse of the Chains for over a decade. They are my jailers, I'm their slave. They cannot harm me, but if I did not obey their commands I would die by walking through that door. I cannot go against their orders in any way, unless they are intended to cause my own death voluntarily."

Jelko took a step back and almost fell to the ground on his knees. If he had been kicked and punched, he would have felt better.

"But I..." he could only say in a faint voice.

"You can't understand now. I'm sorry you've been involved in something you can't even imagine right now. If the two dark

93

elves die, I will no longer have the bond of obedience and I will be able to escape, while still remaining free from the curse in half."

"What should I do, then?"

"Free me from them, then I can explain everything to you. Jelko, please, future events will depend on you and me."

He would have liked to start crying, or maybe not. He would have felt better if he had torn apart everything that was in that dark room.

"They are coming. We will leave in the morning, do not let them find you here. They are about to turn the corner, get out immediately!"

A moment later, Nolan put his head inside the room with the door left open and said in alarm: "Both of them are coming. Lusva and Triny could not hold them off any longer, move! Jelko, take her out and let's go!"

Elyn smiled slightly. She always had a disarming serenity, in any situation. Even when burned at the stake tied to a pole in the main square of Fost, she was like that.

Each time, she seemed to be in control of everything.

"Thanks, Jelko. Trust me, you will see that we'll succeed. Go now."

He had to force himself to recover, nothing had gone as he imagined since he had entered that house. He turned and walked out into the street.

Nolan was incredulous: "The elf! Where is the elf? What happened in there? Damn Jelko, why didn't you take her out?"

"Elyn can't come now" he replied with a lump in his throat, dragging him away.

All four of them found themselves in the shop. It was lunchtime, but no one was hungry.

Jelko told them everything in detail. He was very disappointed with how things had gone, he expected a decidedly different outcome.

The plan devised to bring out the second dark elf had worked perfectly, but that wasn't the ending.

"All we needed was the Curse of the Chains between our feet" Nolan said patting Jelko on the back, "somehow, we'll find a solution. Don't worry."

Triny added: "I've only heard of it. I think it's one of the most risky and complex for those who cast it. I'm not sure, but I think someone spelled an ancient and very difficult ritual. In short, whoever pronounced it against Elyn, was certainly not an apprentice."

"We have to eliminate the dark elves" said Jelko, "and even so, she said that she would only be half-free of the curse, but at least with more calm there would be time to clear up many unknown points."

"She seemed to know well what is happening outside" he continued, "freeing her could also bring us information about the Sleepless Ones we have seen."

Lusva gasped violently. "Have you seen the Sleepless Ones? Where?"

Triny added in alarm: "Are they back?"

"A few days ago, they attacked the caravan with which I was traveling with Nolan and escorted the three to just out-side these walls. They too were part of the group, but obviously they were spared."

Lusva said: "It's a very serious thing! We absolutely must warn everyone before it's too late. Indeed, let's hope some-one has already done so! I remember well the years of their invasions. If they returned, this time they will have organized themselves better."

Jelko got up from his chair and said: "Elyn said they'll leave in the morning, we still have time to think. You and your daughter should go out with us and then take the news to Fost. You will ask about my father, he will believe you when you have explained everything."

"Why not in Kedor, which is just East of here? We can't afford to waste time" Lusva said.

Jelko speculated: "If this town has been targeted, Kedor could be targeted too, given the proximity. Perhaps they have decided to take this area as a starting point or head-quarters.

The Duchy is a little further away and definitely more protected. It shouldn't have been affected by their plans yet, at least I hope not."

Triny said: "Okay, my father and I will take care to deliver the news to the Duchy. It makes no sense to stay here any-more, especially in light of the latest news. We will prepare the wagon, our horse is not fast, but it is always better than traveling on foot. We will do our best."

"In the meantime, we will cover your escape. Then we will deal with the dark elves and Elyn. If all goes well, we will join you somehow or we will meet directly in Fost" said Jelko.

"The problem is how to get out" Nolan added.

Lusva said: "Let's try the same way as when you arrived last night. We will immediately slip behind them when the doors are open for them to pass."

Jelko was looking out the window: "That's what I think too, I see no other solution. The problem is that it will be in the light of day, with more guards around and inhabitants. Maybe they will take us for outlaws and we will find our-selves the adversaries of much more than two dark elves."

Nolan nodded: "And their friends are probably waiting outside for them, even though they shouldn't be in the immediate vicinity. At least we will have a bit of an advantage over the Sleepless Ones."

"We'll help you two too" Lusva said.

"No" Jelko interrupted him brusquely, "your goal as soon as you get out is to run to the Duchy. You won't have to think about us. If it goes wrong, at least you will complete the task at hand. Don't turn around to go back, even if we are in trouble."

"Okay" Triny assured him, "we'll do as you say."

Father and daughter went out the back and went to check the cart they normally used for delivering baked goods.

Nolan approached Jelko at the window: "It won't be easy to beat those two dark elves. You know that, right?"

"Yes, I know, and maybe there will be guards to get in our way too."

"Do you have something in mind? We won't just have to put them on the run, but kill them."

"Unfortunately, I don't. I have a lot of confusion in my head, but we will think of something."

"Yeah, or we'll die" Nolan concluded sitting back down thoughtfully.

They spent the afternoon tidying up the wagon and packing up the food in the backpacks.

They spoke very little, even at dinner.

All four were visibly tense. None of them were used to thinking of the next day as a day of battles or clashes, they were not soldiers in an army.

They tried to go to sleep early to be as rested as possible the next day, but they soon found themselves all in the main room without sleep showing the slightest sign of overtaking them.

They exchanged a few words of comfort in a whisper, silently hoping that dawn would come quickly and put an end to that unnerving wait.

And dawn came.

The cart was ready in front of the shop, which was a stone's throw from the West door from which they had to leave.

Lusva and Triny kept an eye on it, always loading and unloading the usual bags as if they were undecided. They were ready.

Jelko and Nolan had left the backpacks to the two bakers.

They couldn't be clumsy in their movements. If they didn't have time to get them, they would have thrown them to the ground while they were running once they got out.

They had pulled up their hoods to make themselves as less visible as possible. They wandered back and forth along the main road separately, mingling with the citizens who slowly began to populate the settlement.

Elyn and the two dark elves came out shortly after.

She was as usual without any constraint. Evidently the Curse of the Chains was far more effective than any rope on the wrists, and much more discreet by not attracting attention.

When they reached the gate, there were three guards and not two as on the previous evening.

Jelko and Nolan were also ready to run for the door as soon as it opened.

But something was wrong.

The two dark elves were arguing animatedly with the three guards who had lined up, blocking their way to the exit. They had their hands on the hilts of their swords, which were still in the scabbard.

Jelko moved closer, so much so that he was able to hear the tone of the discussion, but without understanding the words.

—The guards this morning are not corrupt!— he thought in amazement.

From a distance, Nolan and the others also exchanged quick, perplexed glances.

The soldiers had no intention of letting them pass, they were loyal to their duty and had to enforce the orders received.

The two dark elves were furious.

They were holding back by force because they were constantly putting their hand to the swords. They had one on each side that day, something that Jelko and Nolan had not noticed previously.

They stopped arguing with the guards, took a few steps back and talked briefly with Elyn, crouching to her height.

She approached the sentries while the two companions remained where they were.

Jelko, who was closest, heard no words. He only saw Elyn staring at them one by one.

Immediately after, one of the guards approached the door.

The others did the same and helped his companion to remove the bolts and the various closing reinforcements.

The door opened.

The two dark elves reached Elyn and together they walked slowly through Meltin's West Gate.

Jelko and Nolan exchanged a quick glance and ran towards the exit.

Lusva did the same. With a few lashes, he forced the horse of his chariot to a rapid gallop in the same direction.

"What are you doing, idiots? Close the doors immediately! Who told you to open them?" one of the guards said.

The other two also seemed to have recovered from a temporary distraction, and worked to try to close the door quickly.

Elyn and the two dark elves were already out and began to move away quickly.

For some reason, they had not recovered any horses to speed up the journey. Certainly, they did not even expect to find the guards to hinder them, unlike the previous evening.

Lusva and Triny were almost behind the door, but the guards were slowly closing it and there was no longer enough room to pass.

"We have to open that damn door more!" Jelko yelled in the direction of Nolan who, like him, was running towards the guards.

One of them stood in the middle, raised both arms and commanded: "Stop! Nobody can pass, by order of the mayor!"

The situation immediately became animated and attracted the attention of several passersby. Two sentries, armed with crossbows, came out from a nearby tower and began to walk along the walls in their direction.

Jelko narrowly dodged the guard who was trying to block his way, threw himself at the closest one, who was intent on closing the door, and knocked him over.

Nolan did the same with the other, charging him like a bull, and gave him a powerful blow with the shoulder, distracting him from his action.

They opened the door more. Lusva's chariot overwhelmed the guard who remained standing and, in a moment, it was beyond the walls.

The two crossbowmen, who had rushed to support their companions, fired their darts. One towards the dark elves, one towards the cart.

Both shots missed the target.

"Go! Go! Don't stop!" Jelko yelled at Triny and her father.

Both of them were moving quickly away.

Nolan started running in the direction of the dark elves, they weren't far ahead of them. Jelko did the same, but paused for a moment to look back to check the situation.

The guards had closed the door and the crossbowmen on the walls had become four by now. They didn't seem to have any intention of going out to chase the fugitives.

More darts flew above their heads.

One hit a dark elf in the back, who fell to the ground and stood up immediately. Perhaps he had armor under his robe, which, although light judging by his fluid movements, had done its duty, even if only partially.

The second dart, however, nearly hit Nolan in the head.

The other two rounds failed completely and dug into the ground.

Lusva and Triny were now out of reach of the crossbow-men, and continued their escape as planned by unloading their backpacks as they ran.

The pursuit also brought Jelko and Nolan beyond the range of the crossbows.

The dark elves slowed to a stop. One of the two proceeded slower, evidently the dart that had hit him had left some mark.

They turned to the pursuers who were almost on top of them, motioned for Elyn to move away from behind them, and drew both swords.

Jelko and Nolan regrouped and did the same, this time walking slowly to catch their breath.

The clash was imminent.

One of the elves spoke and said: "The Chosen One comes with us. Leave while you have time or we will tear you apart!"

Elyn was further away, behind them as she had been ordered.

Surely she could not intervene against her jailers, even if she wanted to.

They swung their swords with great skill, frightening the two boys.

As in a dance, the two dark elves began to slowly move away from each other, bypassing Jelko and Nolan until the latter found themselves almost back-to-back.

"Look over there, Jelko!" Nolan exclaimed in amazement.

Behind Elyn, still very far towards the horizon, a few dozen figures could be seen approaching.

"Don't worry" one of the two dark elves said in a cold voice, "they won't hurt you. When they arrive, you will al-ready be dead!"

The first rushed on Nolan, who parried the blow skillfully and even spared himself from the second blade.

Soon after, Jelko also dodged both of the other dark elf's potentially fatal blows.

The two elves were extremely agile. Unlike mere merchants, as he had known them, they seemed like true masters of the sword.

The ribbons around the hilt of Jelko's sword loosened to reveal it, and the elf in front of him said: "You bastard! Now I remember who you are! I will stick you with that same sword of yours that you so desired that day!"

Nolan screamed. He was hit in the unarmed arm in an attempt to dodge one of the many blows.

Behind the elf who was fighting him, a man was running, brandishing a scythe. He had probably also managed to get out of the chaos just before.

Nolan looked down at his arm and saw blood dripping into his hand.

The elf turned around, hearing someone running towards him from behind and threw one of the two swords at him, hitting him in the chest and killing him instantly.

Jelko was able to parry his opponent's blows quite well, but his counterattacking blows were too predictable and his rival parried them all without any effort.

The Sleepless Ones from the night before could now be clearly recognized, rushing towards the fight behind Elyn.

They were clearly visible and no longer so far away. They moved quickly with their sharp claws glistening in the sun.

The wood elf hadn't looked away for a moment from Jelko and Nolan, who were fighting against her masters, but she could not do anything. She could not go against the curse while they were alive.

Nolan, who was losing a lot of blood, said: "Jelko! I can't take it and the Sleepless Ones are here! I'm sorry!"

They saw Elyn turn to the thirty hungry humanoids who were now a hundred paces from her. She knelt calmly and spread her arms as if to embrace them.

A thin wall of night-black water appeared between her and the running Sleepless Ones. It looked like a dimensional gap.

They could not stop in time and jumped in to get past it.

Elyn fell to the ground as if dead. The ethereal wall was gone, but so were the Sleepless Ones.

"Elyn! No!" Jelko yelled.

He felt the anger rise more and more, his heart pounding and his muscles swelling.

Nolan suffered another blow to his badly injured arm. The elf in front hit him with a kick to the stomach that bent him forward and kneed him in the face. With a thud of breaking bones, he fell back. He never got up again.

Elyn didn't seem to have moved either, they were both on the ground and Jelko was left alone.

The elf that had previously fought Nolan struck Jelko from the back, injuring his leg.

Jelko quickly turned and struck the only sword left with such force that he made it fly away.

He rushed at him like a fury, dropped him on his stomach under him, grabbed his head by the hair and slammed it several times hard on the ground. He stuck two fingers in one eye and tore it out.

The enemy was a mask of blood and Jelko's excitement only grew at the sight.

He rolled on his side, avoiding the blow that the other elf had launched and that almost hit his own companion.

Jelko got up quickly, his eyes were bulging. The rival drew back slightly puzzled to see him and he began his endless line of shots.

The opponent parried them all except one, which hit him in the leg, causing him to fall to his knees. Jelko sent his head flying twenty feet away.

The other had just stood up and had recovered one of the swords. His face was so covered in blood that it was unrecognizable. He struck a blow, but with blood in his face and without an eye, he failed.

Jelko struck him in both legs. One almost broke it off, feeling the blade sticking into the bone.

The enemy fell to the ground, dying on his stomach. Jelko finished him off by sticking his own sword in his groin, until he felt it sticking into the ground beneath him.

He looked around. There was nobody standing and he began to calm down by taking deep breaths. His clothes were stained with blood.

"Jelko..." Nolan said hoarsely, "how is Elyn?"

He ran towards the wood elf and found her on her side. She seemed dead… but no, she was still breathing.

He leaned over her and called out: "Elyn! Elyn!"

She narrowed her eyes. He gently picked her up and walked over to Nolan, who was struggling to sit up.

"You have to heal her, she's still alive!" Jelko said as he laid her next to his injured comrade.

Nolan was already reciting something about himself, speaking incomprehensible words. His wounds stopped bleeding in an instant.

He helped him to his feet.

"Take me out of here. Take me to the woods" Elyn said faintly, her eyes closed. She seemed completely drained.

"Jelko" said his companion, who was slowly regaining col-or, "retrieve the backpacks over there and take us away."

He ran to retrieve the backpacks and weapons, returned to them, picked up Elyn and set off at Nolan's slow pace.

In the distance, there were trees. They would be there in no time.

Behind, the town of Meltin seemed to have fallen into deafening silence.

The surreal atmosphere had enveloped that place again.

No sentries patrolled the walls.

CHAPTER 13 (Arcane Elves and Prisoners)

At the end of the afternoon, they went into a wood. The town of Meltin was just visible on the horizon behind them.

Tired, Nolan leaned with his back against the trunk of a large beech. His wounds were improving, but he still needed time to rest.

Jelko carefully placed Elyn on the grass and sat down beside her, it seemed she was sleeping deeply.

"Do you hear that?" Nolan asked softly.

"What?" Jelko answered, looking around in alarm.

"There is a strange breeze around us. Look over there, not a leaf is moving."

Jelko paid attention and in fact, that light fresh breeze, was only there around them. Just farther away, the air seemed still.

The breeze was pleasant, the days in those places away from rivers and coasts were rather hot and muggy. It seemed to be gently stroking Elyn's straight black hair, uncovering her tattoo of a chrysalis imprisoned by a spider web behind her neck.

Nolan, who was already speaking in a low voice, reached out to whisper something in his companion's ear: "It is the little wood elf who is doing all this. I don't know whether to be scared of her or not."

"I don't know either, we'll ask her a few questions as soon as possible. Let's rest too, it seems to be a quiet place."

Jelko lay down, making himself as comfortable as possible.

Nolan looked at his injured arm, spoke some incomprehensible words again and covered it, leaning against the trunk and closing his eyes.

By sunset, Elyn still hadn't woken up.

The two boys ate quickly and got ready to spend the night.

They decided not to disturb her. She didn't even seem to notice the noise they made while they were arranging things, as they tried to do as little as possible.

Jelko said: "I'll take care of guarding tonight. You rest, you need it. I already rested before and I have no serious injuries."

"Okay, I should be much better by tomorrow morning."

Elyn and Nolan slept all night without ever waking up, Jelko was able to sleep a wink only when he saw one of the two sun peeking out. He wanted to resist, but he couldn't, and he fell asleep as well.

"Wake up!" Nolan was shaking him hard.

"What's happening?"

He looked around, Elyn was gone and so was the light breeze that had accompanied them since the afternoon.

"Hello, my friends!" they heard behind them.

Elyn looked in great shape. Her elegant green and gold dress was flawless, as usual.

"Sorry, I didn't mean to scare you" she said.

"How are you?" Jelko asked.

"Very well, I hope you feel better too."

Nolan looked at his arm, raised it and lowered it several times, it had improved a lot and almost didn't hurt anymore.

Jelko stood up and said: "We must go back to Fost and organize against the Sleepless Ones. My father will be of great help, the two bakers will anticipate the news of their return if they arrive safe and sound."

Elyn replied: "Wait, Jelko. We're not going South to the Duchy. Let's sit down, I owe you some explanations."

They sat in a circle and the two boys exchanged a quick glance.

"The Sleepless Ones are a grave danger" Jelko began, "we must spread the word as much as possible, so that the kingdoms can once again organize themselves against this second threat. If it's not already late."

"I agree" Nolan added.

Elyn, with her usual hypnotic calm, said: "Your two friends will arrive at your destination and do their duty. I'm sorry, but this time the Sleepless Ones are too many. The human armies will only be able to slow their advance, that's why we're headed elsewhere."

Jelko interrupted astonished: "Where are we headed? We have to fight them all together, I don't understand!"

She replied: "I am the Chosen One sent by my people to hunt my twin, he is behind all this. We will have to neutralize him in some way, only then it will really be over. He's somewhere further North, that's where we're headed."

"Which people? The Wood Elves?" Nolan asked.

Elyn smiled softly: "No, the Arcane Elves."

"Impossible!" he exclaimed, almost crossly, "don't fool us, the Arcane Elves are all tall and blond! I don't mean to be rude, but you're not really like that."

She lowered her gaze slightly, looking thoughtful now: "What you see is not my real body, it is the fault of the Curse of the Chains that my brother has inflicted on me."

Jelko said: "But we killed the dark elves. Now you're free, right?"

"As I told you, only halfway. I no longer have the obligation of absolute obedience, but the curse also traps me in a body that is not my own, to make sure that nobody believes me, just like is happening now with you two."

"So you are an Arcane Elf?" Nolan asked with a startled expression.

"Yes" she replied.

"That's why you have those mental powers, not to mention how you made those thirty Sleepless Ones disappear into that dimensional gap!" he added, almost rising to his feet, euphoric.

Elyn continued in a bewitching voice: "The curse casted by a kinsman is much more limiting, my powers are minimized. Every time I try it, I risk a lot and I need a long time to recover."

Jelko said: "And how can we help you then?"

"You have to help me to find my twin, only I can beat him. We will both have to be inside a containment pentacle, there we will be on equal terms again. If I win, I will be free and the Sleepless Ones will be defeated."

"Why is your brother doing this to you?" Nolan asked.

He knew something about that people: "Arcane Elves are peaceful, if I'm not mistaken."

"The thirst for power and dark knowledge has consumed his body and soul. He is no longer who he once was, and we Arcanes must recover him, dead or alive."

Jelko asked: "Why us, Elyn? Why did you tell me in that house in Meltin that things depend on you and me? Why did you lead me here in dreams?"

She looked at him in silence for a moment that seemed eternal, then said: "Because you have a talent, but I can't be the one to reveal it to you."

"But how? And who, then?" Jelko exclaimed.

"Your father will do it. When you are ready."

Jelko gasped. His father evidently knew something that he had never told him yet, and now he was too far away to ask him.

Nolan intervened curiously: "And why me?"

Elyn replied: "You will keep us both alive more than once, my friend! My powers are reduced to a tenth, we will need yours."

She got up and walked away, brushing all the trees she passed by with one hand as if to caress them.

Jelko looked confused and remained silent.

Nolan interrupted that moment by saying: "Do you realize that she is an Arcane Elf? Do you know that with the powers she has, she could disintegrate both of us in an instant? Let alone a Chosen One, then! If you told anyone, they wouldn't believe you, nobody has seen one for centuries. To tell the truth, they would call you crazy, given her current appearance."

"She is powerless at the moment" Jelko said.

"Well, I wouldn't say that. We saw her, think if she were at full capacity! Arcane Elves are mentalists with enormous potential."

"What do we do, Nolan?" Jelko asked getting up too, "I'm afraid, I don't know where this whole story will lead us. It's much bigger than us."

"I know, I'm scared, too. If we follow her, we'll be in a lot of trouble for sure."

Jelko patted him on the shoulder of his good arm: "On the other hand, being torn apart by the claws of a Sleepless One is not a good alternative. And if we don't do anything, sooner or later that is what will happen."

"Come on, let's collect things and go to meet her" he continued.

The two reached the elf further ahead. She barely reached the chin of either. If she had been her true likeness, she would have been taller than both of them.

She still seemed to be contemplating every single tree, one by one, and said: "Aren't they magnificent? They've healed my mental wounds the whole time since you took me to this wood. It's not the first time they've done it."

"Were they that cool breeze?" Jelko asked.

"Of course" she said, "they were worried about me."

"On the other hand, you're a wood elf" Nolan added, "at least for now."

Elyn smiled and said: "Yeah, I'm one of them."

The two boys looked around. For them, they were just trees as there were almost everywhere, yet they felt like so many eyes were on them.

"Elyn" Jelko said, "we will help you find your twin. You will get what you were sent for by your people, and we will get rid of the Sleepless Ones. We have no other alternative to save our people, it seems."

"Yes, we'll go with you" Nolan confirmed.

Elyn looked at them, lightly touched the faces of both with a caress and said: "I'm sorry to do this to you, you do not deserve it. The road will be uphill, but if everything goes well, we will turn around and we can admire everything we have done."

"Together we will make it, if this is our destiny" Jelko said.

Nolan exclaimed: "A name! We need a name to give to the group!"

"The Merchants of Leaves! How about that? I also have a ring with the symbol in my backpack that I made with my own hands!"

"I like it!" the companion answered enthusiastically, "it evokes memories for which everyone should fear us! With Elyn, we will be unbeatable!"

"I wouldn't bet on that at all!" she said, "but Merchants of Leaves sounds right!"

Meanwhile, the elf had begun to walk North. Further on, the forest would end to make way for the great central desert.

"Where are we headed?" Jelko asked.

"We have to meet Ameh Hurak. He's a powerful clairvoyant, I'm sure he'll give us directions to where my brother is."

"Ameh Hurak" Nolan repeated, "I'm not sure, but I think my teacher mentioned him a couple of times. Are you sure he's still alive?"

"No, I'm not sure."

"And what city does he live in?" Jelko asked.

"Nowhere. He's in Argoran, that's where we're headed."

"Great!" Nolan exclaimed, stopping suddenly, "I escaped from that place just a few days ago and now I find it again as my next destination!"

"I know" Elyn said, "but you will enter it as a free man."

Jelko added: "Do you want to put Nolan on? You will be able to tell your grandchildren that you have been to Argoran with the Merchants of Leaves. What more could you want?"

The three began to laugh loudly, the march towards Argoran had begun in the best way.

Meanwhile, somewhere...

"My lord, we have completed the mission. The circle has closed, just like the reinforced doors behind which we herded them."

"Very well" replied the bent and almost deformed elderly man, as he looked out of the window at the ruins of the abandoned city.

The room was almost dark, it was located in a rather low-standing tower with a circular base.

On one side, there was a long worn wooden table with some chairs around it. At the head of the table, there was a larger one with padding and armrests. Hanging on the stone walls, there were shelves with dusty books and a large decorated silver mirror.

In the center of the room, there was a tub also made of stone, with a small black basin beside it with amber water inside.

On the ground, there was a large pentacle that occupied almost the entire round room, emitting a slight blue light.

The one who had brought the news immediately came out wrapped in his raven-black cloak, closing the door behind him.

"Manmur" said the figure at the window, "as you can see, everything is about to happen. Soon, I will be able to found my lineage and abandon the old one to which you still belong. You should have been on my side."

There was a hiss from the great silver mirror, and immediately the image of a tall old elf, with long white hair, appeared and said: "Nothing is yet lost to the Arcane Elves, not as long as our Lady and Chosen One is still alive. So do not believe that you can get away with it, Silven. It won't be as easy as you think."

"My sister is heading to Argoran. The visual delay inside the magic basin is just over a day, it is a place that is far too underestimated. I don't know what she's looking for there, but I can't interfere with events as long as she's in that place. She won't be able to stop me, it's too late now."

He continued: "You made a big mistake when you took her side. I can't forget, I should have been in her place and now you will pay the consequences."

The old elf Manmur replied: "Your parents and ancestors would never have approved of such a betrayal. Free me and let me return to our people, perhaps I can still remedy and do something for you and your salvation. You have become greedy, it is not a characteristic of ours. You have let yourself be seduced by the thirst for power and now your life is confined there, inside that pentacle drawn on the ground."

Silven turned to the mirror where the old wise man was reflected and took a few steps towards him, laughing: "No, you are my bargaining chip, I can't let you go. I need you exactly where you are."

Manmur replied: "You must subject the whole known world to your will, before our people will stop hunting you and abandon you to your fate. Until then, you will always be hunted."

"That's what I'm doing, one day I'll show you what the dungeons of this tower are full of and you'll understand how close I am to my purpose" Silven whispered, "but it's not time yet."

Manmur said defiantly: "Elyn will never let you! Of this, you can be sure!"

Silven suddenly went on a rampage. "She has no power after the curse! How can you think she can beat me in a duel in those conditions?"

The old elf said: "The Chosen One is not alone, her traveling companions hide abilities that no one yet knows."

Silven was face-to-face with the mirror: "And what are these powers that you think might hinder me?"

"No one, Silven. Unfortunately, no one."

Someone knocked at the door.

The shady dark figure from before appeared: "Here I am, my lord. We are ready."

Silven turned to him and said: "Go, two of you will travel fast. Strike as soon as possible, take no prisoners."

"Yes sir" he replied, closing the door again.

Manmur had a dull look, his hopes were very low.

He could not have any influence. Any work of persuasion had been in vain now for a long, long time.

And he was tired of being imprisoned for over a decade.

Silven stared at him menacingly before him and said: "Where were we? It's time to talk, you still have too many things to say that I need to know."

With a gnarled hand, he touched the frame of the mirror.

Inside it, Manmur began to writhe and scream in pain.

CHAPTER 14 (The Ashirs)

"It's starting to get really hot" Jelko said.

The three had left the last wooded area behind them and started rationing the water. A vast, increasingly arid and dusty plain began to open up in front of them. Soon it would give way to the great central desert, which stretched as far as the eye could see.

"How are we going to get to Argoran on foot? After three days of walking from the beginning of the desert, without any precautions, it is impossible, at least to my knowledge" Nolan said, disheartened.

"Wait, we have the rings you took from the caravan guards" Jelko said, "who knows if they can protect us from heat as well as physical attacks."

"Can I see them?" Elyn asked.

Jelko pulled out his ring and passed it to her, the elf slowed down for a moment to observe it calmly.

After having checked it carefully on the palm of her hand, she said: "They are timed, they have a deadline."

"What does that mean?" Nolan asked.

Elyn handed the ring back to Jelko, saying: "It means that you can use them until they are exhausted. The ones you have protect the wearer from all physical and magical attacks and they will surely also shelter you from the unbearable heat of the desert, but by the time we get to Argoran, they will have spent their charge and go back to being simple metal rings."

Jelko asked, puzzled: "So if we use them for the journey, then they won't work anymore at the destination and we won't be protected from possible aggression?"

"Exactly" Elyn replied. As usual, she wasn't worried in the least, unlike the two boys.

Nolan added: "Let's hope for a warm welcome then, but I have some doubts about it."

"You've already done so much for me" Elyn said, "let me take care of it when we get to the prisons. Don't worry, just use the rings. If they run out when we get to our destination, it doesn't matter. Protect yourself from the heat instead, or you won't make it to Argoran alive."

"You seem very calm about it, are all your friends there?" Jelko asked.

"No, not at all" Elyn replied, "but we have no alternative, so worrying too much won't solve the problem anyway. We need to talk to Ameh Hurak at all costs."

"We should get some horses as soon as possible" Nolan said, changing the subject.

"Ehm... I don't know how to ride" Jelko said almost softly.

The friend burst out laughing: "But how? I don't believe it. It can't be true, come on!"

"It's not a joke, I've never learned how. I've never needed to ride, to tell the truth, because I've never left the capital of the Duchy, and those few times I did, I always rode in the carriage of the royal delegation of which my father is part of it."

"At least on the back you will know how to keep up! You don't have to do anything if we tie your mount to mine."

"Well, I do have a mule in Fost. I knew how to ride on his back, but nothing more."

Nolan clapped a friendly punch on Jelko's shoulder and said: "If we go, we will ride two to a horse. Somehow we will, but for now it would be very convenient for us to arrive earlier and avoid three days of marching in this heat."

"If we get out of all this and survive the new invasion of the Sleepless Ones, I swear I'll learn to ride!" Jelko said, "how is your arm?"

Nolan discovered it and moved it as if he were testing something: "Very well, I would say. I don't feel any pain, my God has been merciful and has allowed my magic to work perfectly."

In fact, only a few scratches were visible. What had been a nasty bleeding wound the day before was now almost invisible.

Elyn said: "See? You are a skilled healer. You have done very well, not everyone can heal such serious wounds in such a short time."

The first day was almost over.

The two suns were very low on the horizon, the sand dunes had now taken over the ever-bleak landscape. Only a few rocks stuck out of the sand from time to time.

They had never stopped, except for a very short time to drink and eat, and even then they merely slowed their pace. There wasn't any time to waste. They had to get to Argoran as soon as possible, for their aim was to shorten the journey, which became more and more unbearable with every step.

Despite her petite build, Elyn held up without any problems.

From a distance, she could very well look like a girl between two men.

They spent the first night in a small depression created by high dunes all around. The temperature was acceptable. It was almost cold, in stark contrast to the torrid days. The silence was surreal, only a few gusts of wind broke it from time to time.

The following morning, the coolness of the night, quickly gave way to the increasing heat with the rising of the first sun.

They ate bread and nuts, Elyn always ate very little and seemed troubled by something.

"What's going on, Elyn?" asked Jelko, who had been watching her for a while.

Nolan, who was intent on filling his stomach, also stopped with food in his mouth to look at her worriedly.

She replied: "There is something wrong, but I can't understand what. Here in the desert, I can't perceive things clearly."

Nolan swallowed his last bite and got up, they were still protected by the dunes that seemed to have shifted slightly during the night.

Climbing one of them, he said: "I'm going to take a look from up here."

Elyn and Jelko looked at him, worried. He reached the top of the highest dune around them, shielded himself with a hand on his forehead to protect himself from the intense light and began to rotate, scanning the horizon.

He suddenly lowered himself to lie down on the sand. Everyone held their breath.

Nolan slid to one side and rolled down the gentle slope of the dune, until he returned to the side of the two companions who had remained motionless.

He was very agitated and said: "To the West there are two figures astride something. They are still very far away, but they are coming in this direction."

"What do you mean astride something?" Jelko asked nervously.

"It means they don't look like horses to me, but they are too far away for me to understand what they are. Maybe I'm wrong."

Elyn jumped up and said: "We have to go, let's not waste time."

"Wait" Jelko replied, "they probably haven't seen us, we're sheltered by the dunes here. If we get back on the road in the open air, they'll see us for sure."

"They're our pursuers" she said, "they already know where we are, it's my brother's welcome gift."

Nolan said: "We can try to attack them, there are three of us!"

Elyn replied: "No, not here in the desert, where all magical auras are weak. I would be of no help and they are certainly the best champions he has. We would certainly have the worst of it, they are here to kill us."

"Let's go, then. Quick!" Jelko said.

They quickly climbed the dune to the North. Once at the top, all three looked to the West and saw the two figures still far away proceeding slowly, but inexorably.

"Put the rings on" Elyn said in a calm but firm voice, "it would be better not to stop and to proceed as fast as possible. Those they ride are not horses, they are Ashirs."

"Ashirs? What are?" Jelko asked as he walked quickly, following them behind.

"They are beings summoned from other worlds similar to large lizards" replied the elf, "they have a poisonous sting on their tail. They are slow, but they need neither food nor water and they can walk without stopping as long as there is enough light to do so."

"The Rings!" she repeated.

"Take mine" Jelko told her.

She stroked his arm and said: "Don't worry about me."

She put her hands together as if praying and touched the tip of her nose with her fingers.

Immediately around her body appeared a bubble with colored reflections like those seen in soap bubbles. It was very snug, as if it were a second skin. It shimmered barely noticeably, depending on how it reflected the light when she moved.

Jelko and Nolan put the rings on their fingers. Immediately a grayish bubble, more rudimentary and with metallic reflections, appeared a few inches from their body that enveloped them.

They set off at a brisk pace.

Slowly, the two figures moved, aligning themselves behind them. They seemed neither slower nor faster, as if at the moment they just wanted to keep an eye on them from afar.

"Elyn" Jelko said, "can I ask you something? Actually, I have many questions for you."

"Of course" she replied, "ask me anything you want. If I can answer you, I'll do so very willingly."

"The day I first met you at the market and there was that explosion, you were holding a magic ring that killed and injured all those people. Why? I still don't have any explanation."

"You're right."

"That gesture cannot be traced back to anything sensible. The two dark elves had been joined by two emissaries of the Arcane Elves, in an attempt to somehow free me and they had merged into the crowd. To escape, they staged that explosion and ordered me to hold the object in my hand, so that they knew I would be blamed by diverting attention. They knew that I could not disobey and that I would probably be condemned, but they also knew that, on their orders, I would be able to escape death by mingling in the flames and the smoke."

"But, how is it possible? I heard you scream as you burned, I can't get that image and those screams of pain out of my head. I was haunted by them for days until I hated my father, who lit the pyre you were tied to."

"I know, you are the only one I noticed in the crowd."

"From that moment on, I don't know what has happened to me" he continued, "my life has turned upside down and now I find myself here killing people and monsters."

"I know, Jelko. It wasn't the first time, I suffer as if it were all real until I reach a step away from death. It is precisely at that point that I can escape, but every time it is all terribly true."

Nolan was also listening with interest and said in a soft tone: "Your brother loves you so much that every time he takes you to death without killing you. This is terrible."

"Yes" Elyn said, "he can't kill me with a curse, but it's like he does it every time, and I assure you it's much worse."

"I'm sorry, Elyn" Jelko said, "we have to kill that bastard, what you just told us is atrocious. I'm sorry, I didn't know and I didn't want you to rethink this."

"Don't worry" she said, "after almost fifteen years in this body and in these conditions, I've gotten used to it. Help me find a pentacle face-to-face with him, then I can get my body back and we will fight on equal terms. And if I die, at that point it will be once and for all."

Nobody said anything else.

Jelko and Nolan continued to walk with their heads down.

They were still visibly shaken by what they had just heard from Elyn.

The three walked all day exchanging a few words. Thanks to the protection of the spells they did not feel the scorching heat, but they were fatigued all the same.

Every now and then they glanced back to check those strange figures. They were always there, neither one step closer nor one step further from them.

Paying a little more attention, they could actually see that the mounts were strange and out of the ordinary. They were certainly not just horses.

At sunset on the second evening in the desert, they stopped under the shelter of a small pale rock.

"They stopped too" Nolan said, spying on them.

"Why don't they attack us? What are they waiting for if they have been sent here to eliminate us?" Jelko asked, also leaning over to observe them.

Elyn replied: "I think they are studying us, I fear it will not be long. If we manage to get to Argoran before they do, maybe we will get away with it and we will have a little advantage to think of a plan."

Jelko said lightly: "I've never wanted to get to those damn prisons as quickly as right now!"

"Don't tell me about it!" Nolan echoed.

The elf continued: "They won't do it tonight, not in the dark at least. And the Ashirs will bury themselves in the sand for shelter."

"I'll stay up and check on them" said Jelko, "since I can see them at night, I'm the only one that it makes sense to stay awake. You rest."

"It's a good idea" Nolan replied, "but we should still have a day and a half of travel. Tomorrow it won't be easy to tackle the journey if you don't sleep a wink tonight."

Elyn said: "I'm sorry my friends. I don't have enough power to do anything to help you, much less in this wilderness. If we were in a forest, I would have asked the trees to watch over us."

"If I don't sleep one night, I'll survive anyway. Don't worry" Jelko concluded.

He never took his eyes off their pursuers, he saw that at one point there were only those two human-shaped figures. Their mounts had probably hidden in the sand, as Elyn had said.

—By now my father should have received the message from Lusva and Triny— he thought among many things, —who knows if they are preparing to defend themselves against this new invasion.—

The night was long and his thoughts were many, he certainly could not imagine being catapulted into a matter like that.

He thought that the will of the Gods was really funny at times, reserving destinies that until recently were considered unlikely.

Instead of a comfortable bed in his city, he lay on the desert sand, watching the movements of who-knows-who wanted him dead. And not just him.

Nolan seemed a very jovial big boy, an excellent adventure companion. Maybe if he hadn't risked his life every day, he would have been even more fun. He was a loyal and cheerful type; his presence was pleasant.

The healing powers of his one God were obviously a great comfort, and he hadn't had any second thoughts in offering his help to the cause.

On the other hand, the alternatives were really unattractive: to live a little longer, perhaps a year, but always with the anguishing thought of the Sleepless Ones, who were advancing more and more every day.

As big as the world was, there was no place to hide to escape them. It was really only a matter of time before everyone was probably torn apart by their claws, or by the blades of some corrupt human commander.

Elyn instead was the cause of everything.

Her twin would kill anyone who came between him and her.

He had to eliminate her at any cost, great was his thirst for power and revenge for an allegedly elevated place within the castes of their people.

She had taken it from him, and not even deliberately.

The people of the Arcane Elves did not find him fit to lead, so now he was on a rampage. His sister, on the other hand, was considered much more balanced and predisposed to fill a similar role.

Subduing an entire world was the only way to generate a new lineage, and detach oneself definitively from the people of origin.

Jelko turned to look at Elyn.

She was there on his side, not far away. Unlike his friend, he could hardly even hear her breathe. She was something superior, every gesture graceful, with her elegant movements and persuasive voice.

Everything hinted that she was not of that world.

Who knows what she was really like? Surely tall, blonde and of amazing beauty. Seeing her subjugated by that curse made her strange, small and dark.

She was almost the paradox of herself.

Yet even in that body, she had something magical. She had respect for everything. Jelko barely knew anything about Arcane Elves, but according to what Nolan had told him, they were something supernatural, above any known race.

The night passed quickly.

Jelko did not sleep a wink, but at least he managed to rest his legs to continue the journey the following day. His companions slept through the night.

"Good morning" said Jelko in a calm voice, "how are you?"

"Not bad, I would say" Nolan replied, stretching the muscles of his whole body "were you able to rest a bit? Are our friends still in their place?"

"They never moved. I haven't slept, but I'm fine."

Elyn stood up, quickly adjusted her dress and said: "Let's go."

She was not calm. Since they had entered the desert, she knew that her already weakened powers were even less effective, and knowing that she was constantly being followed, did not make her feel calm because her mentalist perceptions were almost nil.

At first light, they immediately set out and ate quickly as they walked.

Behind them, the pursuers were always at the same distance as observers rather than murderous emissaries.

Elyn threw the protection spell on herself again and the two boys put the rings back on their fingers, evoking the insurmountable bubble.

"It shouldn't be long" Jelko said.

"Argoran will probably be on the horizon tomorrow morning, one last night and then our concerns will be joined by the entrance to the prisons" Nolan added.

"What will you do when it's all over?" Jelko asked him, changing the subject, "will you return to the islands of the Barony of the Dragon, among the raiding pirates?"

"I don't think so" Nolan replied with uncommon seriousness, "by now I have been marked as a heretic there because of the refusal of the official Gods. They are stupid not to believe in my only God, and too many brothers have been killed or deported for having tried to spread the true Creed."

"You don't have any friends or relatives worth returning to, do you?" Elyn asked.

"No, I have no one" Nolan replied, "I have never met my parents. I only remember an old monastery in the mountains to the North, then when I was not even ten years old, they took me to another one closer to the capital called Yers, where I took care of the medicinal plants they cultivated. In the meantime, I followed the teachings of the master healers. My only friends are my brothers, but who knows what happened to them after the persecutions of the inquisitors against us."

"I understand" said Jelko, "I'm sorry. Let's hope we find some peace of mind at the end of this story, I think we all deserve it."

It was towards the end of the afternoon when the protective bubbles generated by the rings suddenly vanished.

"Great!" Nolan exclaimed, "the rings have run out of power."

"Yeah, damn it!" Jelko echoed.

"Damn" Elyn said, "I can't protect you with mine, luckily the suns won't be long in setting. I'm so sorry, you'll have to resist. Just use my water if you need it, I can do without it."

"We'll hold out, one last effort" Jelko said, patting Nolan on the shoulder.

The heat was really unbearable.

It was not difficult to understand why no one had ever managed to survive the second day in those extreme conditions, without any kind of precautions. Argoran's prisoners were purposely given a minimum of supplies for this very reason.

In the distance, they began to see the remains of all those who had tried the desperate escape. As there were no guards to hold them back, it was very common for someone to try to escape, hoping to reach freedom once they crossed the border of the desert.

The rumors were true. There was an expanse of bones and more or less recent remains as far as the eye could see, as reported by the soldiers who periodically transported the new inmates to the prisons.

Jelko was very tired. He hadn't slept the previous night and he was bracing himself with Nolan in the scorching heat, trying to cheat the fatigue.

Elyn looked at them from time to time. Knowing how much they were suffering bothered her, she often avoided meeting their gaze so as not to feel even more sorry for what they had to suffer because of her.

"Hey!" Jelko exclaimed in alarm, "they got off their mounts, but where did they go?"

"I turned around a little while ago and they were there!" Nolan added widening his eyes and wiping the sweat from his forehead, "they can't have disappeared in such a short time, it's not possible!"

Elyn paused and narrowed her eyes.

The two guys were looking at her in concern when she said: "They're coming."

Not far from them, something was moving in the sand in two separate and distinct points, fast approaching.

They could see the surface rippling as if it were a wave of the sea and a light dust rising in correspondence with it.

A few dozen paces from them, a large lizard head suddenly popped up, immediately followed by its whole body. The tail, similar to that of a scorpion, was raised and vibrated menacingly.

It was an Ashir, a being evoked from another dimension, half a lizard with sharp teeth and half a scorpion. Its size was such that it could be easily ridden by those who were able to dominate it.

A little further on, the second abomination also came out of the sand in the same way as the previous one.

"Watch out for their venomous stings!" Elyn yelled, "they have powerful venom and they always strike first with it!"

The two boys immediately drew their swords and stood on guard.

In the distance they saw the two pursuing figures accelerate their pace for the first time.

The Ashir who came out last directed its sting towards Nolan, shot forward and tried to hit him. He dodged it with a swerve to his right.

The lizard, having missed the shot, ejected a greyish liquid that smeared a sleeve of his jacket. The sleeve began to fry and was reduced to shreds in a very short time.

Meanwhile, the other Ashir had approached Jelko, but before trying to hit him, it spit the same acidic grey liquid from the sting of its tail, missing him completely.

When it was close, it stretched its tail, dripping with venom in vain that hit the sand a step away from him.

Elyn started running, screaming: "I have the bubble protecting me! They can't hit me. I'll try to distract them and draw attention to me!"

She ran to meet the one who was on Nolan and began to circle around it. The Ashir seemed intent on hitting the new little threat. Nolan took advantage of it by delivering a blow with his sword, hitting it on the back.

A thick, dark, pitch-like liquid oozed from the wound.

The monster opened its jaws, visibly unnerved. Enraged, it showed its sharp teeth like so many aligned daggers.

A little further on, Jelko seemed to be in trouble.

The Ashir continued to quickly alternate jets of venom with bites that he could barely dodge, and the few blows he could inflict on it were too light and weak.

Its skin was thick and tough.

Meanwhile, Elyn was moving with great agility.

The monster that Nolan was fighting now seemed more interested in her, but it was much clumsier in comparison and could not follow her movement with the same speed with which the elf moved around it.

"Jelko!" his friend suddenly shouted.

Elyn also turned to him, the Ashir's sting was lodged in the middle of his left thigh.

He staggered and fell to the ground on his side, still brandishing the sword of the royal seals, trying to defend himself from more incoming blows.

The monster slowly approached him, opening its mouth full of drool. Its neck retracted slightly as if to take a run and suddenly tried to bite its prey with a snap.

Jelko began to roll on the sand. When he was out of range, he stood up unexpectedly.

He breathed quickly, he shifted his gaze to the Ashir that had hit him. His eyes were bloodshot, just like the blood that came out of his injured leg which, mixed with the grey liquid, corroded part of his clothes.

He began to charge, the lizard hit him with the side of the tail and made him fall.

He immediately got up as if he hadn't felt anything and began to hit it with the usual infinite succession of blows, so powerful as to suggest that the same sword would break at any moment.

In the meantime, Elyn had managed to climb onto the back of the Ashir facing Nolan.

The monster reared up to get rid of that presence as if it had gone mad. The tail with the stinger was wriggling, trying to hit the elf above without succeeding.

It raised itself even more and tried to grab her in its hungry mouth, twisting backwards.

Nolan took advantage of the situation and recited some very brief magic formula, his sword became shinier than usual and he thrust its full length into its vulnerable belly.

Putting all his strength into it, he tried to make a gash in the scaly skin as large as he could.

The sword now shone with a blue light and seemed to cut the Ashir's body as if it were butter. While he was underneath it, he was covered in what was probably blood mixed with guts.

He leaped back to keep the lizard from falling on top of him.

After this fatal blow, Elyn jumped down as soon as the monster hit the ground dying.

They both turned to Jelko, he was still tormenting his Ashir.

He had torn it to pieces, but he kept hitting it furiously with all his force, raging on what was left of it.

At one point he stopped, took a deep breath and fell unconscious to the ground.

"Jelko!" Elyn said, running with Nolan beside her.

Meanwhile, the two pursuing figures had halved the distance.

They were not running. They were just walking quickly and now that they were closer, they could see that they were hooded and dressed in blue. Their features were humanoid.

"Let's take him away!" shouted the elf, "let's get out of here, quickly!"

Nolan carried Jelko on his shoulder, Elyn took care to retrieve his friend's sword and backpack.

He was very white, his breathing barely perceptible, his eyes half closed.

One of the two suns was setting, soon it would be pitch dark.

The two pursuers had not slowed down and with Jelko on Nolan's shoulders, they would not have been long in catching up with them if it had been daylight for a while.

"They won't reach us in time" Elyn said, "but they'll be on us in the morning."

"What do we do? Shall we wait and try to defend ourselves after the night?" Nolan asked as he laboriously carried his half-fainted friend.

"No, they are too strong. At least here in the desert we can't beat them, we have to get to Argoran quickly."

"I don't think we'll succeed, we're too slow that way."

"We will walk again tonight" said the elf, "they will stop and we will gain a little advantage. Even if it won't be much, maybe it will be enough."

"I can try to help you" Jelko interjected in a faint voice.

He was still very pale and could barely keep his eyes open.

The night came and a last glance back suggested that their pursuers would stop to resume the following day.

They were close enough, it wouldn't be hard for them to reach them as they didn't have any weight to carry.

Nolan laid Jelko on the ground. He grimaced in pain, he was all sweaty.

"He has a high fever" Elyn said, "can you do something while you catch your breath?"

"For the wound, yes. For the venom, I don't know. But I can try" Nolan replied, "if it hasn't killed him yet after all this time it has been in his body, maybe he's out of harm's way. But he would still need total rest and some infusions to drink."

Nolan touched the wound in his leg and put his hand on it, when he took it off it was already healing.

"If only I had some medicinal herbs available, I could be more useful."

"You're already doing a lot" Elyn assured him.

"How are you? You never complain" Nolan asked her.

"I'm not hurt, I'm fine."

Nolan turned to Jelko and said: "It's not your time yet, my friend. Are you ready? We need your eyes tonight."

"Leave me here" he replied in a faint voice, "go on alone. You will be faster, there is only a little bit left."

"Well, no! It's the fever that's talking, you're delirious."

Nolan carried him on his shoulders as one does with children and continued: "Try to be lucid, you just need to tell us if we are going in the right direction and if there are obstacles ahead of us. We will proceed slowly, but we cannot stop."

"Okay" Jelko replied, "I'll do my best, it's the least I can do."

Dangling over the shoulders of his companion, from time to time he gave indications on the direction to follow.

They spent the whole night walking, Elyn holding Nolan by the arm trying to help him as he had to support two weights.

"How are you?" the elf asked him.

"I can't feel my legs anymore. If we don't get far enough away from them, by morning and with the prisons out of sight, I won't be of any help in the event of an attack. And unfortunately, I think it will be inevitable. They have put us out of action and exhausted us like real predators."

"Maybe we'll make it, let's not despair" she said.

Nolan continued: "You have to promise me, otherwise you have to run as fast as you can. At least you have to survive."

"Okay" Elyn said, squeezing his arm tighter.

"You lie. You will not, you would rather die with us."

"Exactly" she replied.

CHAPTER 15 (Oasis)

They talked very little all night, listening to Jelko's few directions. As soon as the first sun came up, all three almost exclaimed loudly in enthusiasm.

The injured comrade's indications were correct.

On the horizon, and not very far away, they could see what seemed to be a city.

Argoran was closer than expected, and their pursuers had lost the advantage they had gained during the Ashirs' attack the afternoon before.

"Put me down Nolan!" said Jelko, "maybe I can walk, it won't be long."

He put him on the ground. He seemed to be better, as he was able to stand up. Some strength had returned and even if he proceeded slowly, at least he no longer weighed on his partner.

The two behind them were already on the move. They quickened their pace, they realized they had lost too much ground during the night and wanted to recover.

But it was too late, the three turned when they were a few steps from the city in the only oasis of that desert and they no longer saw them. They had mysteriously disappeared from sight.

"They vanished into thin air" Nolan said in alarm.

Elyn said: "We'll have some respite here, we won't have to worry about them for now. We made it."

Jelko fell to the ground on his knees, he was exhausted: "But it's huge! No one had ever described it like this, it doesn't look like a prison at all!"

Over the decades, Argoran had become a metropolis.

It was probably as big as the capitals of the various kingdoms, certainly more than that of the Duchy of the Seven Lakes from which Jelko came.

It had no real defensive walls; it simply looked like a city through and through. The houses were built with wood and recycled materials from who-knows-what. They were certainly not beautiful, but they gave the place great character.

It stood in a flourishing oasis, it was surrounded by palm trees everywhere, and water gushed from the subsoil that formed a small river and small lakes.

If it hadn't been accused of being a human landfill, where the worst offenders who escaped the death penalty were deported, it would have been a paradise.

From the exact center of the city, rose a flagpole for the sighting of those seen in the galleons, from which the sailor on duty sighted the lands or the other ships, but more robust and tall.

Jelko said to Elyn: "Give me back the sword and backpack. I can manage now, thank you for carrying the burden for me."

She did not object and walked towards a small group of people who, noticing their presence, were going to meet them.

There were four men and a woman.

They were not armed. Theoretically, there were no weapons in Argoran due to a lack of raw materials and the common will of the rulers.

When they reached them, it was the woman who started talking: "Look, look what we have here. Are you lost? We didn't see any transport arriving. They must have unloaded you further than usual, maybe the guards were in a hurry to get home."

Elyn said: "We are not prisoners, we are not lost and we are not looking for trouble. Our friend needs help and rest, plus we need to talk to your Yalla."

The four men meanwhile turned around, looking at them from head to toe, while the woman said: "What a nice morsel you are, who tells you the Yalla wants to talk to you? If he wants to see you, I think he will have other thoughts. It has been a long time since fresh meat of such high quality has arrived."

"This one is half-dead" intervened one of the men who was watching Jelko closely, "why don't we have some fun with the girl in the shed before returning to town?"

Another, almost toothless, added: "Let's eliminate these two and keep only her. We don't need them, unless we want to use them for some heavy work."

"In that case the elf would still be mine" said the woman who seemed to be the one giving the orders, "I want to take a ride first."

The four men grinned at the idea.

"Don't even try, damn it!" yelled Jelko, putting his hand to his sword.

One of the men promptly took his arms and pinned them behind his back. Another punched him in the stomach, making him double over. They released him and he fell to the ground, coughing.

Nolan kicked one of them, but was pushed to the ground by the others, who were immediately on him.

"Enough!" Elyn thundered, her voice turning very harsh for the first time, unlike how her companions had been used to hearing her since they had known her.

Everyone stopped for a moment, surprised. They did not expect such force from a wood elf who looked like little more than a girl.

The woman approached her, challenging her: "How dare you? You're in our house."

Elyn looked her straight in her eyes and said: "You... will take us to the Yalla... and tell your men not to hurt us. Now."

"I'll take you to the Yalla right away" replied the woman, who shook her head as if she wanted to recover from a bad dream, "and you go back to your business without arguing" she said, turning to the men.

One of the men tried to say: "But what..."

"I said... go... away" the woman repeated, looking at them menacingly one by one and articulating her words well.

The four henchmen walked perplexed towards the city and the woman led the way without speaking.

Argoran was very special and unexpectedly beautiful.

Half of it stood on the water.

There was a residential area and, the canals leading to the houses, had small lifeboats at each corner that the inhabitants used to enter them.

On the mainland, however, there were shops of all kinds.

Just like in any city, there were busy people along the streets and children playing. Surely half the residents were born in that place, while the other half were criminals from who-knows-what places in the world.

Argoran was a city teeming with life where many races and stories coexisted by force.

If someone did not know what that place was created for, they could easily think that it was a very normal metropolis with bizarre houses and extravagant architecture. At first glance, it could very well be a little paradise in the middle of nowhere.

Over the decades, the city became huge, reaching a social stability that it had certainly struggled to acquire, after struggles between brigands and prisoners of all kinds were left to slaughter each other for supremacy.

Here, once upon a time, only the strongest survived.

The only difference was freedom. No one could go out even if they wanted to, unless they wanted to have to deal with the endless desert outside.

"This is an incredible place" Nolan commented, looking around with his mouth open. He took Jelko by the arm to support him.

The woman who led them never said a word. Argoran was very large and there were no particular structures to help them to imagine that the Yalla could be near, and they had already been walking for some time.

The many inhabitants they met mainly observed Elyn. In her elegant dress and with her regal bearing, she looked like a princess visiting her subjects.

Instead, Jelko and Nolan did not arouse particular interest in their dirty and now tattered clothes.

Over time, the woman who was their guide must have acquired a certain rank within the society that had been created in Argoran. No one approached them, as if her presence guaranteed a sort of safety to the group.

"I don't know how long I'll resist, I can't take it anymore" Jelko said. He was visibly at the limit of his strength.

"Look, we've arrived" the elf said.

In front of them, the heart of the city was also the center of the oasis.

It was a park around a lake, palm trees were everywhere and grew luxuriant and dense. All around, there were well-tended gardens with flowers of every color. On one side was a wonderful rose garden, a pleasant cool breeze moved the leaves delicately.

The three were amazed to see in the center of it all, in the middle of the lake, a galleon with a very high sighting pole from which they overlooked the whole city and beyond.

"Follow the wooden walkway over the water" said the woman who had guided them there. She turned and left without adding anything else.

A solid walkway wound in front of them until it reached the entrance door on the side of the galleon, almost on the water.

It had a parapet to the right and to the left was a rope supported by wooden poles placed at regular intervals of about five paces. Before reaching the galleon, it turned right and left with gentle curves passing near flowering aquatic plants and shrubs, as if was a tourist route in the middle of nature.

"Jelko" Elyn asked, "can you make it? One last effort."

"I think so" he replied, "I feel like I'm in a rather unusual place."

"Certainly" Nolan intervened, supporting his friend with more strength, "when they sentenced me to serve my sentence here, I would have left with a lighter heart if I had known what it was like."

"You would have been a prisoner left to yourself anyway" Jelko replied, tightening his grip with his arm on Nolan's shoulders.

"This is also true. I wouldn't have existed for anyone anymore, if I had found a place in this kind of society without getting killed for some reason."

After a last curve to the right, which crossed a large and dense bush with red flowers as long as plumes, they found themselves a few steps from the entrance of that singular floating palace, that was the residence of the Yalla of the prison city of Argoran.

The entrance was a large wooden door, like a drawbridge that could be raised if necessary, isolating the ship from the wide platform on the water to which the gangway led.

During the day it was always lowered, it was closed at night.

Two large black-skinned guards controlled the entrance.

They were the only people they had seen up to that moment who had been armed since they entered the city.

They carried a sword at their side and, resting on the ground, they had a crossbow.

"Apparently some weapons can get in here too, contrary to what is believed" said Jelko.

Nolan said: "Maintaining the created order would not be easy indeed without them."

Elyn had spoken very little throughout the long walk through the streets of the city, she only seemed focused on her goal.

When they were within walking distance of the sentries, they made a gesture with their hand to stop.

The elf spoke to them: "We come in peace, we are here to talk to the Yalla. It is very important and we cannot leave without having done so."

A short, bald middle-aged man immediately came out of the door, stopped between the two guards and said: "We know. Leave your weapons there where you are, you are not allowed to enter the galleon with them."

Nolan whispered to Elyn: "Do we trust him?"

"We have no choice" she replied.

The two boys laid their swords on the ground, Nolan helped Jelko because he seemed really exhausted. The fever had risen again and his face was pale.

"Well" the bald man said, "follow me."

He was dressed in clean dark yellow clothes, he was very attentive to the welcome ceremony. With large hand gestures, he indicated the way ahead of them.

A third armed guard, who was inside, followed them at a distance.

The entrance was in the center of the galleon's belly, some well-polished wooden stairs began to go up that led to the upper decks. On each floor there were two guards. Everything was extremely neat and clean, there was nothing out of place.

They didn't even notice a speck of dust and each room was well lit by many torches and oil lamps.

They reached the last deck, Jelko almost fell to the ground, his legs no longer supporting him, when the man who guided them pointed to a door and said: "The Yalla will receive you tonight after dinner. Behind that door there are two rooms, one for the elf and one for the two boys" he opened the door, showing a small corridor, "rest, I will send someone with some food and healing herbs for your friend."

With his usual manner of master of ceremonies, he invited them to enter the corridor. The guard who had followed them began to guard the door and the man said again: "If you need anything, send for me. My name is Tellen."

He closed the door, leaving them alone in the small corridor leading to the two rooms.

Elyn opened one of the doors and said: "Quick, let's put him on the bed" referring to Jelko, who was now clinging to his companion almost as dead weight.

The room was small but well cared for.

Two beds were against the wall in the center opposite the door and a small desk was positioned under a window from which they could see part of the park, where the galleon was located. Next to a small wardrobe, the doors were open and inside there were clean clothes of various sizes. Next to it was a large basin with clean water.

While Nolan was freshening Jelko up and helping him to change his clothes, Elyn went into the other room. It was practically identical, but with the furniture and window reversed.

Shortly afterwards she returned to the two boys' room and approached Jelko, who was already under the covers.

"How do you feel?" she asked him.

He replied: "Much better now that I'm lying down, I couldn't stand up anymore."

"You need rest, they'll bring you something to drink that will help you" she said.

Jelko pointed his elbows to raise himself slightly and said: "They're treating us like important guests, I hope it's not a trap or something to worry about. It's kind of weird, this whole welcome."

Nolan added: "Yeah, I'm not convinced. It's a surreal situation, like the whole city."

Elyn said: "The man from before, Tellen, said the Yalla will see us after dinner. We have all afternoon to rest, we'll know more as soon as we meet him."

"Until then" Nolan interjected, "let's get our strength back, we can't do anything else. Who knows, maybe we'll need it."

"Exactly" she said, "we have no other choice."

"How are you?" Jelko asked her.

"I'm fine. The desert out there was mentally wearing me out, but it's definitely better here."

There was a knock at the door and an elderly woman came in with a tray bearing food and water, with a steaming mug in one corner.

"Tellen told me to bring you this tray. I left the same one in the other room, the mug will help your sick companion."

She set it down on the desk and left, closing the door behind her.

"I'm going to freshen up in there and get something to eat" Elyn said, getting up, "I'll see you later. Meanwhile, let's relax. We need it."

Nolan, in his usual optimistic way, said jokingly: "Well, probably if there is a large basin like this over there, you can even enter it whole in the water."

"I'll try it and let you know!" she said laughing.

Jelko also laughed at the joke and the three said goodbye to each other.

Nolan helped his partner drink the infusion and finally washed himself too, changed his clothes and lay down in bed with a sigh of relief.

The afternoon passed quickly, all three were able to rest without interruption. The place was very quiet. Only the chirping of birds interrupted the silence, making the place even more relaxing.

At dinner time, they found themselves in the boys' room where the elderly woman had brought more food and fresh water.

For Jelko, once again, there was the usual infusion of a few hours before.

He was feeling much better, the fever was almost gone and he had regained a normal color.

"Some idea?" he asked as he calmly ate some bread.

Nolan was the first to reply: "None of them, it's a situation I didn't expect. I don't really know what to think, let's hope the Yalla won't make a fuss when we say we want to talk to this Ameh Hurak, as long as he's still alive."

"He is, I can feel it" Elyn said, "I hope I don't find a hostile person, rather. We can't leave without talking to him."

"We are also unarmed" Nolan pointed out, "and in here I saw several stout guards on the various floors we crossed."

"Let's hope we're lucky and not have to resort to force" said Jelko, "among other things, I'm still weak, even though I feel much better than this morning."

"Let's get ready. The master of ceremonies, Tellen, is about to arrive" concluded the elf.

Shortly after they heard a knock on their door, it opened and the bald little man made a deep bow proclaiming: "Your lordships want to follow me. The Yalla is waiting for them as promised."

The three were ready and finally Jelko and Nolan were wearing clean and scented clothes after several days.

Elyn was in her elegant green and gold dress, flawless and clean as she had always been since they'd met her. Her straight black hair that fell over her cheeks was lightly pointed at the nape of her neck, revealing her face better.

They went out following Tellen, the large sentry standing behind them closed the line.

They went out onto the main deck. From there they could see a large part of the city, confirming its very particular beauty.

The oasis on which it stood looked like a green and blue gem in the middle of a huge yellow patch of sand.

On the prow of the galleon, they saw many guards busy closing and moving crates into what must have been their small barracks.

On the opposite side, the aft, was the bridge, and that was where Tellen was leading them.

As they walked in single file, over their heads, they saw the basket on the very high sighting tree that they had noticed from outside the city. A sentry was on lookout as if the galleon were in the open sea.

"Please, this way" their guide said.

They climbed a small staircase and found themselves on a raised landing with an open door.

The stern structure was quite large and imposing, the only difference from what was the standard of galleons of that size.

Crossing the threshold, the corridor was narrow and long, leading to an atrium that widened to a double door, probably the hall where the Yalla gave audience.

The master of ceremonies opened both doors once again solemnly and made them enter by closing them inside.

The saloon was really beautiful. The wood was light and although the ship itself was well lit, the various rooms were not as bright as this one.

On the walls hung beautiful green and red tapestries, depicting maps of the world alternating with episodes of naval battles.

In the center, there was a long and massive table with chairs around it and lit candlesticks above. The whole room was very bright, thanks to long windows that ran along the sides at the top of the walls until they almost touched the ceiling.

At the back, there was a throne with gold-colored armrests and the back in the shape of a large rudder with silver knobs.

On the sides of it, in a symmetrical way, there were two closed doors.

"Take a seat" said the man who was sitting on the throne.

Between the raised platform on which he was standing and the massive table in the center of the room, there was a wooden bench, which he pointed to with a finger.

The three silently approached to sit down as requested.

The Yalla was a mulatto man, with many tattoos depicting runes drawn on his shaved head.

His build was not as impressive as that of the guards they had met up to then, but his physique was lean and probably very agile. He was not armed and there were no other people in the room, it was just the four of them.

All three were struck by the fact that he must not have been more than fifty years old, they were expecting a much older person.

Jelko and Nolan sat down as ordered, while Elyn, who seemed to know court etiquette better than they did, remained standing next to the bench.

It was she who spoke once they arrived in front of the Yalla after a graceful bow: "We thank you for the welcome we received. We were able to rest properly and eat your delicacies, it was as pleasant as it was unexpected."

"I know" said the Yalla, "Argoran is renowned for something else."

His voice was very mature, he spoke slowly. He was extremely calm and reassuring, his timbre filled the whole room without causing unjustified fear.

Jelko and Nolan did not know how to intervene, the two interlocutors spoke with great mutual respect and the two of them did nothing but nod their heads all the time.

The Yalla said: "You bring very difficult days with you. You can stay as long as you need, you will be my guests."

The elf said: "We will gladly take advantage of this gesture. It will not be lost on us, my people will not forget this. However, we are here because we absolutely have to meet the clairvoyant Ameh Hurak. It is very important, the Sleepless Ones are back and he knows things that would be very useful to us."

"I know who you are, elf" answered the Yalla in a powerful voice, "I saw you arrive even before the city was on the horizon. But before speaking of the seer, there are two people you must see now."

He snapped his fingers and immediately a guard entered from one of the two exits behind him, stood aside and gave way to two very tall elves, so much so that to get through the door they had to stoop slightly.

They were well dressed in white clothes, without weapons, and both positioned themselves shoulder to shoulder on the side of the Yalla's platform.

They knelt in front of Elyn and one of them said: "My lady, we couldn't warn you before. The magical emptiness of the desert didn't allow it. We haven't had contact with Manmur for days now, we fear the worst."

Jelko and Nolan were stunned to say the least, they watched the scene with their mouths open. They were the only ones in there who did not understand what was happening. Even the Yalla seemed to be witnessing a completely normal and expected conversation.

Elyn was disturbed by the news: "This was not wanted. I hope nothing bad has happened to him, otherwise we will no longer have any contact with the place where he is imprisoned. Get up."

The two elves stood up and the one who had not yet spoken said: "We are happy that the two boys have managed to free you as you planned, my lady."

She turned to Jelko and Nolan and gave them a smile as if to thank them.

She then turned to the Yalla and said to him: "I very much appreciate that you have welcomed my two emissaries, the Arcane Elves will be indebted to you. Unfortunately, they bring bad news, Manmur is our most important senior adviser and there is no news of him."

Her interlocutor was very attentive to her words.

Elyn continued: "This is all the more reason for my companions and me to meet Ameh Hurak, and ask to use his clairvoyant powers as soon as possible. There is no more time."

The Yalla stood up for the first time in his midnight blue velvet dress and said: "Elyn of Va'drin, Chosen One and Queen of the Arcane Elves, I am Ameh Hurak. Argoran and I are at your service."

Jelko and Nolan nearly fell off the bench they were sitting on.

CHAPTER 16 (Knights)

They had returned to their rooms and soon found themselves in the two boys' room.

When Elyn came in, no one said a word. They were still too dazed and the candles cast gloomy shadows.

"Why didn't you tell us right away?" asked Jelko, visibly altered, "we risked our lives and spent whole days walking together, it certainly cannot be said that there was not enough time! You are a queen! It's not a minor detail, is it?"

Nolan did not speak, he also seemed hurt by the news learned shortly before in front of those unknown people.

It was the elf who began to speak by breaking that invisible wall that had been created: "I'm sorry, I know very well how you feel and I understand it. It was certainly not my intention to betray your trust. You saved me from the two dark elves, I never would have hidden anything from you if it had not been necessary."

Jelko intervened: "If you trust us, then why is it such a secret? It seems to me that we could at least be informed about what this design of destiny is, since we risked ourselves on the front line like you."

"Please" said Elyn, "I did it only because my brother can interfere with the minds of others. If he had somehow managed to control yours, we wouldn't even be here talking about it."

"I don't understand" Nolan said.

"He probably already knows where we are right now. If he had guessed that you were aware of everything, I think he would not have hesitated to eliminate me through you."

"Not having perceived your knowledge, he sent those two hitmen who followed us until recently outside this city. He evidently failed to manipulate you to his advantage. The more connected our minds are to each other, the more he can interact by switching from one to the other."

Jelko interrupted her by saying: "So, has not knowing and keeping our distance preserved us from greater damage? Do you mean this?"

"Yes, Jelko. The more our minds are aware of common topics and the more they are aligned according to a precise and predictable pattern. I could not risk crossing the desert to get here with the constant threat that he would take possession of you. I would not have been able to survive if you had attacked me, even if against your own will."

"It's starting to get clearer now" Nolan said, as he sat on the bed, visibly more relaxed.

Elyn continued: "I will tell you everything, but you will be more and more exposed. I certainly do not want to have secrets with the two of you. I hope you will forgive me and understand me, I had no other choice."

Jelko breathed a sigh of relief: "Well, it's all solved. You couldn't risk it. After all, what you do is for all of us. We must stand together if we are to try to do something useful."

"I agree" Nolan said.

"What are we to call you now? Queen Elyn?" said Jelko, finally smiling with a joke.

"Stop it" she said, "here, almost without power, and in this body, I am nobody."

She approached the two boys and hugged them tightly: "Thank you for all that you do."

"We are the Merchants of Leaves" said Nolan with his newfound good humor, "we will go on our way, there will be no brothers or Sleepless One who can stop us."

Elyn gently broke away from the embrace: "I wish it were really like that."

"Let's rest" she continued, "tomorrow morning, we will meet Ameh Hurak. If everything goes well, we will know where my twin is hiding and decide how to move. There is not much time. At most, the next day we will have to get back on the road."

Jelko said: "Let's take advantage of these soft beds to get a good night's sleep. I don't think we'll sleep in better places for a while."

"Yes," Nolan added, "it will be better for everyone to rest and regain our strength to the maximum. I'm sure they will come in handy."

The three said goodbye. Elyn returned to her room, slipping out the door almost without making a noise.

Nolan commented quietly as his companion was settling down to sleep: "The queen of the Arcane Elves on a galleon in the middle of Argoran prison. Incredible."

"What a day today! Since this morning, it has not ceased to surprise us" concluded Jelko by blowing out the candles on the bedside table between the two beds.

Jelko had a quiet night. Even before falling asleep, he no longer had a fever. He felt much better thanks to the drinks that were given to him at regular intervals.

When he woke up, Nolan's bed was empty. He thought he had slept too much and began to get dressed, perhaps his friend was eating something with Elyn before meeting the clairvoyant.

It seemed strange to him that they had not woken him up, although perhaps they had not done so to give him more time, since in the clash with the Ashirs, almost two days before, he had been wounded and poisoned.

As he continued to settle down, he approached the small window overlooking the surrounding park. It was not as late as he thought, judging by the position of the suns.

He heard footsteps approaching quickly and Nolan entered the door like a fury: "Jelko hurry! You have to come and see something right away!"

Jelko was alarmed. His friend seemed very agitated, but not worried.

"What's going on?" he asked.

"Come and climb the sighting tree, look east and tell me what you see!"

The two hurriedly left the room. Nolan was practically dragging him by the arm, to make up for the fact that he had just woken up and was taken aback by his abrupt way of doing things.

When they were on the deck of the galleon, Elyn was talking to the master of ceremonies Tellen, to the side, as Nolan pushed him harder and harder.

"Go up!" he said to Jelko, pointing to the tree with the empty basket on top.

"Can I know what's going on?" he grumbled almost angrily.

"Maybe we have visitors, look East."

"The Sleepless Ones?"

"I don't know. I don't think so, that's why I brought you here."

Jelko quickly climbed the pegs of the tree and quickly found himself in the basket. From there he could see well beyond the city limits, the view was excellent in the still clear morning air.

He looked in the direction indicated and saw, far in the distance, many figures moving slowly.

He rubbed his eyes, they had to be knights. Indeed, they certainly were. Looking better, he could recognize the horses.

There were about fifty of them. Those in front carried banners, but they were not visible.

But he noticed something unequivocal: their armor sparkled under the sun's rays and the helmets all had blue plumes. He tried to sharpen his sight as much as possible and it seemed to him that the horses also had vestments of the same color.

"Knights of the Duchy of the Seven Lakes!" he exclaimed to his friend, who had remained down on the deck of the ship.

"What are they doing around here?" asked Nolan.

"I have no idea. I don't think they're headed here, I think they're just passing through. They're going North, from what I see."

"Jelko!" called Elyn, "I think you should go to meet them and ask."

"Come down" Nolan added, "I'm coming with you."

In an instant, he was on the ground. The sight of those knights had made him euphoric. After weeks away from his city, it was like being at home for a moment.

Nolan also seemed excited and said: "Maybe Lusva and Triny have really brought the message successfully, and the raiders are patrolling the area in search of the Sleepless Ones. Something is moving."

"Yes, it must be like that" said Jelko.

Tellen turned to the two who were running to the nearest stairs: "Not from there! Follow me. I'll show you a secret passage that will take you to a tunnel leading directly out of the city in a short time."

"I'll be waiting for you here" Elyn said as they hurriedly passed by her.

The master of ceremonies accompanied them to the hold of the ship.

From there, a door hidden behind crates opened in a dark tunnel. He took a lit torch from the wall and handed it to Jelko, saying: "Always straight, it is not very long."

The two did not respond. With the torch in front of them, they tried to walk as quickly as possible.

When they arrived at the end of the tunnel, they saw that the light from outdoors was trying to infiltrate from above. A small trapdoor half-buried by sand hung over some steps. They climbed them and opened it, finding themselves in the desert with the city behind them several hundred steps away.

It was already hot outside, but they decided to run towards those riders they saw on the horizon, flickering from the heat rising from the sand.

When they were close enough, they slowed down to walk.

There was no longer any doubt that they were soldiers of the Duchy.

"Hey!" shouted Nolan, "wait!"

The knights had already noticed them from afar. Someone from the head of the column gave the order to stop and together with another, broke off galloping towards them.

As they approached, they noticed that, along with what was probably the commander, the other knight was a woman, but without armor, with her hair in the wind and a white cotton dress.

Nolan squeezed his companion tightly by the arm, saying: "But... It's not possible! Triny! It's you!"

"For all the Gods!" she exclaimed as she made her horse stop.

Even the knight who was with her stopped in front of the boys, he really had to be the commander of the expedition.

His armor was much more refined and he was the only one to wear the blue velvet cloak.

He said nothing, nimbly got off his horse and took off his helmet.

It was Faxel.

"Father!"

Jelko ran up to him and hugged him with such momentum that he almost dropped him.

"My son! I feared the worst to the point of believing you dead, until Triny and her father brought me the news of the Sleepless Ones."

Jelko was almost in tears and with a lump in his throat said: "Forgive me, I shouldn't have left like that. I was wrong."

"Our court magician Zimas is there among the knights. He gave me such relief when he said you were alive, even though he didn't know where. I have endured your lack better even though there was nothing certain in his words."

"All my fault. You didn't deserve such treatment, I'm aware of that."

"I left a boy and now I find a man in front of me, this period has made you grow quickly. It must not have been easy, I see that you still bear the signs of it."

Behind them, a man on horseback galloped towards them from Argoran. It was Tellen, who joined them in a short time.

"Argoran welcomes you" he said with his sumptuous manner, "the Yalla begs you to come in and rest before resuming your journey... if you so wish, of course."

Jelko intervened: "Please, father, it is not the prison that everyone has always described. You will realize it yourself. We have been here since yesterday, they are far from inhospitable."

Tellen added: "You can occupy the old barracks of the city. it was used by the garrison before it was abandoned to leave the city-prison to its fate. There are also large stables and everything you need for your horses."

Faxel said: "Just as we were passing by you, Zimas was talking to me about this singular place. We accept the offer, a short break will be convenient for us. We will leave tomorrow, we are going North to Marigard and Han Farn."

"Very well" Tellen concluded.

Faxel mounted his horse and beckoned his riders. They began to move in his direction.

Jelko turned to Triny, she was much better cared for than they had known her in the Meltin's bakery with her father: "Thank you for bringing the message to Fost, you and your father trusted us immediately without many certainties. By the way, how is he?"

"He's fine, he stayed in the capital of the Duchy. We had nothing to lose in Meltin and by trusting you, we did the right thing."

The knights had now reached them.

At the head was Zimas, with his white hair gathered in a large braid and his thick beard also made of many small white braids.

Tellen solemnly announced: "This way!" and headed in the direction of the main entrance of Argoran.

Triny said to Nolan: "You won't want to walk!" pointing to the horse's back behind her.

"Ah! Thank you! You're kind!" Nolan jumped on behind her.

Faxel turned to his son: "Haven't you learned to ride yet? Come on jump up, with this heat there is no need to refuse."

He reluctantly took his father's hand and climbed behind him.

He didn't know how to ride a horse, but deep down he just had to sit.

As they made their way to the pass to the city, Triny said: "Is the elf with you? Did you manage to free her?"

Nolan replied: "Oh yes! It wasn't easy, but we made it. She's inside, but what are you doing here?"

Faxel who had heard, intervened saying: "Zimas wanted her as his adept, he says that she is already very good. When she arrived with her father, she told me something about the elf. I do not understand how she managed to escape from the pyre that day of her execution at the stake, nor what that has to do with all this."

Jelko said: "She is much more than a wood elf. It is one of the things I have to talk to you about as soon as possible, maybe later. Soon we have to see a seer and she will be there too."

"I don't understand" Faxel replied, "tonight, you will tell me everything calmly. First I will be busy arranging horses and riders."

Jelko said quietly to his father: "We have many things to tell each other."

Faxel stretched out his hand and tapped him on the calf: "I know my son. I know."

CHAPTER 17 (Averidia)

Once inside Argoran, the knights headed for the barracks as indicated earlier by Tellen.

As they crossed the city, they too were amazed at how different that place was compared to the clichés that had been told about it.

Probably at the behest of the rulers, the city had to inspire much more terror than it did in reality.

Without any doubt, it was not easy to live there, especially because as soon as someone arrived, they had to elbow each other to have a place in the society that had been created, but it was not impossible either.

Jelko and Nolan got off the horses and, after saying goodbye to Faxel and Triny, they quickly returned to the galleon. Elyn was waiting for them.

"Is everything all right?" she asked.

"Yes" replied Jelko, "they are knights of the Duchy commanded by my father and the court magician. Today they rest here and tomorrow they will leave for the kingdoms of the North to continue to alert everyone."

"Eat something" said Elyn, "I left some food in your room. See you out here shortly, Tellen will take us to the shrine from Ameh Hurak."

Jelko hadn't touched any food since he had woken up, but Nolan had a second breakfast with what Jelko hadn't eaten.

As soon as it was finished, they reached Elyn on the bridge.

Tellen was also ready and walked towards the stairs, making his way.

When they came out of the galleon, it was now mid-morning.

The surrounding park managed to prevent the desert temperatures from soaring.

They retraced the entire wooden walkway on the lake where the ship was located. When they were on the mainland, their guide skirted the shore to a large boulder, behind which there was a narrow path through the increasingly dense vegetation.

They walked in silence, turning right and left, following the path. Now, it was nothing more than ground slightly beaten by the rare passage of someone.

They arrived at a very small clearing.

The trees framed everything. At the top, the fronds touched, creating a roof of branches and leaves. In the center was a dark stone obelisk with a square base standing two men high, with runes engraved on each of the four sides, from the base to the tip.

Some polished stones were placed all around to form a raised platform, probably to ensure that the lush vegetation did not invade even that small space, as well as to raise the small area.

Along the perimeter there were some smoking bowls arranged at regular intervals.

From the back, facing the obelisk, Ameh Hurak wore a black tunic. The lower part of it, which touched the rock pavement, was cleverly decorated to form thin tongues of fire that went up to the knee.

He turned to the newcomers. His face was painted black and red, making the whole figure quite disturbing.

"Welcome" he said, "I have just begun the ritual. It is necessary for the elf to climb up here and stand by my side. All the others remain where they are without moving."

The tone and solemnity of those words left no other choice.

Elyn walked slowly towards the seer and climbed up the small rock platform, positioning herself next to him as indicated.

Immediately, the bowls began to release even more smoke.

Ameh Hurak raised his arms, moving them both above himself and around Elyn's body.

He seemed to draw circles in the air according to a precise scheme.

In a short time, the blanket of smoke was so dense that it obscured the small clearing. In the twilight, the runes engraved on the obelisk shone with an intense red light.

Elyn could barely be glimpsed. Her face had become totally inexpressive, like that of a rag doll. It seemed that she was no longer in that body, the seer continued to pronounce a kind of hypnotizing song as he walked slowly around her.

At a certain point, he came closer to the obelisk with the luminous runes and supported both hands as if to listen to it through them.

The elf made a gasp as if catching her breath after a long apnea, now she looked around disoriented. She calmed down immediately and remained motionless again, carefully turning only her head towards Ameh Hurak behind her.

He was in a trance, continuing to touch the runes and look up at regular intervals, uttering incomprehensible phrases.

Tellen appeared calm, he observed with respect what was happening. Evidently, it was not the first time that he had witnessed such a thing.

Jelko and Nolan were nervous. They had never participated in such a ritual. The situation was rather distressing, it was almost dark with all that fog and the clairvoyant seemed possessed next to Elyn.

The smoke was finally subsiding, with more and more rays of light illuminating the clearing as it dissolved.

Ameh Hurak knelt in front of the obelisk, the runes no longer emitted their own light and everything was returning to normal as when they had arrived.

The bowls of smoke went out, the air became clear and light again. Elyn was still motionless. When the seer stood up, he looked exhausted.

He stood up and approached the elf, holding himself with difficulty and said: "Averidia! It is there that the twin hides. He is in possession of the Fragment of Infinity, the Relic is in that place."

Elyn closed her eyes and sighed, the other three opened them wide with surprise.

A grave silence had fallen on everyone.

Before the invasion, Averidia was known as the mystical city par excellence. It was populated mainly by scholars of all kinds, from magical to engineering arts. It had a huge library located in a low but very wide circular tower near the main square.

Many of the best magicians, artists and builders had studied here.

The city stood on a high and isolated very slender promontory, right on the northern border of the great desert.

From afar and in the evening, when the city lights came to life, it was said to look like a lit torch.

In addition, it had an inexplicable peculiarity. Many scholars tried in vain to give a reason for a strange visual effect that originated here.

From a precise point, just outside the city, looking around you could observe almost the whole world as if you were in front of a map. The distances and proportions were not reliable and real, but it gave a fairly clear idea about its conformation.

The few existing maps had all been drawn starting from this point, on which a small pedestal was then erected to admire this strange phenomenon of optical refraction. At that very precise point, the name of Pedestal of the Cartographer was given.

Following the invasion of the Sleepless Ones fifteen years earlier, it was said that all the inhabitants were exterminated in a single day. Averidia was completely abandoned and never re-populated, becoming a ghost town.

Being almost defenseless, in that period it was first partially destroyed by the demonic horde, then looted by marauders and brigands, in an attempt to steal the great knowledge contained in the renowned library of the city.

Subsequently, various exploratory expeditions were sent from the various kingdoms to recover some important tomes, but none of these were successful.

All returned empty-handed, claiming that not a single book was found in the ruins. It was common rumor that, in reality, these expeditions did not return without anything, but the people did not have to know that anyway.

Elyn moved away from the obelisk down the rock platform, while Ameh Hurak remained motionless where he was.

Tellen beckoned the guys to follow him and all four of them quietly lined up, leaving the small clearing behind.

Once at the galleon, they were left alone on the deck of the ship.

Jelko said: "Averidia, I have always heard of that place. It must have been very fascinating as a place, I never imagined going there now that it is a ruin abandoned and forgotten by the Gods."

"Yeah, neither do I" Nolan added.

"About the Relic" Jelko asked Elyn, "do you know anything about it? I only know that it is a powerful artifact of unknown powers."

Nolan shook his head and also turned to the elf in search of an answer.

Elyn said: "The Relic is also called the Fragment of Infinity, its origin is lost in the mists of time. Its power is to be able to control the masses."

"Human?" asked Jelko.

"Any, human and non-human, as in the case of the Sleepless Ones, if that's what you're wondering" she said.

Nolan said: "Isn't it safe and guarded anymore in Han Farn? According to what the seer said, it seems to be in Averidia too. How did your brother steal it without the alarm spreading? It's not a small thing."

"I don't know" Elyn said looking at them both, "but at least we know that he won't be able to move from there. The Relic physically consumes whoever uses it very quickly, unless one is confined within a magical pentacle that takes time to be set up properly."

Jelko said: "So, from Averidia you can comfortably control an invasion around the world, he just has to worry about getting it done as soon as possible, so that he then has the freedom to move into the conquered lands when his plan is done."

"He will be summoning Sleepless Ones every day" Nolan intervened, "the more they are, the sooner his conquest ends."

Elyn seemed very worried and the two boys noticed.

"We'll make it. We'll help you, you don't have to worry. Everything will be fine" Jelko told her.

She approached the parapet nearby and looked around, admiring the view of the oasis.

"I am afraid. He has already defeated me once, condemning me to this curse. Surely he will fight inside the pentacle where the wear and tear of the Relic has no effect. He is very strong."

Nolan said: "But you too will be within that area. You will return to your real body and with all your powers."

Elyn gazed at them both with her usual serene and sweet look: "I have no other choice, my people are counting on me too. I cannot disappoint them. If I have to die, at least I will do it in my real body and for a just cause. I'm tired of living this way, chasing or running away from someone every day."

The two were rather desolate, and even more so because they could not find the right words to cheer everyone up by now on the ground.

She was an elf, so she was roughly ten times their age, and for fifteen years she had been under the Curse of the Chains as a slave. When she fell victim to it, the two of them were only a few years old. They couldn't imagine how hard it could be to live in that condition.

She seemed very aware of what she was going through.

There would be a fierce fight with her brother. The outcome was completely unknown and she didn't seem at all convinced that it would be in her favor. Moreover, there was no guarantee that they would arrive at the place where he was hiding in time and without obstacles.

Jelko said: "Later I'll see my father, I'll ask him a few things. We might find it convenient to enter Averidia with some knights, I don't think our friend is there alone."

"Good idea" Nolan commented, "if they stop us somehow even before we get to our goal, then all really will be lost."

"I'm so sorry, Elyn" Jelko resumed, "this wasn't what I've always dreamed of doing in my life. I'll do everything I can to protect you."

"It applies to me too" Nolan added.

She took both hands and said delicately: "A dream that doesn't come true doesn't necessarily turn into a lie. I feel safe with you, I'm sure we have some chance."

And she continued: "We will try our best. No matter if it will be enough or not, the important thing is to know that we will have done our best."

The two boys looked down thoughtfully, then Nolan said: "Can't your people do anything?"

"Unfortunately, no. We haven't settled in this dimension yet. That's what we were doing before being opposed, they just manage to send some emissaries from time to time. With or without me, if I don't get the better of them, they'll look for a new world to go to."

"I understand. Even if they want to, they're not in a position to help their queen" he replied.

"Exactly. In these years, they have tried in every way, but they are not physically here. It is already a lot of what they have tried to do to save me more than once."

"Forgive me" she continued, "I need to be alone for a while."

"Of course" Jelko replied, "if you need anything, you can find us here or in our room."

She took her leave of them with a light and elegant bow and walked towards the stern of the ship where their lodges were.

"What do we do?" Nolan asked in a low voice.

"This situation is getting more and more complicated" Jelko replied, "and it gets bigger every day as new things are discovered."

Nolan put his hands in his hair and sighed: "On the other hand, I don't want to stand by. If we don't do anything, this world will be doomed in a very short time anyway. At least we might die having tried."

When dinner time came, the usual old lady brought some food that they ate together on the aft steps leading down to the main deck. It was a beautiful day and everyone seemed to be in a bit of a good mood.

Jelko hurried to finish his meal, impatient to visit his father at the barracks. He had things to clarify and ask, so while the others still had not finished eating, he got up, said goodbye to them and walked away.

By the time he reached his destination, the riders were almost all finished with their meal. Although their stay was only for one day, they were well organized to spend the night.

He immediately identified his father and went to meet him.

"Jelko" Faxel said, "come on, let's take a walk."

They walked down one of the streets that circled the military quarter.

"Father, you said you were headed North to Marigard and Han Farn. Are you looking for something?"

"We are divided into three groups, we are spreading the news of the Sleepless Ones in case it did not reach the local rulers. We ourselves have encountered and eliminated some along the way."

Jelko asked: "Han Farn should have the Relic, right?"

"Why are you asking me this? Yes, of course. Once there, we are instructed to verify its presence."

"What if it isn't there? What would happen?"

"It is very difficult, it is well protected and the news would have gone around the world. But what are you hiding from me? Why do you insist on this subject?"

"The Yalla of this place is the clairvoyant Ameh Hurak. This morning we witnessed a ritual of him involving Elyn, he claims that the Relic was stolen and taken to Averidia."

"What?" Faxel stopped walking and looked at his son astonished, "it can't be true, no one has heard anything about it."

"Looks like it's there now" Jelko added firmly.

Faxel seemed to have taken another blow upon hearing this.

"And for what reason and by whom would it be taken to an abandoned city? How can you be sure what a self-proclaimed thug who is the boss of this place is saying is true?"

Jelko was confused. What his father said actually made sense, even if it was too anomalous.

"Elyn, the elf who is with us, is the twin sister of the one who is currently in Averidia. According to the seer he is in possession of the Fragment of Infinity and is responsible for this new invasion by the Sleepless Ones."

For a moment Jelko had the feeling that his father was looking at him as one observes a madman.

Faxel was silent for a moment and began to walk again: "All this is absurd, do you understand that it is not easy to believe what you are saying? And what role does this Elyn play? You ran away from home after she was burned at the stake, I saw and heard her burn, and now she is here instead?"

Jelko was in trouble. He realized that if he had been on the other side, he too would have had a hard time believing his own words.

"I am Elyn of Va'drin, Queen of the Arcane Elves. What your son is telling you is unfortunately all true."

The elf was behind them.

Faxel whirled around and said: "You're not..."

She interrupted him by saying: "I know, I don't look like one of my people. I am a victim of the Curse of the Chains and this is not my body. If you allow me some of your time, I can explain a few things to you."

All three returned to the barracks, Zimas was called and joined them in one of the rooms.

They talked for a long time.

Elyn told about her people and what her brother was going to do, Zimas confirmed that it could all correspond to reality and Faxel was able to dispel any doubts. Jelko went into the details of her release and of the fact that before meeting the elf, she guided him in dreams.

He also said that he could see in the dark and spoke of the strange euphoria that assailed him uncontrollably when he was forced to fight.

This startled his father.

"I beg your pardon if I didn't believe you right away" he told to Elyn with great respect.

"No problem, I understand that it is not easy to understand. Trust your son. It is my fault that I took him away from you, but it was written in his destiny."

Faxel looked at Jelko and said: "He broke my heart that day, but now it's all clear to me. Tomorrow morning, we will continue North as ordered, then after verifying whether the Relic is there or not, we will join you in Averidia."

Elyn said, looking at Faxel: "There's still something he needs to know."

She stood up. Zimas did the same and they both left the room, leaving father and son alone.

Faxel was staring at the floor in front of his feet. Jelko was looking at him, waiting for something in an embarrassed way.

He slowly looked up at him and said: "Elyn is right, it's time for you to know something I've had to keep from you all this time."

Jelko wanted to talk and say something, but he couldn't.

"Earlier, when you talked about that strange force that takes hold of you and the fact that you can see in the dark, probably coming out of the comfortable and safe city walls, your true instincts awakened after being asleep."

Jelko could hardly sit in the chair: "What do you mean? What instincts are you talking about? I'm becoming more and more aware of them, but I still struggle to control them."

"One moment son, let's take a step back. We need to talk about when your mother died shortly after your birth."

This time Jelko stood up: "My mother was killed during the first invasion, by the demon leaders of the Sleepless Ones! She is not just dead! So you've always told me."

Faxel looked back at the floor.

Jelko approached him, bending over him with a threatening air: "Didn't she go like this?"

"I killed her."

"What?"

"I had to, she begged me herself."

Jelko felt that furious feeling build up inside him again and asked almost screaming: "Why did you kill my mother when I was still just a child?"

"She was a demon, and you are her son!"

CHAPTER 18 (The Sorceress)

Jelko left his father alone in the room. He went out without saying a word and walked in the direction of the galleon, he walked slowly as he thought back to all the conversation he had just before.

The evening slowly began to obscure the streets of Argoran.

The air was fresh, and he seemed to breathe after a long apnea once in the street.

He found friends outdoors on the deck of the ship chatting while observing the oasis, the part of the city that could be seen from there, was lighting up mildly as the night progressed.

Upon his arrival, they immediately realized that something was wrong. He was visibly upset and dark in the face, he barely looked at them and headed for the lodgings.

Nolan went to meet him and said: "Hey! What happened to you? Are you okay?"

Jelko stopped and seemed to recover from a nightmare in which he was absorbed just a moment before.

All three entered below deck and he recounted, like a river in flood, the conversation he had with his father.

Now everything was clear.

The acquired ability to see in the dark, his superhuman strength almost without control, his thirst for blood and the excitement he felt every time he saw it.

By some unknown spell, during the first invasion, his mother herself became a demon shortly after bringing him into the world. Somehow, a part of her new demonic condition had been transmitted to him.

He said that Faxel had to kill her for her own good and under her insistence. Evidently, for his mother, being a demon was not as manageable as it was for him.

"I hope it doesn't backfire" he said in a sad and detached tone, "in which case you'll know what to do."

"I'm very sorry for your mother, coming to know a hidden truth after so long is never pleasant. For the rest, I'm sure you'll learn to live with it" Elyn replied.

"Yeah" Nolan added, "you're already doing it. It seems to me that every time it happens to you, you're more and more aware of it."

It was true. In fact, each time he had more and more mastery of what happened to his body. He could not deny it, even if it hurt him to admit it.

Talking and venting with Elyn and Nolan made him feel better, sharing the weight that he carried on his conscience lifted him quite a bit. At least at that moment, it was of great help and relief.

They agreed that the next morning they would leave for Averidia. The elf said goodbye to them and after making her usual light and graceful bow on the door, she closed it behind her.

Jelko struggled to fall asleep, the thoughts were too many and swirling.

His roommate noticed it, it was not difficult. He tried several times to talk about it, but his friend did not want to know. He answered in an elusive way and with two words he cut the speech short.

After a few unsuccessful attempts, Nolan surrendered and let sleep take over.

Jelko, in the darkness and silence of that small room, felt lonely and upset again. In less than a month, his existence had been turned upside down. There were too many things in such a short time. He retraced almost his entire life, turning a thousand times in bed.

When dawn came, it seemed to him that he had not even turned a blind eye.

"Nolan, wake up!" he said, "we must go."

The friend got up quickly and, like the previous morning, opened the door to get the large jug of clean water and the tray of food that the old lady had left outside.

"How are you?" asked Nolan as he placed food on the table in the room, "have you been able to rest at least a little?"

"Not much, but I'm fine" he replied, lying and trying not to let his inner turmoil shine through.

"It doesn't have to be easy what you're going through and I can understand it, but Elyn and I are with you. If you need to vent, don't worry."

"I really appreciate it, I know I can count on you" Jelko replied.

They ate, washed themselves and went out collecting their few things from the room. They would collect their weapons at the end, the guards had requisitioned them on the first day when they had entered.

They went out on the bridge. Elyn was not there yet and leaned on the balustrade admiring, perhaps for the last time, the view of that strange place.

The elf arrived shortly after, smiling and elegant as always.

"Good morning, my friends" she said, "a beautiful day even today, it seems. Come on, the master of ceremonies left me a message last night. The Yalla wants to see us before leaving."

They headed to the room of the previous days. Tellen was in front of the throne room waiting for them, with his usual pomposity, he welcomed the three and let them in.

As soon as the door closed behind them, the seer stood up from his stuffed throne and said: "Sit down. I am sorry not to have you here in Argoran for a while longer, but I know that you have important things to do and I am not going to waste your precious time."

"Your hospitality has been greatly appreciated" said Elyn, "here we have had the opportunity to rest and heal our wounds, we will not forget it."

Ameh Hurak seemed very pleased to hear those words, nodded his head and sketching a smile. Coming down from the platform on which his throne was placed, he went to get a small casket placed on a table in the corner of the room.

He placed it on the ground in front of them and said: "A small gift before your departure. We do not have much here, but always more than what is thought outside."

He pulled out of the casket three beautiful daggers. He unsheathed one, the new blade shimmered like a gem in that bright room.

The small hilts were finely decorated with engravings of leaves and branches that twisted together, the scabbard was made of black leather.

"For the Merchants of Leaves, I thought they would be perfect" he added, handing them one at a time.

"Our fame precedes us, apparently" said Jelko, bewitched by that really well-made weapon.

From what he remembered, no one had ever mentioned the name they had decided to give to their group, but he did not want to ask questions that might seem inconvenient at that time.

The Yalla closed the small casket and said: "Argoran will always be a safe haven for you as long as I am in charge. Now go, I have taken too much time from you."

Elyn replied: "Your help on where my brother is hiding was fundamental. I knew that Argoran had an important role in this affair, and not only for me."

She turned to Jelko and winked and smiled at him.

"Well" said Ameh Hurak, "as you exit, you will find your belongings and your weapons, Tellen will take you to the stables. As a last gift, I made you prepare two horses. Unfortunately, I could not offer more, they will make you comfortable to make up for the time I have made you lose. Tonight two were stolen, otherwise you would have had one each and one spare."

He accompanied them to the door and without waiting for Tellen to open it, he did it himself. Like a real landlord, he preceded them to the staircase that led below deck and then to the exit.

"May the Gods protect you" he said to them before turning back.

They took their belongings from the guards at the entrance and went out following the master of ceremonies.

"Don't worry" Nolan told Jelko in a joking tone, "you'll get on mine. I'll ride the horse, maybe it's the right time you learn how to do it!"

They retraced the entire walkway over the water until they left the park on which the galleon, the city's command center, was located.

As they walked through the various streets, they passed by one of the city gates and noticed that the knights, commanded by Faxel, were neatly gathering near it.

Evidently they too were about to continue the march shortly thereafter.

Jelko noticed his father a little later.

For the second time, like the day he left home, he had mixed feelings towards him. He had omitted the true cause of his mother's death, certainly to protect him, yet in doing so he was the one who paid the price now.

The stables were not far away, he looked away from the knights of the Duchy and a moment later they arrived at their destination.

Tellen spoke with the groom, who immediately beckoned to one of his helpers. Together they went to get the horses prepared and brushed properly.

It was two horses with black coats, the master of ceremonies pointed them out to the three saying: "Very well, this is what the Yalla promised. Good luck to all of you!"

He made a long bow and left, disappearing shortly afterwards among the people who crowded the street.

Jelko said: "Argoran has weapons and horses, I would like to know why everyone says that no one can get out of here alive through the surrounding desert."

"It's true" Nolan intervened, "I asked myself that too, but I don't think they have many of them either. Probably only the highest castes have access to it, the poorest who have tried are among those remains that we have seen outside here."

Elyn added: "I'm not sure everyone wants to leave here, after all I find meaning in the abnormality of this place where everyone thinks you don't exist anymore."

She climbed on her horse with agility as if she did it every day and added: "Come on, we have to go."

Nolan did the same and helped Jelko get behind him.

The nearest exit was the one where they had seen the knights just before. In the meantime, they had just come out. They were still again, but outside the almost non-existent boundary wall.

The three joined them in no time, they seemed to be waiting for something. In fact, as soon as Faxel saw them, he nodded and approached on foot.

As he walked towards them, with his hand he attracted the attention of Triny who at that moment was next to the magician Zimas, broke away from him and trotted the horse in his direction.

On her shoulder, she had a magic stick. The tip was adorned with three orange stones in a row, set one behind the other up to the top, the latter pointed like a common spear.

When she was next to him, Faxel had now reached out to them and said: "Forgive the intrusion, but we thought that maybe the girl could come with you. She will help you."

Elyn looked at her and closed her eyes for a few moments, Triny opened hers wide and almost fell from her horse if she had not readily clung to the mane.

The elf reopened them and said: "Certainly, an extra hand will undoubtedly help us. Welcome among us, sorceress."

Triny sketched an embarrassed smile. It seemed she could not take her eyes off the elf, as if she were in a state of mystical contemplation.

Just at that moment Zimas reached them, also on foot and said: "Take these amulets, they will give you protection, though it will be very light. Also, if you are away from each other, you will know if your companions are healthy. They emit a slight light and there are four notches, if one or more of these go out... Well, let's hope that doesn't happen."

The magician put them around their neck one by one personally with the only hand he had, accompanying the gesture with a very short unknown phrase.

The amulet was a small glass cylinder three fingers long and a half-finger in diameter, semi-transparent with something like a fog and three dividers that separated the whole into four subparts. They all emitted a slight turquoise luminescence.

"Very well" Faxel added, trying to hasten his speech, "we will try to complete our task as soon as possible. We will not go to Marigard, we will immediately verify the presence of the Relic. After that, if it is not in its place, we will join you in Averidia."

Jelko looked at his father almost defiantly and said: "Your verification will be useless, we already know that the Fragment of Infinity is no longer kept in Han Farn."

He was still bitter from the previous evening, he understood perfectly well that his father could not disobey the orders received.

He had never done so in his life and he had already changed the route by skipping a stage to do it first, taking the risk, but to him it seemed once again to have a hostile figure in front of him.

Faxel looked at him coldly and said: "We'll see, Zimas will somehow get in touch with Triny. If you arrive before us in Averidia, be very careful and, if possible, wait for our arrival."

It was Elyn who ended the discussion by saying with extreme calm and confidence: "I'm afraid it won't depend on us. We will do what has to be done, our destinies will guide us."

She gave a slight blow with her heels to the horse and looked towards Triny and Nolan, so that they too would do the same.

"We are grateful to you, Faxel, I know that your soul is just and loyal" and she overtook him with her traveling companions behind her.

When Jelko passed by his father, he turned the other way, trying to hide behind the back of Nolan who was riding the horse.

He turned around only when they were hundreds of feet away, he saw the riders resume their march in their shining armor. The horses were trotted and, as Faxel had announced, they would try to speed up as much as possible the task assigned to them, to make sure to get to Averidia more or less in conjunction with them.

The discipline of those knights was impressive, they moved as a whole. Even just looking at them, you realized how much self-denial each of them practiced.

On the other hand, the small Duchy of the Seven Lakes was famous for the excellent training and equipment it offered to its soldiers.

All this, combined with the willpower that every man put into it, made the army a deadly weapon, although much smaller than those of the other far larger kingdoms.

"These horses are a divine blessing!" exclaimed Nolan enthusiastically, "by tomorrow night, we will be out of the wilderness thanks to them."

Triny smiled, yet she still seemed embarrassed and uncomfortable about something.

Nolan had been watching her for a while. He clearly had a soft spot for her from the first day they met at Meltin's bakery, and even more, when he saw her again in Argoran following the wizard Zimas.

She was much more cared for and well dressed, her bushy brown hair went down to the middle of her back and moved slightly by the increasingly hot desert wind.

When they met her she was much more masculine, with her hair enclosed in a braid and wearing a large work apron, probably owned by her father.

They proceeded North all morning and much of the afternoon, when Nolan finally broke the ice and said: "Triny, tell us something about yourself. What does it feel like to be an adept of an archmage of the Duchy court?"

She slowed down the horse's pace to flank herself, leaving the elf in the lead and said: "I did not expect it, I like it and I am very curious about magic. I have always devoted myself to studying, since my parents allowed me to do so in the school of the Duchy. Evidently this has not gone unnoticed."

"Then our meeting, although it became risky, brought you luck!" said Nolan.

"Definitely! The day we arrived at Fost's palace, Jelko's father never let us go anymore by assigning us a room that was still free in the servants' wing. In the following days, we got to know Zimas, who wanted to know the details."

"Well, I can understand that. Apart from the news of great importance, he also had a beautiful girl in front of him as an ambassador."

Nolan immediately pinched himself on his leg as soon as he finished saying the sentence. Jelko laughed loudly behind him and Triny became all red in the face.

Elyn also turned around smiling and she blushed even more to see her turn in her direction.

"Forgive me!" Nolan hastened to say, "excuse me all! I did not intend to create an embarrassing situation for anyone! I will keep my mouth shut at least until we are out of this desert, I promise!"

Jelko, who was still laughing, said: "Sure! And how could we believe you? You're not the type who can be silent for more than an hour!"

They burst out laughing again all together at the thought of that blatantly vain promise.

Triny slowly approached the two boys and whispered: "Did you already know who the elf was when we met in Meltin? I learned about it this morning when Faxel decided I would join you."

It was Jelko who answered quietly: "No, we did not even remotely imagine it. We discovered it a few days ago."

They didn't notice that Elyn had stopped her horse and almost went after her with theirs.

"You don't have to be embarrassed by my presence, Triny. Right now, and who knows for how long, I'm nothing more than a wood elf."

The girl returned to being purple in the face and could barely say: "I ask your forgiveness. You are a queen, I did not want to..."

The elf interrupted her and gently took her arm saying: "My name is Elyn, you don't have to think of any pleasantries with me. We're friends from now on, okay?"

"Of course!" replied Triny relieved and enthusiastic.

The elf smiled softly and, immediately after, her face faded and became very worried.

"Hey!" shouted Jelko suddenly, "look down there! Behind us!"

They turned around alarmed and saw them.
Wrapped in a light cloud of dust raised by the horses' hooves, two dark figures proceeded quickly towards them.

CHAPTER 19 (Suspended Life)

"Damn!" exclaimed Jelko as he turned to the pursuers, "they only gave us a brief respite while we were in Argoran."

"Yes" Nolan replied, "those two horses in all probability are the ones that were intended for us, the Yalla had spoken of a theft that took place just this night."

Elyn said: "Let's try to go faster. If we can get to sunset, they won't attack us before it's day again."

They put their horses at a gallop. Elyn was very light and Triny did not weigh much more, but Nolan and Jelko's horse got fatigued first since it had to bring two people.

The two knights behind them were fortunately still far away.

When the first sun set, they had recovered half the distance, but not enough to attempt a possible attack without risking that the darkness would get in the way.

"We have to continue" said Jelko who, not having to ride the horse, constantly kept an eye on them, "I can make my way during the night. Even if we only had to go at the horses' pace, it would still be a nice advantage."

"We will do as you say" replied Elyn, "it seems to me a very good idea. If the clash is as inevitable, as I fear, the more we are out of the desert, then the more I will be able to help."

So that is what they did.

They led the horses slowly throughout the night.

Jelko guided them by paying attention to the small rocks that surfaced more and more frequently.

The desert was slowly giving way to a grassy terrain with rather large boulders, as if anticipating the rolling hills that were expected later, and then becoming in turn real mountains.

They were now located northwest of Argoran, just above the great central desert.

Long before dawn, they unexpectedly had to proceed more slowly. The area they were crossing was now quite rocky and began to increase the difference in height.

When the day came, they believed in vain that they had added distance between them and the pursuers, instead they saw them traveling already in their direction.

With that step, they would have recovered in a short time that small margin lost during the night.

"We have come out of the desert" said Jelko, "they will reach us quickly, perhaps it would be better to find shelter among these boulders and come up with something."

In fact, the two figures on horseback behind them were dangerously close, pressing them relentlessly. It was useless to run away, the breath they felt on their necks made them nervous and the whole thing was definitely distressing.

"We won't be able to escape them" said Elyn, who had turned to look at them, "we'll reach those boulders over there, Triny and I will stand tall and you two will have to defend us from below in case they look for a melee."

She pointed to a group of rocks in front of them. Some were a little higher than the others, they looked like giant steps.

They spurred the horses in the appointed direction when suddenly Elyn's stopped and refused to take a single step.

Its legs began to sink. Under it, the ground was as if it had gradually become softer and softer.

"Damn!" exclaimed the elf, "they have cast a spell on this area. Soon! Get out and run before we get trapped too!"

She jumped off her horse and everyone else did the same.

Jelko turned for a moment and saw one of the two pursuers motionless with his arms outstretched towards the sky.

All three horses began to fidget and move randomly in panic.

From the ground, small roots began to rise, holding them by the hooves. They tried with all their energy to free themselves, but every effort was in vain and slowly they were swallowed up by the ground, still alive, until they disappeared.

By now they could see them well, their enemies were normal human beings. Until recently, they believed that the elf's twin had evoked some mysterious being from who-knows-what dimension for the occasion.

One of them made his horse gallop and braced a bow that they had not been able to see before due to the distance.

The other held a sword in his left hand and what appeared to be a scepter in the other.

"They're coming!" Nolan yelled, "get in, quick!"

The boys helped Elyn and Triny to climb some rocks in order to take a position above them, who instead immediately put themselves on guard at ground level.

The position they were defending was more isolated than the other boulders, they didn't have time to look for something that would at least give them the chance to have their backs covered.

The archer ran his horse around them in wide circles, nocked two arrows and began firing from a distance.

"Watch out!" Jelko shouted.

The arrows were both aimed at Elyn. One broke hitting the rock just below her feet, the other would have hit her in the belly if she hadn't nimbly dodged it by turning to the side.

The archer nocked two more arrows. The quiver attached to the horse's saddle appeared empty, yet each time he pulled out two.

His companion dismounted and from a distance began to wield the scepter, spinning it and drawing strange elongated circles in the air.

Triny, who was on a spur of rock next to the one on which the elf was standing, raised her magic staff in the air. She uttered a formula and the three stones embedded in the tip lit up.

Immediately, two images identical to her appeared beside her.

They performed exactly all the movements she did, she began to move in her small space at her disposal. The two images did the same quickly for a few moments, finally not allowing to recognize which of the three silhouettes was really the girl in flesh and blood and which were simple copies.

Meanwhile, Elyn closed her eyes and concentrated. Immediately, a protective bubble appeared around her, adhering to her body.

Jelko and Nolan continued to be on their guard, the two enemies were not within reach of their swords and did not seem to intend to get close.

Shoulder to shoulder, they tried not to lose sight of either the one in front of them or the other one on horseback, that disappeared from view when the horse continued galloping beyond the rocks on which the girls were positioned.

Two more arrows.

One more in Elyn's direction and one in Triny's, both of which hit.

The elf's protective sphere vanished, completely absorbing the blow. One of Triny's two illusory images disappeared, it was impossible to understand which one she really was.

Luckily this time, he had hit a double of her that immediately dissolved, leaving the arrow on the ground.

At the same instant, a rain of stones began to fall in the area where they were perched.

The enemy with the scepter had finished his ritual. Now he walked slowly towards them, still concentrating so as not to interrupt that shower of stones.

"We have to do something" Jelko said, covering his head with one arm, "we'll get the worst of it at this rate."

"You stay here" he continued to Nolan, "I'll try to distract the wizard in front of us."

Elyn and Triny were hit by some stones, diverting attention from their target on horseback. They suffered some minor injuries, the intent of that magic was mainly not to allow them to concentrate.

Soon afterwards, they realized that all four were protected by something invisible.

The stone that was falling on them stopped hitting them as if they were protected by an invisible shield above their heads.

Triny cried out in amazement: "The amulets! The amulets have been activated!"

Nolan put a hand around his neck and pulled out his own.

He saw that the light fog inside moved swirling, the four cells that indicated the health of the members of the group emitted a strong turquoise light.

The girl began to throw fiery lightning bolts in the direction of the knight, in an attempt to hit him or at least to unseat him.

One of them missed him by a hair.

He underestimated the danger and this time he couldn't nock the arrows. Now he had to worry about dodging the sorceress's blows on that spur of rock.

Elyn stretched out an arm in front of her and opened her palm in his direction and narrowed her eyes. They heard a roar spread right in front of her. In an instant, the shock wave generated hit the rider, making him fall.

The horse got up in fear and ran away.

The archer quickly recovered his bow and began to approach, running from one rock to another, while in the meantime he had found shelter.

The quiver had remained tied to the saddle, so the two arrows he had at his disposal, were also the last ones.

Nolan moved to his left, he had seen that he had been thrown off and that he was getting closer. He had to protect Elyn and Triny in case he got too close looking for a hand-to-hand fight. From above, the sorceresses seemed to have the upper hand.

Meanwhile, Jelko had reached the man with the sword and scepter. The rain of stones behind him was over.

The amulet slipped out of his collar and he too became aware of his vivid luminescence.

His rival was well built. The tunic he wore had no sleeves, his bare arms highlighted his tense muscles, his face was painted half black and half blue.

When he was about ten paces away, the man plunged his sword into the ground and aimed the scepter at him.

He spoke a few sentences.

Jelko felt that his body no longer responded to his commands, he took a few steps then stopped. It was as if someone had filled his boots with lead, as each step required an enormous effort.

His arms also became heavy and sore, his opponent was knocking him out without even touching him. In those conditions, he certainly could not have fought.

His sword fell to the ground.

The enemy pulled his own from the ground and, always pointing the scepter at him, slowly went to meet him.

Elyn fell to her knees, the Curse of the Chains did not allow her to fully dispose of her mental powers. Every time she threw one, she lost more and more strength.

Triny noticed her immediately and ran to reach her and help her, the rocks from which they cast the spells were distinct but easily accessible to each other with a jump.

The image of her, which imitated all her gestures and which she had next to her, did the same, also landing near the elf, a little further on.

She bent down to try to lift her up, when Elyn cried out desperately: "No!"

The archer noticed it immediately, he had never looked away from his goals.

Bending down to try to lift the elf, Triny did not realize that her image did the same, but there was no one in front of it, clearly revealing which of the two figures was the real one.

There was a hiss.

Triny opened her eyes and fell forward with two arrows stuck in her back. The last of her illusory images vanished as her body hit the rock with a dull thud.

Nolan, who had turned to Elyn's desperate scream, had witnessed the whole scene from below. His sword almost fell from his hand, he wanted to scream but no sound came out of his throat.

If the archer had had other arrows, he could have hit him even with his eyes closed.

In the amulets that everyone wore around their necks, one of the four notches began to slowly fade.

Elyn appealed to the few forces left and scrambled to her feet.

Her gaze at the enemy was frighteningly cold. Under normal conditions, she could probably have blown up the archer's head and the rock behind which he was hidden, by the power of thought alone.

She pulled her arms slightly away from her body and opened both hands with the palms facing down.

All the stones that had rained down just before, rose from the ground and began to spin around her quickly, as if she herself were the center of a devastating hurricane.

Nolan was furious, he gripped his sword tightly and charged.

The archer saw him, abandoned the bow and pulled out two long-bladed daggers.

Feeling in danger in that position, he noticed a bigger and taller rock not far away, so he decided to run towards that new shelter.

Elyn unleashed her attack.

She stretched her arms out in front of her as if she were pushing something invisible, and hundreds of stones whirling around her hurled themselves towards her enemy at great speed.

The man was overwhelmed while he was still halfway to his new hiding place. Not even one stone missed him, he fell to the ground unconscious in a bloodbath.

Nolan joined him shortly after and finished him off by cutting off his head, accompanying the gesture with a liberating scream.

Jelko, hearing that heartbreaking scream, sensed that something serious had happened behind him.

He began to breathe quickly and felt a formidable force begin and flow into his body. His opponent's spell was still strong, but he was stronger and began to regain sensitivity in his legs and arms.

The man in front of him noticed it and was taken aback, he was now a few steps away.

Jelko wasted no time in recovering the sword that had fallen to the ground shortly before, he drew the dagger he had received as a gift from Argoran.

The opponent in front of him seemed terrified just looking at him, no one had ever resisted an immobilizing spell like what he had inflicted on him.

The man continued to study him. Jelko's eyes became red with blood, the gloomy look of those who harbor within themselves an instinct and a murderous fury. In that condition he no longer even seemed human. He was just a boy, yet he seemed almost of a bestial nature.

The enemy took two steps back, turned around and began to run away in the opposite direction.

Jelko could have chased him, as the spell had now been broken.

He had an incredible craving for blood and that man running could satisfy his desire. If only he had him in his hands, he would have torn it to pieces.

He decided not to chase him, he preferred to calm down and retrace his steps to see what had happened to his comrades. He did not hear any battle noise coming from his shoulders where he had left them.

He put the dagger back into the sheath of the belt and recovered the sword, the ribbon that wrapped the hilt was now in shreds. He threw it, leaving those symbols uncovered once and for all. He was no longer interested in hiding that detail.

Worried, he hurried along the short stretch of road he had made. As he proceeded, he kept catching his breath to calm down until he reached the rocks they had chosen as their defense point just before.

Elyn was on the ground on her side.

She had no obvious injuries and was slowly trying to sit up, she just seemed to be very tired. Next to her Nolan was on his knees, while he held Triny close, cradling her gently.

He had just carefully extracted the arrows from her back, immediately after he had cast several healing spells. Such an operation would have caused severe bleeding, but he had managed to contain it. The girl did not lose a drop of blood from the still open wounds.

Instinctively, Jelko looked at his amulet, one of the four notches was almost extinguished.

—She is still alive!— he thought.

In the blink of an eye, he went up the rocks on which his companions were standing.

"How are you?" he asked with apprehension as soon as he was among them.

Elyn replied: "Jelko, help Nolan. Triny is very bad, I'll be okay. I'm not hurt."

He turned to his friend, it seemed that he hadn't even heard him coming. He continued to lay his hands on her while saying his litany, as if he were alone with the injured girl in his arms.

Right now he was completely vulnerable, he had no other interest but to save Triny.

The girl was very pale and her pulse was barely perceptible.

Nolan was doing his best and the wounds were no longer bleeding, but she had lost a lot of blood anyway. Under normal conditions, she would have already died.

"Everything will be fine, my friend. You will be able to heal her. Take all the time you need, I am at your disposal."

He looked at Elyn, he knew he was lying.

The light of their amulets was getting weaker and weaker and they were aware that they could not stay in that place for long, it was better to move as soon as the situation stabilized a little.

He sat next to the elf.

She relaxed, rested her head on his shoulder and said softly: "I'm tired Jelko. If Triny dies it will be my fault, because of my fratricidal mission."

"You have no fault" he replied, "you have not chosen your destiny, and you have not even chosen that fool of a brother. We are all in trouble with this second invasion. In reality, you are our only hope."

She sighed, each spell consumed a lot of energy.

Whispering, she said: "As a child, I always wanted to be the queen of my people. It fills me with pride, but I didn't think being one involved all this."

She smiled at the thought and continued: "When I was elected by the Circle of Elders, I certainly could not hold back. The Gods punish those who have wings but prefer not to fly."

CHAPTER 20 (Preparations)

"Damn!" swore Silven, "they are getting closer and closer and my killers have failed miserably!"

From the main tower of Averidia, the tall elf was looking through the water inside the black stone bowl. He made a gesture of annoyance that bumped into it and nearly knocked it over.

From the mirror in which he was imprisoned, Manmur said: "The healer who is with them is much more powerful than he believes, he will most likely save the girl's life."

Silven had called the old elf because he needed to let off steam with someone: "If only I weren't surrounded by incapable ones! If I could do it on my own, I would already have the world at my feet! But no! I can't move from this damned place!"

Manmur replied, as always, very calmly: "You wanted all this, and yours was the decision to cast the Curse of the Chains on our queen. Free her, you still have time. We will ask her for leniency together."

"No!" Silven yelled, "I won't be her subordinate now or ever, I'm one step away from my goal."

He approached the magic mirror remaining inside the pentacle and said: "Rather, what do you know about the other boy who is with her? Days ago, you told me about still unknown powers."

"I don't know anything" lied the old elf, "I guess you just need to worry about the healing powers you just saw."

"Really?" Silven said irritably, "and should I believe you? Your useless presence is starting to tire me, tell me something I don't already know or I will seriously think that you have become a nuisance."

Manmur held his gaze defiantly.

After all those years as a prisoner the thought of being killed did not scare him at all. He would die in order not to reveal anything important that could be used in favor of that Chosen One traitor.

"I'm waiting" Silven urged him.

"I have already told you everything I know, even under torture. I have been locked up here for too long, I no longer have any contact with our people. I am no longer aware of anything. Everything I know, I already told you a long time ago. You yourself made sure that I no longer had any contact with the outside world by locking me up in here."

"Very well" Silven replied with restrained calm, "your arrogance and your lies have come to an end, I think the longed-for hour has come for you. Let's see if once I inhibit all your resistance, you will really have nothing more to hide."

He approached the elf in the mirror, without leaving the slight blue glow that the perimeter of the containment pentacle drew on the wooden floor. Manmur continued to display mastery of his emotions without fear of his last words.

His end was approaching, he would soon be free again in the last dimension with his ancestors.

Silven closed his eyes.

The powers of the mentalist began to flow in his brain in an orderly and very precise pattern. He slowly spread his arms, bending them backwards, his feet detached from the ground by a palm.

The old elf uttered something incomprehensible.

Silven's body meanwhile was bending backwards, vibrating stronger and stronger as if trembling in a high fever.

The Chosen One stretched out his arms in front of him and spread his palms towards the mirror. There was a blinding flash followed by a roar that shook the whole tower as in an earthquake.

Silven opened his eyes. His feet were resting on the floor again, a drop of sweat slipped down his forehead.

He looked around, the black bowl from which he observed the outside world was on the ground in a thousand pieces. The amber water it contained evaporated instantly in a breath of wind.

The magic mirror in front of him had cracked in several places.

There was no one inside.

Triny alternated moments of conscience with others in which she seemed more dead than alive, the group had decided to spend the night on those rocks where they had fought.

"We can't move her from here now" Nolan had said as he continued to take care of her with all of his energy.

The girl's life hung by a thread, the turquoise light in their amulets was barely noticeable at one of the four notches.

Elyn and Jelko positioned themselves on the highest rock in order to have a better view of the surrounding area, they were leaning back-to-back.

On the sides, they were sheltered by small ridges that the rock formed and from which they peeked from time to time to keep the area under control.

There was no movement. From there, it seemed that the whole known world was serene. A little further away, you could see the increasingly higher hills giving way to the mountains.

Here and there, there were small wooded areas alternated with green clearings.

Jelko went downstairs to bring food and water to Nolan.

Once back in his place, he said to Elyn: "Here, let's eat something. Luckily, we still have a lot of food. We don't lack that."

She thanked him with a smile and said: "Rest a bit. Unfortunately, tonight we will need your eyes to watch over us again."

He replied: "Don't worry. Now I'm used to sleeping little, it won't be a problem. Rather, we hope that by tomorrow morning Nolan will be able to move Triny. We stopped too much in the same place."

"Yes" replied the elf, "somehow, we will make it. Tomorrow. We will think about it tomorrow."

Elyn was always very reassuring. Starting from the tone of voice, her words were always extremely balanced and never taken for granted.

She lay down next to him and fell asleep, her almost evanescent presence was imperceptible.

The night passed quietly.

The next morning, Triny seemed to have stabilized, although she never regained consciousness.

Nolan had just finished another healing spell, he was exhausted. The elf was stroking the girl's hair gently when she stopped for a moment and said: "Stay down!"

They immediately ducked where they were standing without understanding what was going on.

Not far away, they heard the sound of many footsteps approaching. They turned in that direction remaining as hidden as possible behind the rocks.

"It's the Sleepless Ones" Jelko said, leaning slightly to get a better look, "many, perhaps a hundred. They're coming this way."

"Down! Down! Don't let yourself be seen!" Nolan exclaimed, "if they find us, they will tear us apart. There are too many for anyone!"

Spontaneously, that Sleepless One battalion was marching in their direction, they didn't seem to have noticed their presence judging by their attitude.

At their head were three different figures without the now known bestial physiognomy.

Jelko said in a low voice: "They seem to be under the control of human beings. So far, I have never seen them take initiative on their own. Even when they attacked the caravan, there was always someone in charge."

Elyn said: "I don't think they're capable of taking over the world on their own. They definitely need someone to rule them, it's likely they're somehow magically linked to their commanders."

"Watch!" Nolan noticed another battalion behind the first.

They counted five in all within a short distance of each other, all commanded by humanoid figures.

Fortunately, no one noticed their presence or even the corpse of the archer they had killed the day before.

Once they passed the rocks on which they were stationed, a little further on they separated, three to the North and two to the South.

"That way is Averidia, they come from that direction. They must have been recently summoned and sent who-knows-where" said Jelko.

It was not long before the last battalion disappeared from sight.

"Nolan" Elyn asked, "we have to go. How's Triny? Can you move her?"

He replied: "With due caution, yes. I will carry her on my shoulder, you will have to try to tie her to me so that she does not escape my grip."

"Okay" Jelko intervened, "I have an idea, wait for me here."

He quickly descended the steps of the rocks and headed for the archer's body, tore off his robes and turned back.

They made strips of it and helped Nolan harness the girl on his shoulders. She groaned and woke up for a moment, opening her eyes and then closing them again soon after.

Her back was slightly uncovered, in correspondence with the wounds of the arrows that had hit her, almost nothing was noticed except for two very small scars that were barely visible.

They set off slowly West, Nolan was slowed down by carrying Triny on his shoulder.

The heat, away from the rivers and the coast, made itself felt, but they didn't seem to notice too much as they were all focused on the destination.

None of them had ever been to Averidia. The mystical city was very famous, and they, like most of the inhabitants of the planet, knew of its existence only through tales and legends that told of its magnificence and excellence in terms of knowledge.

Throughout the day, Elyn continued to divert the group according to her perceptions on whole squadrons of Sleepless Ones.

Along the way, they found woods and passed through them.

The coolness gave them a bit of refreshment, and also, hid them from view of the enemy who kept moving its numerous troops in every direction.

In addition to the five battalions seen in the morning, they counted as many in the afternoon.

On that day, they saw a total of a thousand units moving in different directions, forcing them to lengthen their gear so as not to be seen.

Meanwhile, Triny was recovering.

In the very short stops they made, and helped by his companions, Nolan momentarily got rid of the makeshift harnesses that allowed him to keep the wounded girl firmly in place.

His healing spells were less and less frequent. The amulet they had around their necks slowly began to shine with turquoise light, even at the notch that until the day before was almost extinguished.

Triny was out of danger, but she still needed rest that the group could not give her at that time.

She alternated moments of unconsciousness with others in which she could barely speak, moments in which she asked for water and then returned to a soporific state.

When evening came, they stopped in a small grove.

For some time now, the Sleepless Ones had not been seen marching to their unknown destinations, and they certainly would not have done so with the arrival of the evening.

"Who knows how the kingdoms are doing" said Jelko, "if this is the rate at which troops are sent every day, the invasion is proceeding at full speed."

The companions did not answer. The thought of what was happening in the whole world did not make them comment on that terrible observation.

They helped Nolan lay Triny gently on the grass. The girl was regaining color and just at that moment she opened her eyes and said almost in a whisper: "I'm sorry to get in your way. I was a fool, I should have foreseen it. My first fight with targets in flesh and blood wasn't good."

Nolan, who was really tired, replied: "I think you will remember it for the rest of your life. I'm sure it will be much better next time. You'll see!"

Jelko patted his friend on the back. Turning towards her, he said: "He didn't give up on you for a moment, he worked harder than he would have done for anyone else. I'm sure!"

Triny smiled and squeezed Nolan's hand tightly, hinting at a slight smile.

"You have great willpower" Elyn said to Nolan, "we're lucky to have you among us."

"You are very kind" he replied. Now he could breathe a sigh of relief and rest a bit.

Jelko sat down with his back against the trunk of a tree, put his sword on the side of the grass and tried to relax as the sunset became more and more red.

The elf stood up, began to speak softly and gently touched some trees while she walked from one to the other.

A light breeze began to move the branches and everyone immediately had the feeling that someone was watching them with a thousand eyes.

Elyn went back to the boys and said: "Tonight the trees will watch over us. Let's try to rest, we all need it."

Triny, still in a faint voice, said: "Among my things there is a sealed parchment. Take it, Zimas will contact us through it when the time comes. He gave it to me before leaving Argoran."

"Okay" replied the elf, "now rest. Don't worry about the parchment, we'll take care of it."

Elyn stood next to her and she smiled at her.

The girl was always very in awe of her even though the elf had repeatedly told her clearly not to be, she lay down next to her and gently stroked her brown hair until she fell asleep again.

Even the second sun was setting. As the darkness advanced, the light wind that moved the branches of the trees decreased in intensity until it was barely perceptible.

Nolan, who was exhausted, fell asleep immediately.

Jelko still could not fall asleep and asked the elf in a low voice: "Do you feel anything? The second man sent to kill us has escaped, but I don't think he'll let us continue our journey so easily."

"No, I have no perception of him" Elyn replied, curling up on herself like a cat, "but I doubt he'll go back to my brother without fulfilling his mission. He'd kill him."

He nodded thoughtfully and said: "We'll be in Averidia shortly, I'm afraid of what lies ahead."

She sat up and replied in her usual seductive, calm voice: "Me too. The invasion has begun Jelko, our time is up."

"And how can you always be so peaceful?"

Elyn looked at him intently.

Her green eyes pierced straight into his as she did when she wanted to make mental contact with some of her victims: "I don't know how I do it, but I prefer to think about everything that is beautiful beyond my fears."

CHAPTER 21 (Fragment on the Run)

The knights divided into two groups. They moved away from each other following semi-arches with perfect symmetry.

When they were at the right distance, they maneuvered to get back on the correct trajectory facing each other.

They galloped their steeds and set off to charge.

The battalion of a hundred Sleepless Ones found itself in the middle as the spears lowered. It had no escape.

The soldiers of the Duchy, led by Faxel and Zimas, mercilessly mowed down everything they encountered in their path.

After the first charge that halved the enemy, a second followed that eliminated all the survivors, including the two human commanders.

No knight was injured in the attack, the technique and training had once again borne fruit.

They were not far from Han Farn. Within a couple of hours of walking, they would have entered the city.

And so they did.

In the middle of the afternoon the knights encamped in a small clearing outside the capital of the Dark Kingdom.

Faxel, Zimas and three other escort soldiers hurried through the imposing city walls.

They were greeted with absolute respect by the city guards on the watchtowers, the soldiers of the Duchy were well regarded everywhere, their loyalty and fame preceded them and they never went looking for trouble or lands to conquer.

The captain on duty, who had recognized them by the banners, approached and said to Faxel: "Welcome to the capital of the Dark Kingdom, I hope you have had a good trip."

"We greatly appreciate your courtesy, we come in peace as a delegation in the name of the Duchy of the Seven Lakes. You are certainly aware of the return of the Sleepless Ones, our sovereign asks to be able to confer with you through the court archmage Zimas and myself."

"Come, follow me" said the captain, leading the way.

He was a mighty man in his forties, the same age as Faxel.

His armor, of reinforced leather, was very well made and with fine finishes. The guards they met wore the emblem of their kingdom proudly drawn on their shields: two crossed black swords on a dark red background.

Their kingdom was known for the discipline and rigor with which the king governed his possessions.

Zimas motioned for the three escort knights to wait outside, while they and Faxel entered a gatehouse near the door used as the captain's office.

Inside the room, they were alone. The landlord made them sit on the only two stools there were while he remained standing in front of them.

The captain pointed to a jug of water and wooden glasses on the desk, he motioned for them to be served without compliments and said: "Our king left a few weeks ago with his usual royal entourage, he hasn't returned yet."

"Where was he headed?" Faxel asked.

"Nobody knows" the soldier replied, "but his destination is almost always unknown except to his inner circle. Our security service believes this decreases the risk outside our solid city walls."

The captain looked worried and began pacing nervously up and down the small room.

Zimas intervened resolutely: "Captain, are you hiding something from us? You look uncomfortable."

The soldier stopped and replied: "I'm afraid something has happened. The Sleepless Ones are back and our king is out there somewhere, his prolonged absence is not normal in light of what is happening."

"Is there really no way to be able to track him down? Can't your wizards do anything?" the sorcerer pressed him.

"Not that I know of" replied the man, "our commander-in-arms is also my uncle. He is part of the Council, which for now has thought it wise to tell the population that the king is not well, even if his life is not threatened. All this while waiting to know something more and to hide the reason for his absence."

Faxel said: "I'm afraid his failure to return is related to the invasion, it's not safe for a king to be away from his kingdom at such a time."

"Yeah, that's not like him" the captain added.

Zimas took the floor, cutting off the conversation and asked: "Can we be accompanied by someone to check the Relic? Since we are here, we have the right to verify its presence by our Duchy."

While he was speaking, he pulled out of his pocket the seal of the Duchy of the Seven Lakes as evidence of what had just been said.

"Of course, I will accompany you myself."

They left the gatehouse, motioned to their respective men to wait there, and all three set off following the captain.

The Relic, from the time of the first invasion, was brought to Han Farn to be guarded by mutual agreement with the other kingdoms.

The pact was that any official delegation, sent by the various sovereigns, could check its presence at will whenever they wished.

This ensured a certain security for everyone, since the custodians' request to have seen the Fragment of Infinity was not expected.

The more people were able to verify that it was in its place, the more it confirmed the fact that no one was seizing it improperly.

The city and capital Han Farn was very beautiful.

Almost all the roofs of the white stone houses were colored golden yellow and shaped like a dome. Every street they traveled was well paved, and on both sides were small well-kept flower beds with colorful grass and flowers.

The many flowers, of different species, gave the city a pleasant scent that spread almost everywhere in the air.

Almost everything suggested that the capital was a rather wealthy city, there were very few beggars. Even a small district of the city was set aside for them so that they did not crowd the vain streets, disfiguring their beauty.

The Relic, a stone chalice unique in the world, was barely a palm high and emitted a candid light as white as milk.

The unknown matter of which it was composed was as hard as steel, but light enough to float in water. Inside there were constantly two fingers of a transparent liquid. Each time it was turned upside down, it vanished and evaporated immediately after touching any type of surface.

At the same instant, the same liquid was reformed as soon as the glass returned to a neutral and vertical position.

It was decided, under the expert advice of many archmages of the time, to seal it in a glass box, which, after being appropriately enchanted, became indestructible, despite the fact that the material continued to resemble a very banal crystal.

Legend has it that, during the first invasion that took place fifteen years earlier, many noticed that whenever an undead being was destroyed, a slight glow escaped from its body, and that this flash of light disappeared soon after walking a few steps in a northeastern direction.

At every point in the world, when a Sleepless One was killed, a tiny light, lasting an instant, broke away from the abomination in that direction.

It was also said that a very rich pirate, named Ablar from the Barony of the Dragon, decided to embark on a long journey with his fleet of five galleons to the Fell Islands, and that right there he found the Fragment of Infinity inside a cave by the sea.

When he returned, all his boats were shipwrecked shortly after setting sail, leaving no way out for anyone due to very strong winds, that are said to have been generated by the Relic itself.

The latter, pushed by the waves, was found on the coast of the Dark Kingdom, where a little girl who found it gave it its current name.

To avoid further catastrophic movements, it was decided to keep it in the capital Han Farn with the approval of all the sovereigns, who, to wash their hands, believed that the Fragment of Infinity had chosen that kingdom as its home, so it was better not oppose the will of the Gods.

During the first year, the studies on the Relic were many.

The best experts in magic also came from Averidia, but it was not possible to establish their origin or what power was contained in that mysterious object.

The aura of energy around it went far beyond the knowledge available to anyone.

Attempts to understand its capabilities were in vain.

The conclusion was simply that of tracing the Relic to a powerful artifact, whose origin had been lost in the mists of time, perhaps when the Gods inhabited the planet before all other living beings.

Even at the present time, it was believed that the powers had yet to be revealed in the times and in the ways that the Gods themselves deem most appropriate.

The captain took Faxel and Zimas to an imposing mausoleum of very beautiful white stone, three floors high and within the perimeter of the octagonal walls, next to the government building of the capital.

At the top there were imposing statues of divinities who looked down upon the subjects at their feet. The external walls were divided into large bas-relief rectangles, one for each ruler buried inside, on which the deeds that the kings had performed in life were painted.

"Here rest all our kings" the soldier said proudly, "our use does not include their cremation on a pyre, but mummification."

"So that's where you keep the Relic?" Faxel asked.

"Yes, some crypts have been adapted to allow a small community of monks to be able to live in the nearby rooms. It is a very reliable and duty-bound order that practices self-flagellation, they never leave there. Every ten days they are left with food and water at the beginning of the great staircase that we will see shortly."

The large bronze door with two doors, expertly decorated, was closed. The captain walked over to two guards who guarded the royal palace next door.

He talked to one of them who immediately entered and left shortly afterwards, followed by a fellow soldier with large keys in his hand and a man with a tunic behind him.

They headed for the mausoleum.

The door was enchanted, because the unarmed man whispered a formula, laying his hands on both doors. As soon as the latter finished his litanies, the guard with the keys opened two locked locks with three turns each, producing a great clatter of gears.

The captain motioned for the two to return to their duties and crossed the threshold. He was followed by Faxel and Zimas, who had remained in respectful silence as they witnessed the rituals of the hosts.

The interior of the mausoleum was as beautiful as it was outside. The walls in the lower part were painted in purple red, while at mid-height they were white again.

Huge and wonderful tapestries were scattered almost everywhere, of all colors and depicting still lives, ancient maps, war and hunting scenes.

In the upper part, some arched windows let in the light so that it illuminated the most important images at certain specific times of the day.

Thirty gold-handled torches lined the walls.

At the center of the large circular nave, there was an imposing staircase that descended into the basement to the crypts.

"This way" said the captain, after briefly contemplating that place so sacred to him.

They went down the elegant staircase in silence, until they found themselves in front of a large room lit by torches identical to those on the upper floor. From here departed corridors that led to the various funerary crypts.

"For all the Gods!" exclaimed the captain of the guards, his gaze was fixed on the large extinguished brazier in the center of the atrium.

Faxel stepped back in alarm, yanking Zimas to back him up too. They had neither noticed nor heard anything strange.

The captain ran up to the pyre, examining it and said: "The Sacred Flame is extinguished! It has never been out for as long as I can remember! The guardian monks have a very specific order to keep it burning at any cost!"

"Something does not convince me" Zimas said. He looked around and placed his magic white wooden staff in front of him.

Faxel had his hand on the hilt of his sword and, as the captain continued to obsessively circle the ashes of the pyre, a shadow moved to their right.

"Who is there?" Faxel yelled.

The figure fell to the ground with a thud. The captain was on top of it in a moment and exclaimed in surprise: "He is one of the keepers! He is dead!"

The monk was shirtless, with his wrists slit, and had numerous torture marks and bruises everywhere.

More noises were clearly heard.

Five Sleepless Ones emerged from the corridors in front of them, two attacked the captain and the other three rushed towards Faxel and Zimas.

Behind the undead, five monks with spiked clubs tugged at each other, making their way and also exiting the corridors of the crypts.

The keepers seemed possessed, they had their eyes turned backwards and were foaming at the mouth.

One of them hit the captain in the back, who in the meantime had cleverly killed a Sleepless One. The blow was not lethal, but enough to make him lose his balance, finding himself one step away from the other that he was facing.

He couldn't hit him with the sword from such a short distance. The space between them was too little, so he decided to pounce on him with his bare hands, dropping the weapon.

Faxel positioned himself in front of the wizard to protect him, Zimas in the meantime had cast a spell. A fiery barrier now separated them from everything else, giving them some time to think of a strategy.

On the other side of the wall of fire, the keepers and the Sleepless Ones were about to cross the flames. They wanted to satisfy their compulsive desire to fight against their enemies, who had dared to get too close to their hiding place.

One of the monks jumped over the flames and got burned.

With few remaining clothes and partly charred skin, he rushed on Zimas.

Faxel promptly intercepted him. The keeper parried the blow with the club, but was struck by a kick that knocked him to the ground.

The captain was in trouble, he was facing four and was wounded.

Zimas noticed this. A flash of energy went off from the magic stick that hit one of the Sleepless One, destroying it, just as the soldier stabbed a keeper after having knocked him down and picked up the sword that had fallen shortly before, when he had lost his balance.

Faxel fatally wounded the burned monk who had attempted to attack the wizard. The fiery barrier vanished and Zimas instantly launched another flash of energy, destroying another undead.

"Behind you!" Faxel shouted in the direction of the captain, who was about to be torn by a claw of a Sleepless One who, in the confusion, had managed to take the soldier with it.

He eliminated the monk he had disarmed with a blow, but only managed to partially avoid the razor-sharp claws of the undead. In fact, he was hit in the arm and left leg with a blow from top to bottom.

The captain fell to the ground, continuing to defend himself with his sword as best he could from that position of disadvantage, trying to keep up with his ravenous opponent.

He was a skilled fighter and he would have sold his skin dearly.

Zimas struck a keeper with his stick, knocking him out. He pulled the dagger from his belt and thrust it into his throat, while the monk was still trying to recover from the stunning blow he had just received.

Faxel cut off the head of the last remaining caretaker and went to the rescue of the injured captain, who was struggling to defend himself.

He reached him attracting the attention of the one who was attacking him as he fought the other Sleepless One left.

There were two left in all.

Faxel managed to get his back against the wall. The two undead seemed to disregard the captain on the ground and raged on him, giving him problems.

Zimas raised both arms up and slowly lowered them as if he were laboriously pulling something down from above.

The two Sleepless Ones tried to instinctively cover their faces, as if blinded by a sudden light visible only to them. In that position, they uncovered their hips and Faxel did not miss the opportunity.

With powerful swipes, he hit them both and nearly cut them in half.

The tomb silence that characterized the whole mausoleum until before the battle, returned.

The captain was wounded, but his life was not in danger.

He was breathing heavily. He got helped up by Faxel, to whom he said: "I am indebted to you, we must immediately go and check the Relic. It is in the second crypt after that corridor."

They did not know if there were other monks or Sleepless Ones lurking, so with great caution they advanced in the indicated direction.

The door of the crypt, where the Fragment of Infinity was kept, was open. From that direction came an acrid smell of decomposition, they slowly entered and found what they had already suspected.

The captain leaned against a wall, bewildered. What he saw hurt him more than the wounds he had suffered from the fight that had taken place shortly before.

The room in which they found themselves was small, with white walls slightly blackened by the soot of the torches.

In the center was a pedestal of gray stone on which an open box of magical glass was placed.

On the ground were the corpses of two guardian monks.

The Relic had been stolen.

CHAPTER 22 (Last Steps)

It was mid-afternoon of the following day. Triny was able to resume walking without help, albeit slowly. Nolan often took her in his arms or on his shoulder so as not to tire her.

"Without you, I would have died" she told him on more than one occasion.

He was very proud to hear those words, he had more than a weakness for the girl and carrying her in his arms didn't weigh on him at all.

"My God has been merciful this time too" he repeated with cheerful solemnity, "you should all approach him and leave yours, it doesn't seem to me that up to now they have been of much use."

It was true: every time he invoked his God to perform some healing, it succeeded perfectly. He had already proved this on several occasions and Triny would certainly have died if he hadn't been there to heal her promptly.

Nolan was a goliardic and humble soul, his company was cheerful and easy-going. He never took himself too seriously, although his skills were actually extraordinary and not insignificant. He never gave himself excessive importance.

"Does this God of yours have a name?" Jelko asked curiously.

"No, nobody knows yet what it might be."

"And how can you be so devoted if you don't even know his name? Do you have any pictures of him at least?"

Nolan replied: "We don't need to know his name, it doesn't matter and we don't even know what he's done. No one has ever seen him, so there are no images of him. It might not even have a shape as we mere humans understand it, but to be honest, what does it matter what he's called and how he's made?"

"You're not completely wrong" said Jelko, "in fact, our Gods are depicted in paintings and statues, but deep down I don't think anyone has ever seen them in person, now or ever."

Nolan smiled: "This should be enough for you to answer for yourself about their authenticity!"

"Right, but for that matter, you don't have proof either."

"No, but at least I'm aware that it's not important!"

Elyn listened amused and smiled as the two commented on each other's statements.

Jelko, seeing her interested, asked: "What do you think about it?"

She replied: "What you say is right. I think that whatever God or Gods we believe in, something higher must exist. We ourselves are proof of it with the powers we have, then everyone is free to call him whatever he wants."

The elf continued: "Every time I close my eyes and concentrate, the colors become barely perceptible, but I see around every living being something similar to the concentric circles that form when a stone is thrown into a pond. Some are big, others very small. We are all different and the very diversity of our Creed is the beauty of each of us."

Triny interrupted the conversation abruptly: "Wait! Nolan put me down!"

He carried out the perplexed order and asked: "What is going on?"

"The parchment of Zimas!"

The girl hastened to open her small travel backpack, the sealed parchment she spoke of was vibrating insistently.

He pulled it out and said: "They are contacting us, they must have reached Han Farn and have news of the Relic."

Triny broke the seal and unrolled it by opening it on the grass.

Elyn and Jelko exchanged a glance. The Argoran seer had been clear, they were afraid they already knew the answer that was about to come.

Meanwhile, the magic parchment was darkening, starting from the edges to the center. When it was all black, the faces of Faxel and Zimas appeared more and more clearly.

The wizard said: "The Relic has been stolen. We are heading to Averidia, we will meet there."

Faxel interjected: "The seer was right, but it was still our duty to verify the veracity of his words. He is still an Argoran thug and such news could not be taken seriously without first confirming it."

Jelko realized that, when he answered his father hard-nosed about the fact that he would not need to go to Han Farn, he had exaggerated. In fact, such an event had to be controlled by official sources.

Elyn spoke up and said: "In a day, we will be within sight of the mystical city. We will wait for you and decide on a plan together."

"We have been on the march since yesterday" Faxel replied, "we have nearly three hundred infantry from the Dark Kingdom with us, and another two hundred are gathering in the capital. The neighboring Kingdoms of Karinal and Miriam have also sent some swift troops towards Averidia, while they are recalling the conscripts."

Jelko said: "It might be a good idea if we just sneak in. Maybe with some spell we could move more stealthily and get to the goal without making too much of a fuss."

Nolan added: "Indeed, even if you are a small army, you will not go unnoticed."

The parchment was slowly starting to burn around the perimeter.

Zimas spoke up and said: "We don't have any more time, we'll talk about it in person. Stay hidden near Averidia, I'll try to get in touch with the mentalist and we'll calmly decide on a plan."

The flames enveloped all the parchment, which in a very short time was pulverized and dispersed in the weak warm wind.

"Here we are guys" Nolan said without his usual humor.

Nobody said a word, the tension was palpable. Within a day or two they would meet their fate.

It didn't matter which God or Gods had forged their destinies. At that moment, they all felt infinitely small and frightened. Their young lives had turned upside down in too little time to get used to.

Triny was a girl of humble origins, her parents were both bakers and her mother died a month earlier. She had a high fever for some time and the few treatments that they could give her were not enough.

She had a very determined character. Her propensity for magic had prompted her parents to make sacrifices in order to allow her to study in the magic schools of the Duchy, in the hope of guaranteeing her a better future.

Zimas noticed her immediately, confirming her strong magical skills. Since he hardly ever said it about anyone, it had to be true.

Nolan had long hair and his beard was usually tied in braids with metal ribbons or rings. He was the companion of the group, the one who always wore sarcasm and irony in everything he did. His gaiety was contagious, but rarely out of place or too intrusive.

He knew very well when the situation got serious. In all other cases, he preferred to laugh and make fun of life.

Orphaned since birth, he had grown up between one monastery and another in the Barony of the Dragon, where he had learned important notions about medicinal herbs and defensive spells, both for protection and for healing.

In recent years, he had embraced a monotheistic religion that was frowned upon. The Order was investigated and persecuted, and many of his brothers were executed as heretics. He received a life sentence in Argoran, which for many was even worse than death.

Jelko, on the other hand, was in constant inner turmoil.

He had always lived an altogether peaceful life in the capital of the Duchy. He lacked nothing, but he was also constantly looking for something new. His curiosity was very strong and to get out of his usual routine he had to grow fast.

Faxel had to be his father and mother. He managed very well to fill both roles, managing to educate him in justice exactly as he himself had based his whole life.

For Jelko, his father was all his family, but Elyn had indirectly wreaked havoc in their relationship. Thanks to her, he was able to find out how his mother had really died, from whom he had, to great surprise, inherited demonic genes.

He felt something strange about the elf, but he still didn't know how to give it a precise definition.

For some time, his feelings for Faxel had been mixed. He knew that he always acted for his sake, yet he continued to see him as a hostile figure. Not having escaped the elf's stake and keeping silent about his mother destabilized him, he felt betrayed by the only family member he ever had.

Elyn was the oldest in terms of years. She was over a hundred and fifty years old, but compared to her people, she was still a very young girl, since elves could live up to a thousand years.

None of the other companions were over twenty and, beyond the age dictated by the race, all four of them could be considered peers.

She had been queen for fifteen years, when the first invasion ended, and almost immediately she was condemned to the Curse of the Chains and sent away from her people by her twin brother, who aspired to the throne that she had taken from him.

The election of her sister was unanimously by the Circle of Elders. She loved that role, but she had never requested it.

Her qualities as a mentalist had made her the Chosen One as a child, this was enough for her.

Silven, her brother, never managed to accept his total exclusion from the possibility of becoming king. Unlike his sister, he had hoped for it, and remaining a Chosen One was no longer enough for him, although only those who had particular and extraordinary skills could be one, while still holding a position of prestige within the hierarchy of his people.

His disposition was never deemed fit to lead the Arcane Elves, a nomadic people believed to be superior to any other, moving between dimensions every five hundred years.

It was said that they left the world they settled in much better than they found it.

Elyn had a sweet and kind nature. Her manner was charming and her regal status suited her perfectly, despite the fact that she was not in her real body at the time.

Her rationality had always made her make wise and mature decisions, her serenity accompanied her at all times and was easily visible even from the outside.

She hardly got upset, but when she did, her psionic power almost escaped her control, producing potentially devastating energy.

By concentrating, she could read the minds of almost anyone who was in front of her, even if for a very short time and based on the resistance that the intelligence of the individual put up.

The sunset was upon them.

She raised her eyes and looked towards the horizon. Among all the members of the group, perhaps she risked the most of all.

She was the one with the lowest chance of survival since it had to be her, and only her, to fight her brother to the death.

She could finally break free from the curse only by killing him in person.

No one else would have been powerful enough to deal with it.

She was the queen of the Arcane Elves.

As she was in charge of that task, she would never shirk her duty. Symbol's world and the dimension in which her people were suspended, depended on the outcome of that fight.

Her fate was a strange one: from newly elected queen to slave in a very short time, from Chosen One with formidable powers to almost nothing, she also risked her life through exhaustion by using the little energy of which the curse had not been able to deprive her.

The landscape around her was enchanting.

A tear ran down her face and fell into the grass, no one noticed.

Now, she had to be stronger than ever.

CHAPTER 23 (The Torch Off)

They walked all the following day.

When it was evening, they found themselves in a small and dense wood.

In that area, the trees were quite frequent, which was considered quite rare and precious considering the usual hot and sultry days almost all year round.

Triny was much better. She only felt some pain in her back, depending on the movements she made, but all in all she was almost healed from her injuries.

For the past three days, they had not seen any movement of troops.

The Sleepless Ones perhaps went through other paths, or the evocation from their dimension was for some reason suspended at the time, considering that the ritual itself required time and a considerable magical commitment.

The wood in which they were located began to thin out and a new great plain would soon open up.

Jelko looked over the last tree almost by chance and saw it.

"Here we are guys" he said with a lump in his throat to his companions who were just behind him.

They joined him and all together remained in silence to observe that isolated promontory on which Averidia stood.

The spur of rock was rather thin. If the mystical city had still been inhabited, the lights would have become visible as the suns set and the evening advanced.

From a distance it was clear why it was said that it looked like a lit torch. The shape of the promontory and the city itself at the top recalled its shape, creating the idea perfectly.

But no, Averidia was now extinguished by the last invasion.

Now it was just a heap of ruins forgotten by the Gods.

"That's where a lot of things will be decided" Elyn said, "no matter how it goes, we've all done our best. It was an honor to have met you, I would have liked to have met you in better circumstances."

"Do not say that!" Nolan exclaimed, "all is not lost, We still have a role and cards to play."

Usually, it was he who raised the morale of the group, but this time he could not find the right words to have that effect.

Triny, who was finally beginning to feel less awe of the elf, approached her and hugged her: "We'll do it, and you will defeat your brother by getting free once and for all."

Jelko also stood beside her and said: "Soon my father's knights with the soldiers of the Dark Kingdom will be here to give us a hand. Somehow we will manage, we are not alone. You will see that everything will be fine."

"You're right" Elyn replied, not believing what she was saying.

While she felt inside that she was lying, she managed to say that sentence with a decisive and reassuring tone. They were all involved in that story because of her.

Somehow the invasion would still have touched them closely sooner or later, but it was still her relationship with her twin that was the trigger for what was happening. All of this made her feel terribly guilty.

"At this point, I think the first invasion also had to do with your brother" Jelko said.

"We Arcane Elves believe so too" Elyn explained, "but he didn't have the Relic with him. It was almost a mild attempt to test the ground. At the time, we were still uncertain about who would be the successor to lead our people. Now it's different, he's smarter and he's got the Fragment of Infinity with him. Moreover, hatred of him has grown out of all proportion."

Triny said: "So many people died even then, I don't dare think what might happen this time."

"That's what we're here for!" Nolan intervened, "we will be able to get rid of that damned madman, and we will go together around the world to discover its beauties as soon as possible!"

"You are an incurable optimist" Jelko told him smiling.

Everyone looked at each other and felt for a moment relieved of that tension, mixed with uncertainty that had been created in seeing Averidia reduced in those conditions.

In that ghost town, somehow they would have to enter shortly among a thousand unknowns. Their mood was understandably in turmoil.

Elyn said: "Please, we are still far and hidden. I want to run and roll on the grass of this forest like when I was a child, let's see who gets there first before it gets dark!"

She started running, the others put down their weapons and backpacks and followed her.

"But how the hell can you be so damn nimble and fast?" Nolan yelled after her.

Jelko, who was laughing, said: "Our healer will surely arrive last, I can feel it! Get moving, lazy one!"

He easily passed him, leaving his partner to close the line.

Triny laboriously reached the elf: "Try to catch us if you can!" she said, turning around.

The girls were faster, even though Jelko was a little behind.

They came to a small clearing without trees. Elyn dropped to the ground, lying on her back and began to laugh. The others as they reached her did the same, Nolan arrived last.

The four of them were next to each other, the sunset colored the horizon with shades from red to orange. They laughed like they had never done before.

Then silence.

Elyn said: "How beautiful is life as a free person? I haven't run on grass like this for a very long time."

"You're right" Jelko replied, "and to think that it takes so little."

"Yeah" Triny and Nolan said in chorus.

"You know what?" continued the elf, who at that juncture seemed simply a girl and no longer a queen, "I think my brother has a tool to be able to observe us, with which he studies our moves. If he is using it even now, I want him to see us exactly like this, lying on the ground, happy and smiling."

"Well said!" Triny beamed.

They lay down until just before it was completely dark. They felt less tense, they had finally eased the tension a little.

They got up and went back to get their things where they had left them just before. Jelko took one last look at the mystical city before night hid it until the next morning.

"But…" he barely managed to say.

"What have you seen?" Triny asked.

"Don't you also think you see a slight glow coming from Averidia?"

In fact, a barely perceptible luminescence could be seen overhanging the most central part of the city. It was located in a very specific point and radiated only in the immediately adjacent areas.

"There is evidently something that sheds light" Nolan said, "it's strange that a light source is left on. Even if it is barely visible and nobody ever passes through these parts, it is still risky for those who do not want to be noticed."

Jelko said: "Perhaps there are preparations underway that cannot be postponed until tomorrow morning."

They settled down for the night right near the end of that wood, so that they were sheltered and could still keep an eye on that faint glow that didn't seem to go out, and for which they could not offer a plausible explanation.

They kept a tiny lit candle sheltered from their backpacks, so that it illuminated only a small area between them and their faces were barely visible to each other.

"I don't really know what that could be" Elyn said, still looking in that direction.

While they were preparing for the night, no one spoke. They were all troubled by trying to understand what that anomalous light on the city was.

"I have to go and see."

"Jelko, no!" Triny exclaimed in concern.

"We have to take advantage of it" he said with the resolute tone of someone who does not allow replies, "I can see in the dark and they can't. I can go up and take a look."

Elyn sighed, looking down after hearing that statement. She knew that he would not back down, but she was afraid of the risk he would take. Yet he was right, his night vision was a huge plus that was worth taking advantage of.

Jelko was already on his feet. Nolan looked at him helplessly and said: "Needless to say, pay close attention. You don't know the streets of that place and we don't know what's in there."

"I know" Jelko replied as he adjusted his sword at his side, "but if I could get any information, it would also be very useful for the incoming knights and soldiers to come up with a plan when the time comes."

"That's true" Nolan said.

Elyn got up almost silently and went to hug Jelko: "Please, be careful."

"Don't worry" he said, "I'll be back before dawn trying to get as much information as possible. If you see me first, it will mean that I wasn't able to get too close. I won't take unnecessary risks, rest assured."

They saw him pass a couple of trees a few steps away from them, then night enveloped him.

The only access to reach Averidia was the path that spiraled up to the promontory on which it was perched.

The place where his companions had stopped was not close.

He had to walk a long way out in the open, there were only a few trees and shelters here and there.

By now, he had mastered his ability to see in the dark. He watched in every direction as he strode cautiously towards the path. There could always be some magic spell or trap that could reveal his presence, however unlikely that was.

His thoughts were on that object that Elyn had mentioned, through which her brother could observe anyone at any time.

He promised himself that as soon as he noticed something potentially dangerous, he would immediately come back.

He came to the base of the rocky promontory and started up the path.

Probably when the city was still inhabited, it was much better kept. The road was partially paved, but the grass and brambles had filled the spaces between one stone and another. It could still be seen that it was a wide path that had once been well cared for. On the other hand, it was also the only access to the city.

Going up, he noticed that in many points, the road was free from weeds, a sign of the continuous and repeated passage of many people over time.

He sensed that after fifteen years, the path could not be so beaten if no one had passed since then.

It was to be expected, all confirmed the origin of those Sleepless Ones' battalions seen in recent days. They had all passed this way.

He managed to get to the top in a short time, his every gesture was carefully thought out to make as little noise as possible. He felt his heart in his throat, his friends were far away and they would not have been able to come to his aid if something happened to him.

The road led to a guard bastion, the only one in the whole city since it had no other entrances. The two large doors were uprooted on the ground, covered with ivy and weeds.

He crossed it and moved to one side of the main road, skirting the ruins of the abandoned houses. Many were still standing and only a few had actually collapsed or demolished, all of which made one think of a ghost town rather than a city of old ruins.

There was no noise, the city was immersed in silence.

A few more steps and he saw further on that glow that he noticed with his companions from the woods where they camped.

—I'm on the right track!— he told himself.

As he got closer, he was increasingly visible and he had to pay more attention. His advantage of seeing in the dark began to fade and the intensity of the light increased as he approached its own source.

Still there was no noise and nothing moving, yet there must be something down there.

He saw a tower.

It was not very high, but it had a very wide and unusual circular base. In front of it, a large pale stone building emerged from the half-light. Probably it was the great library in which it was said that absolute knowledge was contained, starting from the origins of the world of Symbol.

Initially it was all contained within the tower, but over time it was necessary to build a second structure as documents, books and knowledge, increased.

Some parts of it had collapsed and almost all the windows had broken shutters.

The road led him to one of the main squares of the city, but he stopped. It was too risky to go on, even if he didn't see a soul and heard nothing. The light, that came from something in front of the tower and was not visible from there, was starting to become too strong.

He noticed his own shadow and felt like he was naked.

He immediately entered a house that he was skirting, taking shelter. He could not continue. If there had been someone from there on, he would have been visible.

From this close, the slight glow had given way to an intense white light.

—I'm a stone's throw from that thing— he thought, —I can't leave right now without finding out what it is.—

The house was three floors high, he went up the dusty inner stairs hoping to find at least one window from which he could see something more.

And so it was.

A small terrace was facing right in the direction of the tower.

He just put his head out and noticed something he had never seen before.

In the center of the square overlooked by the library and the tower, there was a large obelisk of black stone. Next to it was a large tree without leaves emitting an intense white light, like milk.

It seemed to be made of glass, the trunk was impressive and gave the whole tree a majestic image. It was almost as tall as the obelisk next to it, which in turn was about four floors high.

The light was blinding from so close. While he watched it in amazement, he noticed that from one of the highest branches, another very small twig, as long as an arm, developed right then and there.

He imagined that the luminous glass tree was alive and that it was growing even at that precise moment under his eyes. This was extraordinary and unimaginable.

With a start, he noticed that at its feet a figure was moving quickly in the direction of the gate of the tower.

It ran across the square.

He tried to sharpen his sight as much as he could, to at least understand if it was a human being or not.

It was a man. His face was painted black and blue and in his right hand he held a scepter.

He recognized him. He was one of the two hitmen Silven had sent to kill him and his companions, the one who escaped just after trying to beat him.

The entrance to the tower was not visible from his position, but he clearly heard the door close, so he sensed that he had entered.

He waited a little longer, dawn was not near.

He wanted to see if there was any other movement, but he saw no one or noticed anything else worthy of note. The silence was deadly, there was no trace of the Sleepless Ones.

He waited a little longer, but he didn't want to risk it. To go back there was a long way to go and doing so at the crack of dawn was not wise.

He furtively retraced the path backwards, carefully checking every street and anything he could discover and report to the soldiers about the strategic makeup of the city; at least the part from the entrance to the obelisk square, which without any doubt was the most important.

He passed the entrance bastion and began to descend the road that led to the base of the promontory.

He tripped over something, a stone rolled down the side of the road. He crouched down from the noise he had made unintentionally and noticed that the stone, he had just bumped into, uncovered a root.

He waited to study the situation, he was already halfway down the road and the noise was not loud enough to be heard from a great distance.

He got back on his feet. With amazement, he noticed that the root was beginning to emit a very slight white light. A little further on another did the same. The light was barely perceptible and could not be noticed, if not at a very short distance.

—They are the roots of the tree coming up here! How is it possible? I'm very far away!— he thought, amazed.

He told himself that he absolutely had to report that detail to those who knew something about magic, as he was not an expert on the subject.

He hypothesized that the roots might descend to the base of the rocky spur and then sink into the soil of the surrounding plain, but it was actually impossible for any tree of non-magical origin.

He quickened his pace.

When the first sun began to lighten the horizon, he was just a few steps from the woods and entered it still with the favor of the darkness that was slowly dissolving.

He felt someone move, Nolan and Elyn had heard footsteps and got ready to react.

"It's me!" he said to be recognized.

Triny, who had remained motionless, breathed a sigh of relief at hearing his voice.

He told everything he had seen while they were having breakfast, paused on the fact that he hadn't noticed anyone but one of the hitmen, then described that bright tree explaining his theory of improbably long roots.

Suddenly they heard the sound of trampled leaves.

"Get down" Jelko barely whispered.

Nolan drew his dagger and listened.

They looked around slowly. The wood was quite dense, but apparently there was no one there, or it was very well hidden.

Triny held her breath, Elyn closed her eyes and concentrated.

The others spotted her and looked at her silently, waiting for her mental powers to line up for an answer.

"Stop!" the elf said after a few moments that the others never seemed to pass by, "it's a deer, it's coming towards us."

From behind a nearby bush, the horns and then the whole body of the animal came out.

It seemed agitated. It moved its head up and down impatiently, moved in one direction and then immediately retraced its steps, never taking its eyes off the boys.

"It wants us to follow" Elyn said, "come on, it will take us somewhere."

"Are you sure?" Nolan asked, "it's just a deer, and who knows where it might lead us."

"Yes" she replied, "I'm sure of it."

They gathered their things and began to follow it.

The deer always stood in front of them at a safe distance, but often turned to check that it was being followed. If the group slowed down, it did the same. It didn't seem to want to lose eye contact with them.

Time passed and Nolan said: "It's already mid-morning, let's hope we've done the right thing by moving away from Averidia to follow a deer."

"Apparently, we're there" Elyn said.

The animal suddenly began to run to the right until it disappeared in a short time swallowed by the woods, in front of them the trees thinned out and then left room for a sweet valley.

They were exactly on the opposite side, they approached the last trees and passed them and saw a camp.

The soldiers and knights commanded by Faxel and Zimas were in front of them, intent on setting up some tents. Along the perimeter, some were patrolling the area.

They went out definitively, showing themselves to the nearest patrols. Zimas immediately noticed and joined them on horseback: "I don't have enough mental powers to contact you. I had to resort to a more elementary form of life, I hope it was to your liking."

"The deer!" Nolan exclaimed.

"I will lead you" said the magician, dismounting and walking with them.

The soldiers were well organized, in the higher areas of that small valley there were patrols that could enjoy a better view.

Further down and out of sight, the rest of the troops were hidden. There were not many, but the knights of the Duchy, united with the Dark Kingdom infantry, could worry anyone regardless of the number.

Faxel met the group followed by the captain he had met a few days earlier in Han Farn.

"Welcome!" said Jelko's father, "let's not waste time, we can't afford to stay in this place for long. It's the best we've found, but I don't like it. I'm happy to see you safe and sound."

Faxel led everyone to a tent located in the center of the camp.

Inside, it was almost empty. There was only a rectangular table, some candlesticks and some stools.

"Take a seat" he said, pointing to the sessions, "we have to discuss what to do, the king of the Dark Kingdom left weeks ago and never returned. As already mentioned, the Relic is no longer where it should be."

They talked for a long time, advancing different theories.

Jelko began to tell what he had seen in Averidia the previous night. Everyone froze at every word, as that silence in the city worried them.

"Did you notice if that tree was powered by something? Was the Relic inside?" Zimas asked, "I'm afraid it has to do with controlling the Sleepless Ones."

Elyn said: "What if it was the tree that kept the contact with all the monsters summoned alive? The roots could magically connect with the feeble minds of the Sleepless Ones around the world, through the power of the Relic."

Nolan said: "You told us about the power to control the masses of the Fragment of Infinity. At that point, the tree would make sense and the hypothesis be valid."

Zimas added: "It could magically expand its area of influence to even the most remote places through everything it touches with its roots without being noticed, as if it were an amplifier that expands its power through the hidden passage of the same underground. The control of the masses had long been discussed by the archmages. According to them, it represented one of the hypotheses about the various unknown powers that the Relic could have."

One of the knights of the Duchy asked to enter, he was carrying a letter.

Faxel opened it and said: "Very well, by tomorrow afternoon some troops from the Kingdom of Miriam and Karinal will be here as promised."

Jelko said: "I have been in an abandoned house in Averidia for most of the night. I have not seen any Sleepless One, I believe they are summoned and sent immediately without being stationed there."

"The city seemed deserted to me" he added after a pause.

The captain of the Han Farn guards spoke up and said: "Maybe it is true. So as not to be too conspicuous here, there could only be the command center with a few guards to defend it. It is a rather isolated place where there are no important passageways, not even for trade."

"I have some doubts about it" said Zimas, "anyone would be a fool to be found so unmanned."

"But it would be easier to move from one place to another in case of escape" Faxel commented, "few travel fast and access to Averidia is only one and therefore easily controlled."

The magician said: "If we attacked with all the troops, we would be spotted immediately, whoever stole the Relic is not a fool. He would find a way to escape with the help of magic, even if we barred the only way out."

"We'll have to do something more discreet" Elyn said, "while knowing we have our backs covered in case of need."

"I have an idea" Jelko spoke in a firm, mature voice.

Elyn closed her eyes and sighed, she knew what he was going to say by exposing himself.

"Only the four of us will enter, with the favor of the night as I did."

Everyone turned to him without saying a word.

He continued: "If we managed to surprise whomever is inside the tower, it would be much faster and more discreet, without the risk of escape after seeing entire battalions surrounding the promontory."

He fell silent. Everyone under that tent knew it was the best solution, even if the riskiest.

It was impossible to bring troops into the city without being noticed, its very conformation enjoyed an excellent and long-range view.

There was not much to add.

Faxel became very serious, his son was at risk personally and although their relationship had become stormy in the last period, it was still all he had left.

He got up and said: "You will come in tonight, we will start moving in small groups inside the woods as early as this afternoon. By mid-morning tomorrow, we will be ready and waiting for your signal. Try to stay hidden for a while after dawn, to give us time to prepare as best we can."

"How are we going to contact you?" Nolan asked.

"Any visible magic is enough" Zimas replied, "you will have all our eyes on you. There are two wizards among you, it won't be difficult for them."

"Before you leave, however, come with me" said the captain, "we will give you light armor that will protect you, without making your movements awkward."

"Good" Jelko said firmly. In the midst of those commanders, he seemed much older than he really was.

They got up in silence, no one knew what to say. The soldiers certainly had colder blood than anyone else under that tent.

The four boys seemed too mature and calm given the situation they would face.

Elyn went out first, the captain of the Han Farn guards hastened to raise a flap of the tent to facilitate her. She turned and elegantly bowed to all present.

Jelko, on the other hand, went out last.

Faxel deliberately extended his exit and when they were the only ones left inside the tent, he said: "Good luck, son. Everything will be fine. When we meet tomorrow, it will be to celebrate victory."

"Or we will go back to our fathers' house in the last dimension," he replied.

CHAPTER 24 (The Chrysalis)

They returned to the opposite side of the forest where they had initially camped and waited for the sunset to arrive.

The armor that the captain of Han Farn's guards had given them was really light, while providing decent protection.

They helped each other to put it on. The only one who did not wear hers was the elf, who thanked the captain and said: "If I manage to be inside the pentacle with my brother, I will return to my original body. I cannot wear such small armor or waste time to take it off."

She carried only the dagger that the Yalla had given to all of them.

They didn't talk much, they were visibly tense but they tried not to let it shine through to avoid catching each other's feelings of uncertainty mixed with fear.

"It's time, let's go" Elyn said a moment before the second sun also disappeared below the horizon.

Her voice was as usual very reassuring, everyone exchanged glances and tried to smile but no one came up with anything more than a grotesque grimace.

They held hands for as long as it took to get to the bastion of Averidia's front door.

Jelko proceeded slowly, trying to avoid the few obstacles that could make his companions stumble.

Silence was everywhere.

They could barely hear their footsteps on the grass and their breaths.

They passed the city gate.

Jelko tried to retrace the same steps of the previous night to get to the house where he had found shelter. According to him, the view from there was good, then they would study in detail the way to enter the tower.

Among the hypotheses discarded, there was also that of trying to do it at night, but in the square, the magic tree emitted too much light.

If there had been any hitch, it would have been necessary to call the soldiers hidden in the woods. They would not have been able to quickly reach Averidia in the dark, and above all they could not fight with a torch in their hands or worry about fighting where there was more light for the troops.

It was vital to not take unnecessary risks. They did not know the place of the clash, having not been able to carry out a strategic reconnaissance of the battlefield.

They reached the house.

Now everyone could see what surrounded them coming out of the darkness of the night of the world of Symbol. The light that emitted the tree was very intense and they hurried to enter and climb to the upper floors.

Elyn took a quick look from the terrace, putting only her head out, then went back inside the shelter and said: "It's as I imagined. It's a Luxia tree, they look like crystal and they are hollow. I'm sure that the Relic is inside, they need to keep a magical object to live and grow."

"But then, if we somehow brought it down" Jelko said, "would the control it exerts over the Sleepless Ones end?"

"Yes" she replied, "the artifact that it guards most of the time is destroyed with the death of the tree. The bond would be broken."

"And how do we tear it down?" asked Nolan.

Elyn replied: "It is immune to any physical attack and very resistant to magical ones, despite its fragile appearance."

"Zimas and I will focus on it then" Triny said.

The elf nodded and said: "That's probably the best thing."

Elyn seemed confused for a moment: "It all seems so strange to me. I can't perceive anything, It's like being in an empty bubble, there have been no vibrations since I set foot in Averidia."

"What do you mean?" asked Jelko, "couldn't it just be an uninhabited city?"

"Yes, of course, unless the Luxia tree combined with the Fragment of Infinity can interfere in some way."

Triny said: "In fact, there seems to be just desolation. We haven't seen any movement since we've been here and Jelko didn't notice anything yesterday, either."

"Let's wait for tomorrow morning and we'll know" Elyn concluded, "there will be enough light, we'll try to enter the tower. Maybe it would be better if you stayed here, in case of need, we will need someone who can send signals to Faxel and Zimas, and only something magical can be clearly visible from so far away."

"I would like to come with you and be more helpful" Triny said.

"You are useful to us here" Jelko spoke, "if we could not warn the soldiers for some reason, they would never know that we were in trouble and we would have no escape. You will join them and with Zimas you will have to worry about the tree. Nolan and I will cover Elyn as we try to reach Silven in the tower, hoping that he is there and that he does not escape from us."

"Okay, I'll do as you say" the girl confidently said.

They continued to keep an eye on the obelisk square throughout the night. There was no movement.

"What if the hitman you saw coming in, came to escort Elyn's brother away from here?" Nolan speculated.

Everything actually suggested that city was really abandoned.

The morning came quickly.

Just before the second sun rose, Triny lurked on the terrace leaning out only with half her face so as not to be seen.

The three companions greeted her and took courage by taking to the street, they crossed it and skirted the walls of the opposite houses up to the corner overlooking the square.

It was completely empty.

The light of Luxia's tree was still strong. Its glow was more reddish, despite the fact that the daylight began to prevail overwhelmingly.

They looked around at every step, Elyn was in the middle between the two boys.

At one point, Nolan said: "Wait, I saw something between the tree and the obelisk."

The comrades immediately stopped with their hearts in their throats, Jelko put his hand on the hilt of the sword.

They were a few steps from the door and disappeared from the view of Triny who managed to oversee a good part of the square, but not the entrance area of the tower.

"I'm going to see" Nolan added as he was already walking towards the obelisk, "we cannot risk that there is something that observes us even before entering."

"Where are you going? Wait!" said Jelko, trying not to shout. Nolan was already halfway there.

He and Elyn watched him with their backs against the wall of a building that bordered the tower.

Triny also kept an eye on him as he returned to her field of vision.

"Elyn, come and see! Maybe I have found the Relic!" said the healer in a low voice and beckoning with his hand to reach him.

Jelko and the elf looked at each other in amazement, Nolan seemed really excited by that discovery.

"Soon!" he continued, "if we could get it out of here, we could break the link with the Sleepless Ones. Let's take advantage of it now that there is no one!"

"Let's go and see" said the elf, and they quickly walked toward their companion.

When they were close to him, they saw clearly that inside the Luxia tree, suspended at half the height of the trunk, there was a chalice that emitted the same light seen so far.

Jelko exclaimed: "Damn! Is that the Fragment of Infinity?"

He barely noticed that Nolan was holding Argoran's dagger in his right hand, with a snap he was behind Elyn and immobilized her by pointing the blade at her throat.

"Get away!" he cried, shouting in his direction, his eyes out of his orbits.

"Nolan!" said Jelko.

"I said get away or I'll kill her right now!"

"But what the hell are you doing? Are you crazy? Damn traitor!" shouted Jelko, pulling out his sword as Nolan pressed the blade even harder into Elyn's neck.

She said: "Look up there Jelko!"

He turned around.

From one of the small windows of the tower a tall, blond elf was clearly moving his lips as if speaking while maintaining eye contact with Nolan, but nothing could be heard from where they were, in the center of the square between the tree and the black obelisk.

A trickle of blood began to descend from Elyn's neck.

"Run away! Save yourself!" she cried, "I can't do anything! Go away!"

Jelko didn't know what to do, Nolan was out of control and clearly not himself.

His friend seemed to try to counter the mental domination that Silven was inflicting on him, his blade approaching and moving away from the elf's throat as in an arm-wrestling contest.

Jelko yelled with the anger of the helpless: "How can I save myself? Do you think I could live with myself leaving you here to die? I followed you from the first dream, I have no way out! Don't you understand that I can't abandon you right now?"

The door of the tower behind him was heard opening.

The assassin with his face painted black and blue came out with a scepter in one hand and a sword in the other.

"It's not over yet!" Nolan shouted in a moment when he seemed to be cleared up, and then tightened his grip on Elyn again.

There was a flash of red light coming from their shoulders.

Triny had cast a spell that struck Nolan in full, swinging him backwards.

Five more followed in quick succession, this time shot in the air and clearly visible to anyone in the area of Averidia.

The sorceress was signaling to Faxel's troops to intervene as soon as possible to help them.

And so it was.

The knights of the Duchy came out first from the forest in which they were hidden, it made no sense to enter the city on horseback. The father of Jelko and Zimas were at their head.

Immediately behind, the infantrymen of the Dark Kingdom led by Han Farn's captain proceeded at a fast pace.

Nolan sat down and began to cough loudly.

Elyn approached him as Jelko retreated towards them and remained on guard, the warrior magician went to meet them slowly by skillfully twirling his sword.

They heard some bestial noises.

In a short time, the whole square was immersed in them.

A Sleepless One appeared from a street of the square that had apparently been deserted shortly before. A lot of them arrived, it seemed that they were going through a portal.

They understood that the entire perimeter of the square was an illusion of the same, but deserted. Sleepless Ones appeared everywhere, surrounding them, as if crossing an invisible barrier behind which they were hidden from anyone's sight, which perfectly reproduced the entire area but in an uninhabited version.

It seemed they were crossing a huge tent, with the city depicted perfectly as seen from the square.

As the illusion was overcome, a slight flicker could be noticed, like the one seen looking at an image beyond a flame or a heat source.

In a short time, the entire square of the obelisk was filled with razor-sharp claws, ravenous jaws and guttural verses of hundreds of Sleepless Ones.

"Stay here next to me!" cried Elyn.

The din of all those monsters was almost deafening.

Meanwhile, Nolan stood up and said: "What the hell happened to me? I don't even remember how we found ourselves in the midst of all these damn monsters! What do we do? Where are the soldiers?"

"You were going to slit Elyn's throat!" replied Jelko, "Silven was mentally controlling you."

"What?" Nolan exclaimed, amazed and embarrassed at the same time by what he had done.

Elyn stretched out her arms in front of her by spreading both palms of her hands and began to rotate.

As she concluded the circle, a dome-shaped black smoke barrier appeared around them ten steps away.

Nolan also began to pronounce magic formulas, now his armor and that of Jelko began to shine with a very light blue light.

The barrier just created by Elyn did the same.

"We hope that the soldiers will come to our rescue soon" she said, "there are too many and we will not be able to keep them away for long with that barrier."

From the outside, the Sleepless Ones had begun to rage against that impassable wall with more and more insistence.

Failing to cause obvious damage, however, they were crazy with anger.

Triny was terrified.

No one seemed to care about her. She was well hidden and all the attention was turned to the center of the square, but seeing that scene made her legs tremble. Her friends were under a dark dome, similar to the smoke that develops after setting fire to the brushwood in the fields.

Around them, the square was filled with angry Sleepless Ones.

She could do nothing but wait for the arrival of the troops.

From there she had no view of the outside of the city, so she could only hope that her signals had been received.

The dome was semi-transparent, she could barely see that Elyn and Nolan continued to maintain their magical contact.

As a sorceress, she knew very well that they could not do it for much longer.

For the elf, who was subjugated by the Curse of the Chains, the effort was even greater, although her magical abilities were extraordinary.

Elyn and Nolan continued to concentrate, but they began to get tired. Jelko felt that within a short time, the protective dome would disappear.

He began to control his body, his breathing became faster and his muscles began to stiffen and swell. His heart already accelerated further to a thousand beats per minute.

In the multitude of the Sleepless Ones, he could no longer see the warrior magician. The aggressors crowded as if they were hungry from days of fasting and pursuing a wounded and bleeding prey.

He was ready and was sure of it. If he died, he would take many dozens of those monsters with him. He also knew that when the dome of magical smoke dissolved, none of his friends would have escaped.

Some tongues of fire fell from the sky, hitting the Sleepless Ones.

Zimas and Faxel had finally arrived.

Behind them, the soldiers had already begun to charge, breaking into the square teeming with abominations.

The interest of the monsters shifted to the troops, at least they could be hit.

They stopped raging against the impassable barrier and began to move towards the entrance of the road, that gave onto the square from which the soldiers came.

Triny burst into tears, her emotions were really uncontainable. She took courage by wiping away her tears as she saw Zimas fighting by casting spells.

She ran out of the house where she was and joined the magician who, in the meantime, was set back from the front line and told him: "It's a Luxia tree! Elyn said we need to focus our magic on that. If we could break it down, the link with the Sleepless Ones would be lost."

"And so be it" he replied, not at all surprised or agitated.

The soldiers were fighting with all their strength and great skill, but the enemy was much more numerous. Faxel killed one almost with every shot, but for each of them that was shot down, two more came.

They had managed to gain ground until the middle of the square, but they would not have resisted for long. The Sleepless Ones were more than triple and could not be fatigued.

Faxel and some other knights joined the boys.

Elyn and Nolan finally interrupted their concentration and the protective dome vanished instantly, they were both exhausted.

"Take shelter behind us, soon!" said Jelko's father.

He had never yet seen his son fight and was amazed, the demon that was in him was really scary. His blows were almost all scored with such power as to leave no escape to the victims.

A Sleepless One suddenly came out of the shoulders of another and hit Faxel in the leg and then stuck a claw to his side.

He fell to the ground. Jelko and other knights shielded him, while from the rear they dragged him away with weight.

Nolan had already eliminated some of them and at the moment he had two on him. One he managed to destroy almost immediately, while the second instead gave him more trouble.

Elyn looked up at the sky above her, raised both arms and closed her eyes.

She began to sway left and right as if she were dancing. Her lips were barely moving, she uttered a few spells in a low voice.

A distant, small black cloud was rapidly approaching.

Triny and Zimas stood in a spot far from the center of the fight, protected by a square of soldiers around them.

They began to cast spells on the glowing tree.

Each time they hit it with energy darts and tongues of fire, it went out for an instant as if it were feeling the blow, only to return to shine like a moment before.

The wizard warrior with the scepter made his way through the enemy ranks.

He swung his sword, killing a Dark Kingdom soldier while he was turned from behind to fight a Sleepless One.

Jelko saw him and his anger grew even more. His father had just been badly injured and carried away bleeding, he went towards him like a fury.

Time passed.

The soldiers were exhausted, the fighting was lasting longer than expected and they did not expect to be in a clear numerical minority. Faxel had fallen and they didn't know if he was alive or dead.

They managed to overcome that disadvantage by almost equalizing, now they were fighting one on one, but they were stalled due to fatigue and morale that began to falter.

Soon after, news broke that the captain of Han Farn's guards had been torn apart by the claws of the Sleepless Ones after a heroic fight. The troops were almost on course.

From the tower, Silven began to hit the soldiers with small lethal fiery balls, each of them killing a soldier with an explosion.

What from a distance seemed to be a cloud, was over the square in an instant and descended on it.

With amazement, everyone realized that it was formed by thousands of dark insects a finger long. They pounced on the eyes of the Sleepless Ones, some were blinded and others tried to protect themselves as they could.

The soldiers took advantage of this and before the insects vanished into a breath of wind, they had halved the number of enemies by hitting them to death at that moment of unexpected difficulty.

Now it was they who had the numerical superiority.

Elyn walked towards the gate of the tower, walking proudly as if she were at an important parade in the midst of her people.

A Sleepless One came up to her brandishing its sharp claws in the air. She looked at it intensely, stopped, and the monster fell dead a few steps from her.

When she reached the door, before entering it, she turned towards the square that had become a battlefield. There were hundreds of dead on the ground of both rows.

Jelko, Nolan and Triny were watching her as they fought.

Elyn gave one of her reassuring smiles, and they thought they heard one of the few easily recognizable elven words inside their heads: "Thank you."

The door slammed shut as she passed.

No one ever saw that little wood elf again.

The numerical superiority revived the attacks of the friendly troops, Zimas and Triny approached Jelko escorted by seven soldiers and the magician said: "Enter the tower, we'll take care of it here."

The warrior mage was almost on Jelko, he had thrown some protection and enhancement spells on himself, the soldiers of the escort blocked his way.

Nolan joined them after taking out other attackers.

"Don't waste time! I said we'll take care of it here, for all the Gods!" pressed Zimas.

Without the captain and Faxel, he was in charge now.

The three boys stood shoulder to shoulder and ran towards the gate of the tower.

They opened it and entered.

Inside, silence dominated the scene. It seemed to be hermetically sealed, despite the fact that there was a battle going on outside.

The entrance was very wide, the tower was low but very wide.

Its shape was unusual, as was all Averidia.

On the ground, some banners had fallen on the dusty floor.

Some wooden benches were overturned and others were stacked against a wall, the few windows left the whole environment wrapped in the dim light.

A small door probably led to a service exit at the back.

There were two stairs, one very wide that went up, and one rather narrow that went down into the basement.

"Listen!" said Triny quietly, standing still and stretching out her ears.

Just in the direction of the ramp that went down, they could hear a repeated and dull noise, like something heavy slamming.

"It's as if someone is knocking animatedly" Nolan said, "and that he wants to come in at any cost."

"Here! We are down here!"

"It's a trap" said Jelko, "let's go up, we don't have time to go and see."

Nolan approached the staircase and craned his neck to look.

He said: "I see a reinforced door. It's right there, it won't take long. Help could come in handy."

"Okay" Jelko agreed, "let's be on the alert and act quickly."

In a moment, all three were in front of that door just below the level of the ground. The staircase continued and was lost in the darkness a little further on.

"Damn, it's tightly closed" Nolan said, who had already tried to force it.

Triny said: "Get back, I'll try to open it."

She casted a spell and the three large hinges crashed to the ground with a clatter.

The reinforced door fell towards the inside of the room it sealed.

Something indescribable was before their eyes.

A dozen well-dressed men, wearing jewels and heavy gold rings, were piled in there one on top of the other.

Half of them wore a crown.

They were the rulers of Symbol's world, held like beasts.

Their gazes were lost in the void, some did not even seem to realize what was happening. One kept hitting his head with a fist, another tried to scratch the wall with broken and bleeding nails.

Nolan recognized the ruler of the Barony of the Dragon from which he came. It was he who was knocking and asking for help until recently, he seemed to be the only lucid person among all the other prisoners.

"I am indebted to you" said the man who had banished his monotheistic Order.

"Get to safety, you'll have to fend for yourself" Jelko said as he recovered from his amazement.

Silven had imprisoned them all: sovereigns and prime ministers were lured and then captured to squeeze their minds, in order to steal information useful to his cause. Moreover, with the various lords absent, he would most likely have found less resistance to his plans of conquest. The various peoples should first reorganize their leaders.

Among them was also the king of the Dark Kingdom.

Silven had managed to bribe him by having the Relic delivered, behind the vain promise of enormous glory and power.

Jelko walked up the few steps and said, turning to his comrades: "Come on, affairs of state do not concern us at this time."

"My dear twin sister" said Silven, "you are unrecognizable inside that ridiculous body."

The door to the last room at the top of the tower was open and Elyn had just entered it.

"It's time to conclude what began fifteen years ago, in one way or another" she replied.

Silven moved away from the only open window from which he, until recently, had checked the outcome of the battle by casting deadly spells on the soldiers from above.

He was inside the containment pentacle.

There he could dispose of all his powers and appear in his young body.

Outside of it he was frail and feeble, looking like an elder consumed by the same power he had always sought for most of his new renegade life.

The pentacle took up most of the room, drawing a large five-pointed star on the ground with a slight blue luminescence.

"Come in, take a seat inside it" Silven said calmly, pointing with his hand at the magic symbol it was in, "I can't kill you while you're under the Curse of the Chains."

Elyn stopped just a step away from the blue border.

He continued: "You haven't folded in all these years as a slave, it's time to end it another way and once and for all. If you enter, you will return to your real body and I will finally be able to eliminate you forever. The choice is yours, to try to be free again, or to remain who you are now for the rest of your days."

She stared at him, she could not speak.

For a moment, she remembered when as children they played in the lawns outside the house. A tear ran down her face.

"Come on, we'll be on equal terms. Show me what the queen of the Arcane Elves, as well as Chosen One, can do. You should have built up enough grudges against me, you can finally get rid of me. I'm here, come in. One last effort is missing."

She took that last step and entered the magical pentacle.

The blue glow of the perimeter was accentuated by increasing in intensity. Her body was enveloped by a white light, so intense that Silven had to look away so as not to be blinded.

The wood elf was gone.

Now, inside that pentacle, was the queen of the Arcane Elves.

Elyn, like all the elves of her people, was tall and blonde. Her hair long up to the shoulder blades was slightly wavy. Some strands formed dreadlocks adorned with thin strings of colored cloth and silver rings.

Her eyes were blue and she was really lovely in her perfect and young body.

She wore a long black and purple dress. Along the hems of the sleeves, neckline and along the hips, small runes with golden threads were drawn. It was very stylish.

"I didn't want it to end like this" she said, "it's time to go home, Silven."

He gestured with his hands and immediately two tongues of fire left in the direction of his sister.

She dodged both, her athletic and sinuous body was very agile.

Elyn drew a circle in the air and a shimmering shield appeared around her, narrowed her eyes for a moment and launched a small black orb.

Her magic was predominantly that of the void, so almost all her attack spells were typically of energy black as night.

Silven dodged her spell and it hit a chair leaning against the wall, shattering into pieces with a small explosion.

She clasped her hands in front of her as if she were pushing something invisible. A dark shield of vibrating energy began to form and rapidly expanded to cover her entire height, starting from the floor.

The elf generated something very similar with the same ritual, but his shield seemed to be made of fire.

They both remained in that position so as not to frustrate what they had just created, they closed their eyes at the same instant and each concentrated on trying to possess their rival's mind.

The shields generated in front of them pulsed violently as if they were alive.

Depending on the energy they subtracted to try to control the mind of the other, they decreased their diameter and then returned to their maximum size shortly after.

Silven pushed his fiery shield forward with the thought of his without taking a step, Elyn sensed it and, still keeping her eyes closed, did the same.

At a certain point, the two magical barriers were less than a palm away from each other and began to fry noisily.

The few chairs scattered around the room were thrown against the walls as if attracted by them, moving as far as possible from the center of the room where the two energies almost touched.

The two shields barely touched and an explosion threw both duelists backwards, breaking the mental contact they had created.

Silven reached out to a wall where a stiletto was hanging, this broke away from the wall crossing part of the room in mid-air and in an instant it was in the elf's hand.

Elyn pulled the dagger she received, as a gift from Argoran, from her boot.

With her free hand, she generated a shock wave that caused everything that was resting on the shelves in the room to fall.

She closed her eyes and the books, the candlesticks and some bowls began to lash out at the elf hitting him.

He tried to protect himself by shielding himself with his arms and hands.

She was on top of him and thrust the blade into his belly.

"You'll never get me!" he yelled with all the breath he had.

The anger he felt was clearly in his face.

Silven was bleeding, but he managed to move to one side and pushed his twin away. He squeezed the stiletto tightly and tried to hit her.

Elyn dodged a few blows, but one of them landed.

However, it only destroyed the magical protection she had summoned upon herself at the start of the fight.

She came out unscathed from that fight. Her brother, instead, was wounded on the ground.

Elyn walked away and took the opportunity to go to the window to see what was happening in the square.

The soldiers were still fighting. Zimas continued alone to cast spells against the magic tree, which seemed to begin to feel his blows. Each time he hit it, it stayed off longer and longer before returning again to emit its increasingly amber light.

Out of the fray, she clearly noticed Faxel. He was alive and receiving first aid from some healers who were part of each battalion as usual.

His brother's warrior mage lay dead not far from Zimas.

Suddenly her vision blurred.

Silven was again trying to control her mind. She turned and saw him standing with his back to the wall, his eyes rolled back, his fists clenched, the sword on the ground in front of him, his feet in a pool of blood.

For a moment it seemed to Elyn that she was dreaming.

She saw the green meadows of her childhood, the rolling hills and the streams that flowed at their feet. A little girl was running trying to chase two butterflies. It was her.

From the sky, pieces of rusty chains began to rain, the little girl began to scream and run towards a house. The sky became dark and it was almost night. She kept running, but the house was moving further and further away until it became a dot on the horizon.

There was no one around, only her and the darkness that gradually enveloped her. She began to scream louder and louder, she was terrified.

That scream was also heard in reality.

The soldiers who were fighting turned for a moment towards the tower. The Sleepless Ones were now decimated. The tower was shrouded in a dusty cloud, as if that cry had shaken it and made it tremble from the top to the foundations after an earthquake.

Elyn came to her senses.

Silven kept chanting something she had never heard before.

She didn't know those words he was saying, but she clearly felt the strength was leaving her as she did fifteen years ago, when he gave her the Curse of the Chains.

The elf was in a trance. Around him an aura of protection enveloped him completely, his feet detached slightly from the ground.

Elyn heard a noise coming from outside the room, someone came in.

The sight of her came and went, her legs began to give out and she had to lean against the wall.

"Save yourself, my queen!" Manmur yelled at her.

The elf was amazed to see him. She wanted to say something, but she couldn't speak. Silven didn't even notice and continued with his spell as if nothing had happened.

"You still have time for one spell!" the old elf said to her, "we can't stop him now, before it's too late and he takes away all power. Teleport out of here, his spell will hit me since I'll be the only living being in the room."

Elyn could really make one last move, get out of there or stay and do something else.

She decided on the second hypothesis, aware of the risk she was running.

Manmur sensed her intentions and cried out in despair: "No! No!"

Tongues of fire began to circle all around Silven's body.

His tone of voice was higher and higher, his words more and more pronounced and harsh. It was as if he were in the middle of a pyre without taking any damage.

The old elf ran towards his queen, stepping between her and her twin.

In that instant, Elyn said something in a low voice.

A blinding flash replaced her figure for a moment. A large globe of black light was seen starting from the square at the last window of the tower.

It struck Luxia's tree.

It caught fire immediately, but the flames were blue and black. Its light became white and then ceased.

Shortly thereafter, the fire of void magic went out. Now it was no longer bright and looked like a simple glass sculpture in the shape of a tree.

On the ground, a goblet broken in two pieces had rolled near a root.

The Sleepless Ones froze as if petrified, the soldiers took advantage and killed almost all of them.

Some started to run away emitting guttural noises, but no one chased them.

The square was free from abominations. Silence fell upon it, the monsters were gone.

A soldier said almost timidly: "They have broken the magical bond, they are gone!"

Another next to him added loudly: "It's all over! We won! The queen of the Arcane Elves did it!"

As if from the stands inside an arena, the victory cry of all the survivors rose in unison.

Many beat their sword against their shield, the din and shouts of exultation filled almost the entire deserted city of Averidia.

Others began to shout: "For the queen! We are safe!"

Jelko, Nolan and Triny were inside the tower halfway up the stairs when they clearly heard those words. Outside, the battle was over, the enemy had been defeated.

"She did it!" Triny said with a big smile.

"She could only go like this" Nolan added enthusiastically, "I had no doubt!"

Jelko said: "We're almost there, let's go and take her in triumph! Come on!"

They ran even faster than they were already doing, they didn't even feel tired anymore.

They reached the door like furies and entered.

Near the window, on the ground, there were two Arcane Elves.

Elyn was sitting with her back to the door through which the three boys entered, she held the head of a dying old elf on her lap.

"I would have liked to serve you again my queen" said Manmur, "it would have been an honor for me."

The elf turned to her companions who had just entered.

They had never seen her with that appearance. They were speechless, although the fight just took place, was always in order as when she was a wood elf. Her beauty was wonderfully amazing, her dress impeccable.

Her face was wet with tears.

She lowered her gaze to the face of the old elf she was supporting on her lap, and said to him: "The honor was mine."

Manmur closed his eyes, a tear from his queen falling down his cheek as she hugged him tightly to her.

The broken mirror in which he was imprisoned broke off the wall and fell to the ground.

Triny burst into tears, the two boys did not know what to say and were silent.

From the window, the soldiers could still be heard cheering for the hard-won victory at a high price. They did not realize that it was almost sunset, the battle had lasted a whole day.

Reinforcement troops from the other kingdoms were due to arrive in the afternoon, but they had not yet appeared.

Elyn raised her head and looked at them one by one, and finally said: "I failed, get me out of here, please."

"The soldiers have won! The Sleepless Ones have escaped and broken their magical bond! Luxia's tree has gone out!" Jelko said not understanding why Elyn was saying those words.

"My brother ran away" she said, "he couldn't kill me. Manmur sacrificed himself for me, I didn't beat him."

She began to sob, they had never seen her so fragile. They had always known her to be strong and sure of her every gesture.

She now was there on the ground, the queen was no longer a slave. She had taken back her real body, yet she was so helpless at that moment. She just looked like a normal girl.

"Please take me away" she said again. She was visibly out of strength.

Triny ran to meet her and hugged her tightly. The two boys immediately went after her and gently helped the elf to get up.

"Let's get out of here, quick!" Jelko said, "let's go through the small door we saw in the entrance hall, it will take us to the back without attracting too much attention. For now, it is not necessary for everyone to see her."

Elyn tried to stand up.

Supported by the two boys, she couldn't and Jelko decided to pick her up: "Let's go" he said.

"Let's go to the Pedestal of the Cartographer" Nolan added, "there we will be just out of the way. We will be able to keep an eye on the city and the soldiers without being noticed, thus avoiding their celebrations by staying on the sidelines for the moment."

The Pedestal of the Cartographer, as previously mentioned, was an artificial platform from which, due to strange and inexplicable refraction games, it was possible to see a large part of

Symbol's world even if the distances and proportions were not correct. It was like having a map in front of the eyes.

It was located not far from the only entrance to the city, on a small rock raised above the surrounding area.

They quickly went down the stairs to the atrium of the tower, Nolan opened the door and took a look outside: "All clear, there is no one."

Elyn clung to Jelko's neck. In no time, they were out of town and reached the pedestal.

It was almost dark. From there, the view of the world was truly something unusual and never seen before.

Triny said: "Look over there, what is that red glow?"

It was not easy to understand what it was. Nolan turned a little more to his right: "There is something similar there too, and not far from there."

The elf whispered to Jelko: "Put me down, I want to try to stand up."

He and the others held their breath.

Elyn narrowed her eyes barely as she watched all those reddish flashes increase in intensity and number. Everywhere they looked, there were new ones in every direction.

Everyone was afraid to know what the queen of the Arcane Elves was about to say.

Their nightmare materialized.

"It's the villages and towns around the world that burn" Elyn said, "I'm sorry my friends, the Merchants of Leaves have a long way to go. Our journey isn't over yet."

A slight gust of wind gently moved her hair to one side, exposing the back of her neck.

The tattoo of the lugubrious chrysalis imprisoned by a web, which she had behind her neck, was gone.

Now, instead of it, there was a beautiful colorful butterfly.

Well, now I have to go. Today here in Argoran is a strange day. I feel that something is about to happen.

That day, I managed to escape by a hair by teleporting myself with the few remaining energies.

My sister, instead of saving herself with the last spell at her disposal, had attempted to destroy the Relic inside Luxia's tree.

And she succeeded.

I would have killed her if that damn Manmur had not stood in the way.

Meanwhile, I felt that the bond with my subjects had vanished. I wouldn't have survived if I had been there again.

I was too weak.

Although the Sleepless Ones were now out of control, the second invasion of Symbol's world began.

And... if you have patience, I will take you with me again on the path of this story.

Many thanks for reading this book!

Web site	www.ilmondodisymbol.it
Facebook	Il Mondo fantasy di Symbol
Instagram	armando.bizzarri

Printed in Poland
by Amazon Fulfillment
Poland Sp. z o.o., Wrocław
19 September 2022

bf94ab93-018e-4f6f-934d-c321d09744a4R01